THE CORPSE IN
THE WAXWORKS

THE CORPSE IN THE WAXWORKS

A Paris Mystery

JOHN DICKSON CARR

With an Introduction
by Martin Edwards

Poisoned Pen
PRESS

Published by Poisoned Pen Press, an imprint of Sourcebooks, in association with the British Library
P.O. Box 4410, Naperville, Illinois 60567-4410
(630) 961-3900
sourcebooks.com

The Corpse in the Waxworks was originally published in 1932 by Harper & Brothers, New York and London.
"The Murder in Number Four" was originally published in the June 1928 issue of The Haverfordian.

Library of Congress Cataloging-in-Publication Data

Names: Carr, John Dickson, author. | Edwards, Martin, writer of introduction.
Title: The corpse in the waxworks : a Paris mystery / John Dickson Carr ; with an introduction by Martin Edwards.
Description: Naperville, Illinois : Poisoned Pen Press, [2021] | Series: British library crime classics | Originally published, 1932.
Identifiers: LCCN 2021004365 (print) | LCCN 2021004366 (ebook) | (trade paperback) | (epub)
Subjects: GSAFD: Mystery fiction.
Classification: LCC PS3505.A763 C6 2021 (print) | LCC PS3505.A763 (ebook)
 | DDC 813/.52--dc23
LC record available at https://lccn.loc.gov/2021004365
LC ebook record available at https://lccn.loc.gov/2021004366

Printed and bound in the United States of America.
SB 10 9 8 7 6 5 4 3 2 1

CONTENTS

INTRODUCTION

"Bencolin was not wearing his evening clothes, and so they knew that nobody was in danger." So opens John Dickson Carr's *The Corpse in the Waxworks* (also known as *The Waxworks Murder*), the fourth novel to feature the *juge d'instruction* Henri Bencolin. The setting is Paris, the narrator is the young American Jeff Marle, and the epigraphs include a passage from Poe's "The Masque of the Red Death" beginning: "Be sure they were grotesque." Masks are a recurrent theme in this story, while there is no shortage of grotesquerie.

Bencolin, accompanied by Jeff and young Captain Chaumont, meet a man called Augustin, proprietor of the Musée Augustin, home to a waxworks. Chaumont's fiancée, we learn, was last seen alive entering the museum; her murdered corpse has just been found floating in the Seine. When the little group enters the museum, they discover another woman's body, in the arms of a wax satyr.

A waxworks makes a splendidly eerie setting for a mystery novel. Carr, who was just twenty-five years old when the book was published, exploits the macabre potential with gusto. Augustin describes, "The purpose, the illusion, the spirit of a waxworks. It is an atmosphere of death. It is soundless and motionless. It is walled off by stone grottos, like a dream, from the light of day; its noises are echoes, and it is filled with a dull green illumination, as though it were in the depths under the sea… All things are turned dead, in attitudes of horror… Marat is stabbed in his bath. Louis XVI lies with his head under the guillotine knife. Bonaparte dies, white-faced… This silence, this motionless host in the twilight, is my world."

The infamous Club of the Silver Key is evoked in equally vivid fashion. Secretive, select, and expensive, it's a place where men and women "cross in [the] great hall, which is dimly lighted and muffled with thick hangings—and they all wear masks." And as Bencolin explains to the owner, Galant, in the passage leading to the club, directly behind the waxworks museum, Claudine Martel was murdered.

Not for the first time in his short career, Carr also gave his chapters highly atmospheric titles: for instance, "Confidences Are Exchanged Over a Coffin," "Death in Silhouette," "A Dead Man Pushes Open a Window," "Stabbing as a Sporting Proposition," and "One Card for Cyanide." Yes, this is a young man writing, full of energy and joyful self-confidence.

As Carr's biographer Douglas Greene puts it, "Poe's ghost seems to be present at every scene." There is no locked room puzzle or impossible crime scenario in this particular story, but for Greene, a perceptive commentator, it "is probably the most tightly plotted of the Bencolin books. The crime and the setting are perfectly integrated, the plotting convoluted, the puzzle element beautifully handled, and the final solution surprising." The Bencolin series represents a wonderful literary apprenticeship: Greene concedes that the mysteries may not always be realistic, "but they are colourful, picturesque, terrifying, and compelling."

This novel was first published on March 23, 1932; the UK edition was retitled *The Waxworks Murder*, for reasons which are unclear. The following year, Carr introduced Dr. Gideon Fell in *Hag's Nook*, and the year after that Sir Henry Merrivale, his other long-running series detective, appeared in *The Plague Court Murders*. Jeff Marle returned in the non-series novel *Poison in Jest*, set in the United States, while *The Four False Weapons*, published in 1937, marked Bencolin's last bow. Carr had, it seems, decided that the satanic protagonist of his early stories no longer suited him; his writing style had matured, and as Bencolin retired from his official position and mellowed, he became a rather less striking character.

John Dickson Carr (1906–1977) remains to this day one of the legendary figures of Golden Age detective fiction. He is renowned for the ingenuity of his puzzle-making, and was cited as an influence by David Renwick, the television writer responsible for creating the highly successful British TV series *Jonathan Creek*. But there was more to Carr's work (as there is to Renwick's scripts) than twisty plotting. He wrote with a gusto that reflected his genuine passion for the well-crafted detective story, a passion evident in his famous essay "The Grandest Game in the World."

He was proud to be the first American-born writer to be elected to membership of the Detection Club in 1936, and before long he was appointed as Club Secretary. In collaboration with his friend, fellow Detection Club member John Rhode, he wrote *Drop to His Death*, also known as *Fatal Descent*; he also based another series character, Colonel March, on Rhode. An Anglophile who married an Englishwoman, he lived for many years in Britain, and even contemplated becoming a British citizen, but ultimately returned to the United States in 1958.

Carr continued to publish novels until 1972; his last book, *The Hungry Goblin*, featured Wilkie Collins as a protagonist. It is probably fair to say, though, that his best work was produced in the thirties and forties. Many locked room aficionados regard *The Three Coffins*, known in the UK as *The Hollow Man*, as the finest of all impossible crime novels. His other masterpieces include *The Black Spectacles* aka *The Problem of the Green Capsule*, *Till Death Do Us Part*, and *The Judas Window*.

The inherently artificial nature of fiction about seemingly impossible crimes means that they are well-suited to treatment in a short story, a form at which Carr excelled. His "The House in Goblin Wood" and "The Gentleman from Paris" are especially notable examples of his work in this form. This book includes as a bonus an early Bencolin short story, "The Murder in Number Four," set on a haunted train and concerning a bizarre "locked railway compartment" mystery.

In collaboration with Adrian Conan Doyle, Carr produced a book of Sherlockian pastiches, *The Exploits of Sherlock Holmes*. He also achieved considerable success with radio plays and as a writer of nonfiction, publishing a biography of Sir Arthur Conan Doyle and a well-regarded study of the seventeenth-century murder of Sir Edmund Godfrey. To this day, however, this versatile writer remains most famous as the undisputed king of the locked room mystery.

—Martin Edwards
www.martinedwardsbooks.com

THE CORPSE IN
THE WAXWORKS

"Be sure they were grotesque. There were much glare and glitter and piquancy and phantasm… There were arabesque figures with unsuited limbs and appointments. There were delirious fancies such as the madman fashions. There were much of the beautiful, much of the wanton, much of the bizarre, something of the terrible, and not a little of that which might have excited disgust. To and fro in the seven chambers there stalked, in fact, a multitude of dreams."

— *THE MASQUE OF THE RED DEATH*

"And we, all our lives, like Jules, are incurably romantic. We shall go, therefore, to our first ball at the Opéra because it, too, will endeavour to revive the romantic age… And it will be the same. In the crystal cups on the buffet tables, the same golden sunlight of champagne swims and sparkles. Beneath the black mask, and below the broad concealing hat, still shine the bright eyes of danger."

— GEORGE SLOCOMBE

1

A GHOST WITH A BROWN HAT

BENCOLIN WAS NOT WEARING HIS EVENING CLOTHES, and so they knew that nobody was in danger.

For there is a legend about this man-hunting dandy, the head of the Paris police, which is known and believed in all the night haunts from Montmartre to the Boulevard de la Chapelle. Your Parisian, even one with cause to fear detectives, prefers them to be picturesque. Bencolin had a habit of lounging through the *bottes de nuit*, the fashionable ones which begin as you ascend the rue Fontaine, or the murkier places clustering about the Porte St.-Martin. Even those worst regions which lie tucked behind the left-hand side of the Boulevard St.-Antoine and which visitors seldom hear of, find him drinking beer and listening to the whining, tinny lurch of tango music under a thick heat of tobacco smoke. That, he says, is what he likes. He likes to sit obscurely at a table with a glass of beer, in a gloom of coloured lights, hearing the loudest jazz music possible—to dream whatever dreams go on behind the hooked eyebrows of Mephistopheles. It is not quite a true statement, because his presence is rather less obscure than a brass band. But he does not talk; he just smiles in a pleased fashion, and smokes cigars all night.

The legend, then, says that when he wears on these occasions an ordinary sacque suit, he is out for pleasure alone. Observing this costume, the proprietors of doubtful cafés become effusive, bow low, and, as like as not, offer him champagne. When he wears a dinner jacket, he is on the trail of something, but he is only speculating and watching; the proprietors, though uneasy, can give him a good table and offer a short drink like cognac. But when he walks in evening clothes, with the familiar cloak, top-hat, and silver-headed stick, when his smile is a trifle more suave and there is a very slight bulge under his left arm—*messieurs*, that means trouble, and be sure that everybody knows it. The proprietor does not offer any drink at all. The orchestra gets a little off key. The waiters drop a saucer or two, and the knowing ones, if they have a favourite girl with them, hasten to get her out before somebody pulls a knife.

Curiously enough, this legend is true. I have told him that it is beneath his dignity as *juge d'instruction* to adopt this procedure. It does not, strictly speaking, come under the head of his duties at all, and could just as well be done by a minor inspector. But I know that to tell him this is useless, for he enjoys it immensely. He will continue to enjoy it until some quicker blade or bullet drops him in a gaslit alley in God knows what ugly neighbourhood, with his opal studs flat in the mud and his swordstick halfway out of its sheath.

I have accompanied him occasionally on these evenings, but only once when he wore a white tie. In that instance the night was very rough until we got the chain on the wrists of his man. I had at least two holes in a new silk hat, and I cursed and Bencolin laughed, until finally we handed the noisy gentleman over to the gendarmes. On the night in October which begins this chronicle, therefore, I listened with what my brethren call mixed feelings when Bencolin telephoned to suggest an outing. I said, "Formal or informal?" He replied that it was to be very informal, which was reassuring.

We had followed the pink lights of the boulevards out to that garish, grimy, roaring section round the Porte St.-Martin where brothels abound and somebody always seems to be digging up the street. At midnight we were in a night club, basement level, with considerable drinking ahead of us. Among foreigners, particularly my own countrymen, there is a persistent belief that the French do not get drunk. This hilariously funny statement, I remember, was being discussed by Bencolin as we crowded in at a corner table and shouted our order for brandy above the din.

It was very hot in here, though electric fans tore blotches and rifts in the smoke. A blue spotlight played over the tangled shadows of dancers in darkness; it made ghastly a rouged face which appeared, dipped, and then was swallowed by the heaving mass. Moving in rhythm with a long-drawn bray and thud, the orchestra pounded slowly through a tango—that music which rips the bowels from a concertina and then sinks to a whisper of brass. Another brassy cry of horns, another rise, stamp, and fall, and the murmuring dancers swished in time, their shadows reeling on the blue-lit walls. Shopgirls and their escorts yielded to it with closed eyes, for the tango, of all dances, has the most wild and passionate beat. I watched the strained faces appearing and going, as faces swept by a black wave, under a light now turned green; and some looked drunk, and all looked weird and nightmarish; and, through lulls in the uproar, when the accordion-wail broke, you could hear the small, spiteful whir of the fans.

"But why this place in particular?" I asked. With a flourish and a clink of saucers, the waiter had whirled our drinks across the table.

Not raising his eyes, Bencolin said: "Don't look up now, but notice the man sitting two tables away from us in the corner. The one who is so obviously keeping his eyes away from me."

Presently I looked. It was too dark to see distinctly, but once the green edge of the spotlight picked out the face he indicated. The man had his arms around two girls, and was laughing between them. In the brief weird glare I saw the gleam of black brilliantined hair; I saw a heavy jaw, a crooked nose, and eyes which looked fixedly into the spotlight. It did not fit into this prosaic atmosphere, but I was at a loss to tell why. Seeing those eyes glare and turn away in the beam, it was curiously as though you had flashed a light into a dark corner, and a spider there had jumped and scuttled away. I thought I should recognize him again.

"Quarry?" I said.

Bencolin shook his head. "No. Not at present, anyhow. But we *are* waiting for an appointment here... Ah, there's our man! He's coming towards the table now. Finish your drink."

The figure he indicated was squirming through the ranks of tables, clearly bewildered at the surroundings. It was a little man with a big head and limp white whiskers. When the green light shone in his eyes he shut them, and tripped over one of the parties at a table. He was growing panicky and his eyes besought Bencolin. The detective motioned to me; we rose, and the little man followed us towards the back of the room. I shot a glance at the man with the crooked nose. He had dragged the head of one of the girls to his breast; he was rumpling her hair with one hand, absently, while he stared unwinkingly after us... Close by the orchestra plat-form, where the blare was deafening, Bencolin found a door.

We were in a low whitewashed passage, with an electric bulb burning murkily over our heads. The little man stood before us, his head partly on one side, his back bent, blinking up nervously. His red-rimmed eyes, which were pale blue, had an uncanny habit of seeming to grow round and then shrink, as with the beat of a pulse. His scraggly moustache and fan of white whiskers were much too large for the bony face; his cheek bones were shiny, but his bald head looked as though it had been covered with dust. Two tufts of white hair stuck up behind the ears. He wore a suit of rusty black, much too large for him, and he seemed nervous.

"I do not know what monsieur wants," he said, in a shrill voice. "But I am here. I have shut up my museum."

"This, Jeff," Bencolin told me, "is Monsieur Augustin. He is the owner of the oldest waxworks in Paris."

"The Musée Augustin," explained the little man. He tilted his head and stiffened unconsciously, as though he were posing before a camera. "I make all the figures myself. What! You have not heard of the Musée Augustin?"

He blinked at me anxiously, and I nodded, though I certainly had not. The Grévin, yes, but the Musée Augustin was a new one.

"Not so many people come as in the old days," said Augustin, shaking his head. "That is because I will not move down on the boulevards, and put up electric lights, and serve drinks. Pah!" He twisted his hat savagely. "What do they think? It is not Luna Park. It is a museum. It is *art*. I work as my father worked, for art. Great men complimented my father on his work—"

He was addressing me half defiantly, half beseechingly,

with gestures of earnestness, and twisting his hat again. Bencolin cut him short by leading the way down the corridor, where he opened another door.

At the table in the middle of a gaudy room, whose windows were muffled with shabby red draperies, and which was obviously used for assignation purposes, a young man jumped up at our entrance. Such places have a sickly atmosphere of small lusts and cheap perfume, and there comes to the mind a picture of endless meetings under a light with a dusty pink shade. The young man, who had been smoking cigarettes until the stale air was almost choking, looked incongruous here. He was tanned and wiry, with short dark hair, an eye which saw distances, and a military carriage. Even his short moustache had the curtness of a military command. During the time he had to wait, you sensed, he was nervous and at a loss; but now that something concrete had presented itself, his eyes narrowed; he became at ease.

"I must apologize," Bencolin was saying, "for using this place for a conference. Nevertheless, we shall have privacy... Let me present, Captain Chaumont, Monsieur Marle—an associate of mine—and Monsieur Augustin."

The young man bowed, unsmiling. He was apparently not quite accustomed to civilian clothes, and his hands moved up and down the sides of his coat. As he studied Augustin he nodded, with a grim expression.

"Good," he said. "This is the man, then?"

"I do not understand," Augustin announced. His moustache bristled; he drew himself up. "You act, Monsieur, as though I had been accused of some crime. I have a right to an explanation."

"Sit down, please," said Bencolin. We drew up chairs round the table over which burned the pink-shaded lamp, but Captain Chaumont remained standing, feeling along the left side of his coat as though for a sabre.

"Now, then," Bencolin continued, "I only wish to ask a few questions. You do not mind, M. Augustin?"

"Naturally not," the other answered, with dignity.

"You have been owner of the waxworks for a long time, I understand?"

"Forty-two years. This is the first time," said Augustin, his red-rimmed eye wandering to Chaumont and his voice growing quavery, "that the police have ever seen fit to—"

"But the number of people who visit your museum is not large?"

"I have told you why. I do not care. I work for my art alone."

"How many attendants do you have there?"

"Attendants?" Augustin's thoughts were jerked back on another tack; he blinked again. "Why, only my daughter. She sells tickets. I take them. All the work I do myself."

Bencolin was negligent, almost kindly, but the other man was staring straight at Augustin, and I thought I detected in those eyes which saw distances a quiet hatred, a deep hurt, and despair. Chaumont sat down.

"Aren't you going to ask him...?" the young man said, gripping his hands together fiercely.

"Yes," Bencolin answered. He took from his pocket a photograph. "M. Augustin, have you ever before seen this young lady?"

Bending over, I saw a remarkably pretty, rather vapid face looking out coquettishly from the picture: a girl of nineteen or twenty, with vivacity in the dark eyes, soft full lips, and a weak chin. In one corner was the imprint of Paris's most fashionable photographer. This was no midinette. Chaumont looked at the soft greys and blacks of the photograph as though they hurt his eyes. When Augustin had finished studying the picture, Chaumont reached out and turned it face down. He leaned into the yellow pool of light; the brown face, bitten and polished as though by sandstorms, was impassive, but a glow burnt behind his eyeballs.

"You will please think well," he said. "She was my *fiancée*."

"I do not know," said Augustin. His eyes were pinched. "I—You cannot expect me to…"

"Did you ever see her before?" Bencolin insisted.

"Monsieur, what is this?" demanded Augustin. "You all look at me as though I—What do you *want*? You ask me about that picture. The face is familiar. I have seen it somewhere, because I never forget. People who come into my museum I always study, to catch"—he spread out delicate hands—"to catch the expression—the shade—in living people—for my wax. Do you understand?"

Earnestly he regarded each of us, his fingers still moving as though the wax were under his hand. "But I do not know! Why am I here? What have I done? I harm nobody. I only want to be left alone."

"The girl in this photograph," Bencolin said, "is Mademoiselle Odette Duchêne. She was the daughter of the late Cabinet Minister. And now she is dead. She was last seen alive going into the Musée Augustin, and she did not come out."

After a long silence, while Augustin ran a shaky hand over his ridged face and pressed his eyeballs heavily, the old man said in a piteous tone:

"Monsieur, I have been a good man all my life. I do not know what you mean."

"She was murdered," Bencolin responded. "Her body was found floating in the Seine this afternoon."

Chaumont, looking fixedly across the room, supplemented: "Bruised. Beaten. And—she died of stab wounds."

Augustin regarded those two calm faces as though they were driving him back against a stone wall, slowly, with the prods of bayonets.

"You don't think," he muttered at last, "that *I*—?"

"If I did," said Chaumont, smiling suddenly, "I would strangle you. That is what we want to find out. But I understand that this is not the first time such a thing has occurred. Monsieur Bencolin tells me that six months ago another girl went into the Musée Augustin, and—"

"I was never questioned on that!"

"No," said Bencolin. "The place was only one of the spots she was known to have visited. We thought you, Monsieur, above suspicion. Besides, *that* girl was never found again. She may only have disappeared voluntarily. So many of these cases are like that."

In spite of his fear, Augustin forced himself to meet the detective's gaze calmly. "Why," he asked—"why is monsieur so certain she went into my museum and never came out?"

"I will answer that," Chaumont interposed. "I was engaged to Mademoiselle Duchêne. At present I am at home on a furlough. We became engaged a year ago, and I have not seen her since then. There has been a great change."

He hesitated.

"That does not concern you. Yesterday Mademoiselle Duchêne was to have tea at the Pavilion Dauphine with Mademoiselle Martel, a friend of hers, and myself. She had been behaving—oddly. At four o'clock she phoned me to say that she must break the appointment, giving no reason. I phoned Mademoiselle Martel, and found that she had received the same message. I felt that something was wrong. So I went immediately to Mademoiselle Duchêne's home.

"She was just driving away in a taxi when I arrived. I took another cab—and followed."

Chaumont drew himself up stiffly. Rigid muscles had tightened down his cheek bones. "I see no reason to defend my actions. A *fiancé* has his rights... I grew particularly interested when I saw her coming to this district. It is not good for young girls to be here, daytime or not. She dismissed the taxi in front of the Musée Augustin. It puzzled me because I had never known her to be interested in waxworks. I debated with myself whether to follow her in; I have my pride."

Here was a man who never exploded. Here was a man who was growing into that austere mould which old France fashioned for her soldiers who were also gentlemen. He looked at us in turn with an opaque stare which defied comment.

"I saw on the signboard that the place closed at five. It was only half an hour. I waited. When the museum closed, and she had not come out, I supposed she had gone by another entrance. Besides, I was—angry—at having been made to stand in the street all that time—without result." His head bent forward, and he looked up at Augustin with brooding steadiness. "I learned today, when she had not come home, and I went to investigate, that the museum has no other entrance. *Well?*"

Augustin edged his chair back.

"But there is!" he insisted. "There is another entrance."

"Not for the public, I think," Bencolin put in.

"No... no, of course not! It goes out on a side-street; it communicates with the back walls of the museum, behind the figures, where I go to arrange the lights. It is private. But monsieur said—!"

"And it is always kept locked," Bencolin went on, musingly.

The old man threw out his arms with a sort of witless cry.

"Well? What do you want of me? Say something! Are you trying to arrest me for murder?"

"No," said Bencolin. "We want a look at your museum, for one thing. And we still want to know whether you have ever seen that girl."

Rising shakily, Augustin put his withered hands on the table and leaned almost in Bencolin's face. His eyes were enlarging and shrinking in that queer, almost horrible illusion.

"Then," he said, "the answer is yes. Yes! Because there have been things going on in that museum, and I do not understand them. I have wondered whether I am going mad." His head bobbed as though he were lowering it to butt forward, like a goat.

"Sit down," suggested Bencolin. "Sit down and tell us about it."

Chaumont reached across and pushed the old man gently into his chair. The latter sat there nodding for a moment, tapping with his finger against a bearded lip.

"I do not know whether you can appreciate what I mean," he told us, presently. The voice was eager and shrill. You felt he had long wished for a confidant. "The purpose, the illusion, the spirit of a waxworks. It is an atmosphere of death. It is soundless and motionless. It is walled off by stone grottos, like a dream, from the light of day; its noises are echoes, and it is filled with a dull green illumination, as though it were in the depths under the sea. Do you see? All things are turned dead, in attitudes of horror, or sublimity. In my caverns are real scenes from the past. Marat is stabbed in his bath. Louis XVI lies with his head under the guillotine knife. Bonaparte dies, white-faced, in the bed of his little brown room at St. Helena, with the storm outside and the servant drowsing in the chair..."

The little man was speaking as though to himself, but he plucked at Bencolin's sleeve.

"And—do you see?—this silence, this motionless host in the twilight, is my world. I think it is like death, exactly, because death may consist of people frozen forever in the positions they had when they died. But this is the only fancy I permit myself. I do not fancy that they *live*. Many a night I have walked among my figures, and stepped across the railings, and stood in the midst of them. I have watched Bonaparte's dead face, imagining that I was standing actually in the room of his death; and so strong was my fancy that I could see the night light quivering, and hear the wind, and the rattle in his throat…"

"This is damned nonsense!" Chaumont snapped.

"No…let me go on!" Augustin insisted, piteously, in his queer far-away voice. "Messieurs, I would feel weak after a thing like that; I would bathe my eyes and shiver. But, you understand, I never really believed that my figures really lived. If one of them ever moved"—his voice rose shrilly—"if one of them ever moved under my eyes, I think I should go mad."

That was the thing he feared. Chaumont made an impatient gesture once more, but Bencolin silenced him. The detective, bearded chin in his hand and eyes heavy-lidded, watched Augustin with growing interest.

"You have laughed at people in the waxworks," the old man rushed on, "when they accosted wax figures and thought they were real?" He looked at Bencolin, who nodded. "You have also seen them when they thought some real person, standing about motionless, was made of wax; and you have seen them jump and cry out when the real person moved?—Well, in my Gallery of Horrors there is a figure of Madame Louchard, the axe-killer. You have heard of her?"

"I sent her to the guillotine," Bencolin answered, briefly.

"Ah! You understand, Monsieur," Augustin said, with some anxiety, "some of my figures are old friends. I can talk to them. I love them. But that Madame Louchard... I could do nothing with her, even when I was modelling her. I saw deviltry shape itself into the wax under my fingers. It was a masterpiece. But she scared me." He shuddered. "She stands in the Gallery, very demure, very pretty, with her hands folded. Almost she seems a bride, with her fur neckpiece and her little brown hat.

"And one night, months ago, when I was closing up, I could have sworn I saw Madame Louchard, in her fur neckpiece and her little brown hat, walking along the green-lit Gallery..."

Chaumont struck the table a blow with his fist. He said, despairingly:

"Let us go. The man's mad."

"But, no; it was an illusion... There she stood, in her usual place. Monsieur," Augustin told Chaumont, looking at him steadily, "you had better listen, because this concerns you. Mademoiselle who disappeared, you say, was your *fiancée*. Good!... You ask me why I remember this *fiancée* of yours. I will tell you.

"She came in yesterday, about half an hour before closing-time. There were only two or three people in the main hall, and I noticed her. I was standing over near the doorway which leads down into the cellars—where I have the Gallery of Horrors—and at first she seemed to think I was made of wax, and looked at me curiously. A beautiful girl. *Chic*. Then she asked me, 'Where is the satyr?'"

"What the devil," rasped Chaumont, "did she mean by that?"

"One of the figures in the Gallery. But listen!" Augustin leaned forward again. His white moustache and whiskers, his shining bony face, his pale-blue eyes, all quivered with earnestness. "She thanked me. When she had started downstairs, I thought I would go up to the front and see how near it was to closing-time. Just as I went, I looked behind me. I looked down the stairs…

"The greenish, very dim light was shining on the rough stones of the walls on either side the staircase. Mademoiselle was almost at the turn; I could hear her footsteps and see her picking her way carefully. And then I could have sworn I saw another figure on the staircase, following her down in silence. I thought it was the figure of Madame Louchard, the dead axe-killer from my Gallery, for I could see her fur neckpiece and her little brown hat."

2

THE GREEN LIGHTS OF MURDER

THE DRY, SHRILL, SING-SONG VOICE STOPPED. CHAUMONT folded his arms.

"You are either a thoroughgoing rascal," he said, crisply, "or else you really are mad."

"Softly!" interposed Bencolin. "It is more likely, Monsieur Augustin, that you saw a real woman. Did you investigate?"

"I was—frightened," the old man answered. He looked miserable and on the point of tears. "But I knew nobody like that had been in the museum all day. I was too terrified to go and look that figure in the face; I thought I might—see—a wax face, and glass eyes. So I went up and asked my daughter, who was on duty at the door, whether she had sold a ticket to anybody answering the description of Madame Louchard. She had not. I knew it."

"What did you do then?"

"I went to my rooms and drank some brandy. I am subject to chills. I did not leave them until after closing-time…"

"You were not, then, taking tickets that day?"

"There were so few people, Monsieur!" the old man

responded, snuffling. He went on in a dull voice: "That is the first time I have mentioned the matter. And you tell me I am mad. Perhaps. I don't know."

He put his head down in his hands.

After a time Bencolin rose, pulling on a soft dark hat which shaded his long, narrow, inscrutable eyes. The furrows were deep from his nostrils down past his bearded mouth. He said:

"Let us start for the museum."

We guided Augustin, who seemed half blind, out again into the din of the café, where the tango music burst forth again with an almost unnerving shock. My mind went back to that first man whom Bencolin had pointed out here, the man with the crooked nose and the queer eyes. He sat in the same corner, a cigarette glowing with pale fire in his fingers; but he sat with the rigidity and glassy stare of a drunken man. His companions had deserted him. He contemplated a large pile of saucers on the table, and he smiled.

When we mounted the stairs to the street the garishness of the square was somewhat dimmed. The great stone arch of the Porte St.-Martin rose up black against sharp autumn stars; a wind rasped at the tattered brown raiment of trees, and pushed dead leaves on the pavement with a scratching sound as of small nervous feet. A few café windows were alight, against which you could see the shadows of waiters stacking chairs. Two policemen, in gloomy conference on the corner, saluted Bencolin as we crossed the Boulevard St.-Denis and turned down the Boulevard de Sebastopol to the right. We saw nobody. But I had a feeling that we were watched from doorways, that people were pressing back against the walls, and that behind the tiny chinks of light from closed shutters, a subdued and stealthy activity paused, momentarily, as we went by.

The rue St.-Appoline is a short and narrow street, its blinds drawn furtively. A noisy bar and dance-hall bangs away at the corner, with shadows whisking past its murky curtains; but beyond it no gleam showed save a lighted red numeral, 25, on the left. Directly opposite this we stopped before a high doorway with twisted stone pillars and doors bound in iron. A begrimed sign, gilt lettering almost illegible, read: "Musée Augustin, *Collection of Wonders. Founded by J. Augustin, 1862. Open 11 a.m. to 5 p.m.—8 p.m. to 12 p.m.*"

In response to Augustin's ring, the doors were opened in a clanking of bolts. We stood in a small vestibule, apparently open to the public during the day. It was illuminated by a number of dusty electric bulbs, set into the ceiling to form the letter A. On the walls more gilt lettering testified to the extraordinary quality of the *horrors* to be found within— appealing to that love of the gruesome inherent in the French soul—no less than the educational value of seeing the Spanish Inquisition practising *torture*, the Christian martyrs thrown to the *lions*, and a number of celebrated people *stabbed, shot*, or *strangled*. The naïveté of these announcements did not lessen their allure. The man must be dead and buriable who does not respond to a healthy curiosity about things morbid. Of all our company, I noticed, the sober and common-sense Chaumont seemed to look at these announcements with the most appreciative glance. His dark eyes took in every word when he thought we were not watching him.

But I was looking at the girl who had let us in. This must be Augustin's daughter, but she did not resemble her father in the least. Her brown hair, which she wore in a long bob, was pulled behind her ears; she had heavy eyebrows, a straight nose, and brown-black eyes of such a snapping, electrical, probing quality of watchfulness that they seemed to start out from her head. They ran over her father as though she were surprised he had not been run down and hurt by a car in the street.

"Ah, Papa!" she said, in a quick voice. "These are the police, eh? Well, we have closed up and lost business for you, Messieurs." She frowned on us. "Now I hope you will tell us what you want. I hope you have not listened to Papa's nonsense?"

"Now, my dear, *now!*" Augustin protested, soothingly. "You will please go in and put on all the lights in the museum—"

She interrupted in a brusque voice: "No, Papa. You do that. I want to talk to them." Then she folded her arms, looking at him steadily until he nodded, smiled in a foolish way, and went to open the glass doors at the back. Then she went on: "Step this way, if you please, Messieurs. Papa will call you."

She led us through a door at the right of the ticket-booth, communicating with living-quarters. It was a sitting-room, dingily lighted, running chiefly to lace, tassels, gimcrack ornaments, and an odour of boiled potatoes. There she took up her position behind a table, still with folded arms. On the table lay a roll of light blue tickets, obviously for the museum.

"He is much of a child," she explained, nodding towards the museum. "Speak to *me.*"

Bencolin told her the facts briefly. He did not mention what Augustin had told us; he spoke in an almost careless manner, conveying that neither the girl nor her father could have had anything to do with the disappearance. But, studying Mlle. Augustin, I realized that this was the very thing which made her suspicious. She regarded Bencolin's heavy-lidded eyes, wandering about the room absently, with a fixed look which became somewhat glassy. I thought that her breathing grew a trifle quicker.

"Did my father—comment on this?" she demanded, when he had finished.

"Only to say," Bencolin answered, "that he did not see her leave."

"That is correct." The fingers of the girl's folded arms tightened round her biceps. "But *I* did."

"You saw her leave?"

"Yes."

Again I saw that play of muscles along Chaumont's thin jaws. He said: "Mademoiselle, I dislike to contradict a woman, but you are mistaken. I was outside the whole time."

She looked at Chaumont as though she were noticing him for the first time. She looked him up and down, slowly, but the battering of his eyes did not move.

"Ah! And how long did you remain, Monsieur?"

"Until at least fifteen minutes after closing-time."

"Ah!" the girl repeated. "That accounts for it, then. She stayed to chat with me on her way out. I let her out after the doors were closed."

Chaumont clenched his hands in the air, as though he were faced with a glass wall behind which this woman, unassailable, stared back, unwinking.

"Well, in that case, our difficulties are solved," murmured Bencolin, smiling. "You chatted with her for fifteen minutes, Mademoiselle?"

"Yes."

"Of course. There is just one point we of the police are not certain of," Bencolin said, wrinkling up his forehead. "We believe some clothes are missing. How was she dressed when you spoke to her?"

A hesitation. "I did not notice," Mlle. Augustin replied, quietly.

"Well, then," cried Chaumont squaring himself, "tell us what she looked like! Can you do that?"

"An ordinary type. It would fit many."

"Light or dark?"

Another hesitation. "Dark," she said, rapidly. "Brown eyes. Large mouth. Small figure."

"Mademoiselle Duchêne was dark. But she was fairly tall, and she had blue eyes. God in heaven!" snapped Chaumont, clenching his hands again. "*Why* won't you tell the truth?"

"I have told the truth. I may have been mistaken. Monsieur must realize that many people go through here in a day, and I had no special reason to remember this one. I must have been confused. My statement remains: I let her out of here and I have not seen her since."

Old Augustin came in at that moment. He saw the frozen tension in his daughter's face, and spoke hurriedly:

"I have put the lights on, Messieurs. If you want to make extensive examinations, you must use lamps; the place is never bright. But proceed. I have nothing to hide."

Bencolin halted in an irresolute manner as he was turning towards the door. At that moment Augustin's elbow brushed the shade of the lamp, knocking it sideways so that a strong yellow light ran up the detective's face. It emphasized the high cheek bones, the moody eyes with their hooked brows drawn down, running restlessly about the room...

"This neighbourhood!" he muttered. "This neighbourhood! Have you a telephone here, Monsieur Augustin?"

"In my den, Monsieur; my workroom. I will take you to it."

"Yes, yes. I want it immediately. But one thing more. I think you told us, my friend, that when Mademoiselle Duchêne first entered the museum yesterday she asked you a curious question—'Where is the satyr?' What did she mean by that?"

Augustin looked slightly hurt.

"Monsieur has never heard," he asked, "of the Satyr of the Seine?"

"Never."

"It is one of my finest efforts. A purely imaginative conception, you understand," Augustin hastened to explain. "It deals with one of the popular Parisian bogies, a sort of man-monster who lives in the river and draws down women to their death. I believe it has some foundation in fact. There are records here, if you care to examine them?"

"I see. And where is the figure?"

"At the entrance to the Gallery of Horrors, near the foot of the stairs. I have been highly complimented—"

"Show me the telephone. If you care to look around the museum," he told the rest of us, "I will join you there shortly. Now, if you please."

Mlle. Augustin sat down in an old rocking-chair beside the lamp and took a work-basket from the table. Her bright black eyes fixed on a needle she was threading, she said, coldly:

"You know the way, Messieurs. Do not let me disturb you."

She began to rock energetically and to work on a purple-striped shirt with the needle, pushing the bobbed hair behind her ears, settling herself with an expression of outraged domesticity. But she watched us.

Chaumont and I went out into the vestibule. He took out his case and offered me a cigarette; we studied each other while we were lighting them. The place seemed to confine Chaumont like a coffin. He had pulled his hat down on his brows, and his nervous eye roved, seeking an enemy.

He said, suddenly, "You are married?"

"No."

"Engaged?"

"Yes."

"Ah! Then you can understand"—a fierce gesture—"what this means. I am not myself. You must excuse me if I am upset. Ever since I saw that body…! Let's go in."

The very quiet of the place made me shiver. It smelt damp; it smelt—I can only describe it this way—of clothes and hair. We were in an immense grotto, running back nearly eighty feet, and supported by pillars of grotesque fretwork in stone. It swam in a greenish twilight, emanating from some source I could not trace; like greenish water, it distorted and made spectral each outline, so that arches and pillars seemed to waver and change like the toy caverns inside a goldfish bowl. They appeared to trail, slowly, green tentacles, and to be crusted with iridescent slime.

But it was the motionless assemblage here which filled one with dread. A policeman stood stiffly at my elbow; you would have sworn he was a real policeman until you spoke to him. Along the walls on either side, behind railings, figures looked out. They stared straight ahead, as though (I could not help the fancy) as though they were aware of our presence and were deliberately keeping their eyes from us. A little yellowish light made them stand out in the green gloom. Doumergue, Mussolini, the Prince of Wales, King Alfonso, Hoover; then the idols of sport, of stage and screen, all familiar and fashioned with uncanny skill. But these, you felt, were only a reception committee—a sort of gesture at respectability and everyday life—to prepare you for what lay behind. I started a little at seeing, on a bench down the middle of the grotto, a woman sitting motionless, and near her a man huddled in a corner as though he were drunk; I started, with a knock at my heart, until I realized that these also were wax.

My footsteps echoed as I walked down the vault hesitantly.

I passed within a foot of that figure slumped back against the bench, straw hat over its eyes, and I felt an almost overpowering impulse to touch it, for assurance that it could not speak. To be watched from behind by glass eyes is quite as bad as being watched from behind by real ones. I heard Chaumont wandering about; when I glanced over my shoulder, I saw him contemplating dubiously the drunken figure on the bench...

The grotto opened into a rotunda which was almost completely dark but for the faintest of glows round its models. Over the archway a hideous grinning face looked down at me. It was a jester leaning over as though to touch me with his bauble, and winking. My footsteps caused the bells of his motley to tremble, jingling, ever so slightly. Here in the dark rotunda echoes assumed a dead and empty heaviness; the smell of dust and clothes and hair was more pronounced; and the wax figures took on a more lurid unearthliness. D'Artagnan preened, hand on his rapier. A giant in black armour, axe uplifted, glimmered from the shadows. Then I saw another archway, dimly lighted in green, with a flight of stairs going down between stone walls to the Gallery of Horrors...

The mere inscription of it, above the archway, caused me to hesitate. The word was definite; you knew what to expect, and, like all starkly definite things, I did not know whether I wanted to face it. That staircase suggested walls pressing you in with the terrors, so that you might not be able to escape. Here before the stairs, I remembered, old Augustin had seen Odette Duchêne going down, and he thought he had seen moving after her that horrible phantom without a face, the woman with the fur neckpiece and the little brown hat... It was much colder, descending the steps, and the footfalls had flat mocking reverberations which rushed ahead as though somebody were jumping down the treads ahead of me. Suddenly I felt alone. I wanted to turn back.

The staircase turned sharply. Against the rough and green-lit wall a shadow rose up, and my heart thumped in my chest. A man with humped shoulders, his face shaded by a mediae-val hood, but with a long jaw which carried a suggestion of a smile—this gaunt model crouched against the wall. In his arms, partly covered by the cloak, was the figure of a woman; an ordinary man, except that in place of an outthrust foot he had a cloven hoof. *The satyr!* An ordinary man, except that the artisan had caught with subtle genius a suggestion of the foul and the unholy, of gaunt ribs and smiling jaw. It was as well that the eyes were shaded...

I hurried past the leprous thing, down the tortuous corridor to where it opened into another rotunda on a lower level. Here were groups of figures in scenes, each in its compartment, each a masterpiece of devilish artistry. The past drew breath. A pallor was on each, as though you saw it through veils, yet you saw behind it into its own time. Marat lay backwards out of his tin bath, his jaw fallen, the ribs starting through his bluish skin, a claw hand plucking at the knife in his bloody chest. You saw this; you saw the attendant woman seizing an impassive Charlotte Corday, and the red-capped soldiers, their mouths split with yelling, smash through the door; all the passion and terror cried soundlessly there. But behind this brown room you saw the yellow September sun-light falling through the window, and the vines on the wall outside. Old Paris seethed again.

I heard the sound of something *dripping*...

Panic seized me. Staring round at all those other groups beneath their pallor—at the Inquisitors working with fire and pincers, at a king under the guillotine knife, and the fury of the soundless drums—I felt it as contrary to nature that they did *not* move. They were more ghastly, these shadowy people, than as though they had stepped forth in their coloured coats to speak.

It was not my fancy. Something was falling, drop by drop, slowly...

I hurried up the stairs in a tumult of echoes. I wanted light, and the knowledge of human presence in this choking stuffiness of wax and wigs. When I had reached the last turn of the stairs I tried to recover composure; I would not be frightened out of my wits by a lot of dummies. It was ridiculous. Bencolin and I would have a good laugh at it, over brandy and cigarettes, when we had left this evil place.

There they were, Bencolin and Augustin and Chaumont, just coming into the upper rotunda as I ascended. I steadied myself and called out. But something must have shown itself in my face, for they noticed it even in that dim light.

"What the devil ails you, Jeff?" the detective asked.

"Nothing," I said. My voice told them it was a lie. "I was— admiring the waxworks—down there. The Marat group. And I wanted to see the satyr. It's damned good, the whole expression of the satyr, and the woman in his arms—"

Augustin's head jerked on his neck.

"*What?*" he demanded. "What did you say?"

"I said, it's damned good: the satyr, and the woman in—"

Augustin said, like a man hypnotized: "You must be mad—yourself. There is no woman in the satyr's arms."

3

BLOOD IN THE PASSAGE

"There is a woman now," said Bencolin. "A real woman. And she is dead."

He held the beam of the big flashlight on the group, while we crowded about him.

The wax figure of the satyr was tilted slightly against the wall, there on its landing at the turn of the stairs. Its arms were curved and cupped in such a way that the small body of the woman had been laid there without overbalancing it. (These figures, I have since learned, are built up on a steel framework and can support a heavier weight than she.) Most of her weight was distributed on his right arm and against his chest; her head had been pushed inwards, partly under the arm, and the coarse black serge of his cloak had been pulled up to hide her cheek and the upper part of her body... Bencolin directed the beam of his light downwards. The satyr's leg, covered with coarse hair, and his cloven hoof also, were stained. Blood had gathered in a widening pool about the base.

"Lift her out of there," Bencolin said, briefly. "Be careful; don't break anything. Now!"

We eased out the light burden and straightened it on the stone landing. The body was still warm. Then Bencolin threw the light on her face. The eyes were brown and wide open, fixed in a stare of pain and horror and shock; the bloodless lips were drawn back; and the tight-fitting blue hat was disarranged. Slowly the light moved along her body...

At my elbow I heard heavy breathing. Chaumont said, in a voice he tried to make calm, "I know who that is."

"Well?" demanded Bencolin, not rising from his kneeling position with the flashlight.

"It's Claudine Martel. Odette's best friend. The girl we were to have tea with on the day Odette broke the appointment and... O, my God!" Chaumont cried, and beat his fist against the wall. "Another one!"

"Another daughter," Bencolin said, speculatively, "of an ex-Cabinet Minister. The Comte de Martel. That's the one, isn't it?"

He glanced up at Chaumont, apparently calm; but a nerve twitched beside his cheek bone, and Bencolin's face was as evil as the satyr's.

"That's the one." Chaumont nodded. "How—how did she die?"

"Stabbed through the back." Bencolin lifted the body sideways, so that we could see the blotch on the left side of the light-blue coat she wore. "It must have pierced the heart. A bullet wound would not make so much blood... Ah, but there'll be the devil to pay for this! Let's see. No signs of a struggle. The dress isn't disarranged. Nothing at all—except this."

He indicated a thin gold chain about the girl's neck. On it she had apparently worn a pendant of some sort, and kept it inside the bosom of her frock; but its ends had been snapped off, and the pendant, whatever it had been, was gone. A part of the chain had been caught under the collar of the coat, so that it had been prevented from falling.

"No…certainly not a struggle," the detective was muttering. "Arms limp, fingers unclenched; a swift, sure blow, straight to the heart. Now where is her handbag? Damnation! I want her handbag!—they all carry one. Where is it?"

He flashed his light about impatiently, and it chanced to flash across Augustin's face. The old man, who was huddled up in a grotesque way, plucking at the satyr's serge robe, cried out as the beam struck his eyes.

"Now you are going to arrest me!" he shrilled. "And I had nothing to do with this! I—"

"Oh, shut up!" said Bencolin. "No, wait. Stand out here. This girl, my friend, has been dead less than two hours. At what time did you close up here?"

"Shortly before eleven-thirty, monsieur. Just after I received monsieur's summons."

"And did you come down here before closing up?"

"I always do, monsieur. Some of the lights are not turned off at the main switches upstairs; I must attend to a number of them."

"But there was no body here then?"

"No! Nothing!"

Bencolin looked at his watch. "Twelve forty-five. A little over an hour since you were down here, say. I gather that this girl could not have gained admission through the front door?"

"Impossible, monsieur! My daughter would open it to nobody but me. We have a special ring as a signal. But you can ask her…"

The flashlight's beam shifted across the floor of the landing; it moved along the base of the wall and up the wall itself.

The figure of the satyr stood with its back to the extreme rear wall of the museum—that is to say, parallel with the front—so that one turning the bend in the staircase saw it sideways. At the junction of this wall with the one which followed the steps downward again, Bencolin's light halted. A dim green bulb was placed in this corner so as to illumine the side of the satyr's hood cunningly; it did not reveal any difference in the stone of the wall, but the bright flash-lamp showed that a portion of the wall was wood painted to resemble stone.

"I see," muttered the detective. "And that, I suppose, is the other entrance to the museum?"

"Yes, monsieur! There is a narrow passage which goes down to the Chamber of Horrors behind these walls, where I can get at the hidden lights from the inside. Then there is another door, beyond it…"

Bencolin turned sharply. "Leading where?"

"Why—why, to a sort of covered passage going to the Boulevard de Sebastopol. But I never open the door to *that* passage. It is always locked."

Slowly the beam moved from the foot of the wooden door to the base of the statue. It was starred in a crooked trail with splashes of blood. Stepping carefully to avoid them, Bencolin approached the wall and pushed it. A section of the dummy stonework swung inwards. I was close behind him, and I saw that it concealed a stuffy cubbyhole, with a flight of stairs going down towards the Chamber of Horrors, and, parallel with the dummy woodwork, another heavy door. On my sleeve I felt Augustin's trembling fingers while Bencolin examined with his light the lock of this outer door.

"A Yale lock," he said. "And the latch isn't caught. This door has been used tonight, anyhow."

"You mean it's open?" Augustin cried.

"Stand back!" Bencolin said, irritably. "There may be footprints in this dust." He whipped a handkerchief out of his pocket, twisted it round his fingers, and turned the knob of the outer door.

We were in a low stone passage, still parallel with the back of the museum. It was apparently a sort of alleyway between this house and the one next door; some forgotten builder had roofed it over with tin and wooden supports, so that it was not more than seven or eight feet high. Of the house next door we could see only a blank brick wall, and, far down to the left, a heavy door without a knob. The left-hand end of the passage terminated also in a brick wall. But towards the right of the dark tunnel we could see a little light filtering in from the street; we could hear a swish of tyres and a dim honking of traffic.

In the middle of the damp flagstones, directly in the path of Bencolin's light, lay a woman's white wash-leather handbag, its contents scattered. I remember how the figured black design on that bag stood out against the white, and the silver catch glimmered. Over against the brick wall opposite, its elastic band torn from one side, lay a black domino mask. The flagstones at the foot of the wall were splattered with blood.

Bencolin drew a long breath. He turned to Augustin.

"And what do you know of *this*?"

"Nothing, monsieur! I have lived in my house for forty years and I have not been through this door a dozen times. The key—I do not even know where the key is!"

The detective smiled sourly. "And yet the lock is fairly new. And the hinges of the door are oiled. Never mind!"

I followed him down to the entrance which led to the street. Yes, the stone-flagged passage had a door, too. But it was open, entirely back against the wall. Bencolin let out a low whistle.

"Here, Jeff," he told me, softly, "is a real lock. A spring lock, but the burglar-proof variety known as the Bulldog. It can't be picked in any way. And yet it's standing open! Damn it!—I wonder..." His eyes roved. "When this door is shut, the passage must be completely black. I wonder if there's a light? Ah, here we are!"

Indicating a small, almost invisible button, at a height of about six feet in the brick wall, he pressed it. A soft illumination from up among the wooden supports glowed through the dingy passage. He let out an exclamation, and instantly shut it off.

"What's the matter?" I demanded. "Why not leave it on? You'll want to examine those things—"

"Be quiet!" He spoke swiftly, with a suppressed eagerness. "Jeff, for once in my career I have got to interfere with the nice procedure of the Sûreté. They would want to photograph and examine; they would comb this passage until dawn. And I must risk the consequences; I can't let them do it... Quick, now! Close this door." He eased it softly shut. "Now take your handkerchief and gather up that handbag and its contents. I must make a quick examination of the rest."

Ever since he had entered here he had been moving on tiptoe. I followed his example, while he bent at the wall just above where the floor was splashed with blood. He was muttering to himself as he began to scrape at the floor there, and brush upon an envelope something that glittered in the ray of the flash-lamp. Taking care that I overlooked nothing, I gathered up the handbag and its contents. A little gold compact, a lipstick, a handkerchief, several cards, a letter, an automobile key, an address-book, and notes and change of small denomination. Then Bencolin motioned me to follow him, and we went back through the museum door, through the dummy wall, and back to the platform of the satyr.

But the detective paused at the dummy wall, squinting up at the green light in the corner. He frowned in a puzzled way, and glanced back to the two doors; his eye seemed to be measuring.

"Yes," he said, half to himself, "yes. If this"—he tapped the section of the wall—"were closed, and the door to the passage were open, you could see that green light under the crack…" Swinging towards Augustin, he said, sharply: "Think well, my friend! Did you tell us that when you left the museum at eleven-thirty or thereabouts you turned off all the lights?"

"Certainly, monsieur!"

"*All* of them? You are sure, now?"

"I swear it."

Bencolin knocked his knuckles against his forehead. "There's something wrong. Very wrong. Those lights—that one, anyhow—must have been on. Captain Chaumont, what time is it?"

The change was so abrupt that Chaumont, who was sitting on the stairs with his chin in his hands, looked up dazedly.

"I beg your pardon?"

"I said, what time is it?" the detective repeated.

Puzzled, Chaumont took out a big gold watch. "It's nearly one o'clock," he answered, suddenly. "Why the devil do you want to know?"

"I don't," said Bencolin. The man struck me as being slightly out of his head, and therefore I knew he was closest on the track of a discovery. "Now, then," he went on, "we will leave Mademoiselle Martel's body here for the moment. Just one more look…"

He knelt again by the body. It had ceased to terrorize; with its vacant brown eyes, its disarranged hat, and its curious posture of comfort, it seemed less realistic than the wax figures. Picking up again the thin gold chain about the girl's neck, Bencolin studied it.

"It was a sharp yank," he said, illustrating with a tug at the chain. "The links are small, but they're strong, and they snapped completely."

As he rose to lead the way upstairs, Chaumont interposed:

"Are you going to leave her down here alone?"

"Why not?"

The young man passed a vague hand over his eyes. "I don't know," he said. "I suppose it won't hurt her. But she always had so many people around her—when she was alive. And the place is so dingy! That's what I loathe about it. It's so dingy. Do you mind if I stay down here with her?"

He hesitated, while Bencolin looked at him curiously. "You see," Chaumont explained, holding his face very rigid, "I can never look at her without thinking of Odette… O God!" he said, tonelessly, and then his voice broke, "I can't help it…!"

"Steady!" said Bencolin. "Come upstairs with us. You need a drink."

We went back up across the grotto, out by way of the vestibule, and into Augustin's living-quarters. The decisive creak of the rocking-chair slowed down as Mlle. Augustin looked at us, biting off a thread. She must have seen by the expression of our faces that we had found more than we looked for; besides, the leather handbag was rather conspicuous. Without a word Bencolin went in to the telephone, and Augustin, fumbling in one of the cupboards of the gloomy gimcrack room, brought out a squat bottle of brandy. His daughter's eye measured the large drink he poured out for Chaumont, and her lips tightened. But presently she continued to rock.

I felt uneasy. A clock ticked, and the strokes of the chair beat with squeaky savagery. I felt that I should associate that room forever with the smell of cooking potatoes. Mlle. Augustin asked no questions; her whole body was stiff and her fingers moved mechanically. The forces of some outburst were trembling and gathering round the blue-striped shirt she mended. Drinking a glass of brandy with Chaumont, I saw that his eyes were fixed on her, too... Several times her father started to speak, but we all remained silent and uncomfortable.

Bencolin returned to the room.

"Mademoiselle," he said, "I want to ask—"

"Marie!" her father broke out, in an agonized voice. "I couldn't tell you! It's murder. It's—"

"Please be quiet," said Bencolin. "I want to ask, mademoiselle, when you turned on the lights in the museum tonight?"

She did not spar by demanding to know what he meant. She put down the sewing with steady hands, and said, "Shortly after Papa had gone to see you."

"What lights did you put on?"

"I threw the switch which controls those in the centre of the main grotto and the staircase to the cellars."

"Why did you do this?"

She regarded him placidly, without interest. "It was a perfectly natural action. I thought I heard somebody moving about in the museum."

"You are not a nervous woman, I take it?"

"No." Not a smile, not a curl of the lip; though all nervousness, you knew, was with her a subject for contempt.

"Did you go to investigate?"

"I did…" As he continued to look at her with raised eyebrows, she went on: "I looked through the main grotto, where I thought I heard the noise, but there was nothing. I was mistaken."

"You did not go down the staircase?"

"I did not."

"How long did you keep the lights on?"

"I am not sure. Five minutes, possibly more. Now will you explain to me"—she spoke out very sharply, and half raised herself in the chair—"What is the meaning of this talk of murder?"

"A girl," Bencolin told her slowly, "a certain Mademoiselle Claudine Martel, has been murdered. Her body was placed in the arms of the satyr at the turn of the staircase…"

Old Augustin was plucking at Bencolin's sleeve. His bald head, with the two absurd tufts of white hair behind the ears, was cocked up at Bencolin like a dog's. The reddish eyes widened and shrank beseechingly.

"Please, monsieur! Please! She knows nothing of this—!"

"Old fool!" the girl snapped. "Stay out of this. I will handle them."

He subsided, stroking his white moustache and whiskers with an expression of pride in his daughter, but begging her forgiveness. Her eyes challenged Bencolin again.

"Well, mademoiselle? Is the name Claudine Martel familiar to you?"

"Monsieur, are you under the impression that I know the names, as well as the faces, of all the casual visitors to this place?"

Bencolin leaned forward. "What makes you think Mademoiselle Martel might have been a visitor of this place?"

"You say," the other responded, grimly, "that she is here."

"She was murdered in the passage, behind this house, communicating with the street," said Bencolin. "She probably never visited the museum in her life."

"Ah—Well, in that case," the girl shrugged, reaching for her sewing again, "the museum can be left out of it. Eh?"

Bencolin took out a cigar. He appeared to be considering this last remark of hers, a wrinkle between his brows. Marie Augustin applied herself again to the sewing, and she was smiling as though she had won a difficult passage at arms.

"Mademoiselle," the detective said, thoughtfully, "I am going to ask you, in a moment, to step out and look at the body in question… But my mind goes back to a conversation we had earlier this evening."

"Yes?"

"A conversation concerning Mademoiselle Odette Duchêne, the young lady we found murdered in the Seine."

Again she put down the sewing. "Ah, zut!" she cried, striking the table. "Is there never to be any peace? I have told you all I know about that."

"Captain Chaumont, if I remember correctly, asked you for a description of Mademoiselle Duchêne. Whether due to a faulty memory, or some other cause, your description was incorrect."

"I have told you! I must have been mistaken. I must have been thinking of something else—somebody else—"

Bencolin finished lighting his cigar and flourished the match.

"Ah, precisely! Precisely, mademoiselle! You were thinking of somebody else. I do not think you ever saw Mademoiselle Duchêne. You were called on suddenly for a description. So you took the risk; you spoke very rapidly, and obviously described somebody else who was in your mind. That is what causes me to wonder—"

"Well?"

"—to wonder," Bencolin went on, thoughtfully, "why that image was at the back of your brain in the first place. To wonder, in short, why you gave us so exact a description of Mademoiselle Claudine Martel."

4

HOW A CERTAIN MYTH CAME TO LIFE

BENCOLIN HAD SCORED. YOU COULD SEE IT IN THE slight droop of her lip, the holding of her breath, the fixed expression of her eyes, momentarily, while her agile brain sought for loopholes. Then she laughed.

"Why, monsieur, I don't follow you! The description I gave might have fitted anybody—"

"Ah! You admit, then, that you never saw Mademoiselle Duchêne?"

"I admit nothing!… As I was saying, my description would fit a thousand women—"

"Only one of whom lies dead here."

"—and the fact, the coincidence, that Mademoiselle Martel happens to look something like the person I described, is nothing more than a coincidence."

"Softly!" urged Bencolin, making an admonitory gesture with his cigar. "How do you know what Mademoiselle Martel looks like, mademoiselle? You haven't seen her yet."

Her face was red and angry. Not, you felt, because of any accusation against her, but because Bencolin had tripped her up. Anybody who was a little faster than she at verbal rapier-play would infuriate her. Again she tossed back the long bobbed hair from her ears, smoothing it behind them with savage jerks.

"Don't you think," she suggested, frigidly, "you have tried your shyster-lawyer's tricks on me long enough? I am through!"

Bencolin shook his head in a paternal fashion which irritated her the more. He beamed. "No, but, really, mademoiselle! There are other questions to be discussed. I cannot let you off so easily."

"As a policeman you have that privilege."

"Exactly. Well, then. I think we must admit, offhand, that the deaths of Odette Duchêne and Claudine Martel were connected—very closely connected. But now we come to a third lady, a more enigmatic figure than either one of them. She seems to haunt this place. I refer to a woman whose face nobody has seen, but who appears to wear a fur neckpiece and a brown hat. Tonight, in speaking of the matter, your father advanced an interesting theory…"

"O, Holy Mother," she snarled. "Have you been listening to that dotard's nonsense? Speak up, Papa! Did you tell them—all that?"

The old man straightened up with curious dignity. He said: "Marie, I am your father. I tried to tell them what I thought was the truth."

For the first time that night the cold common-sense whiteness of her face was warmed by an expression of tenderness; her black eyes grew pinched and filmed. Stepping over softly, she put her arm around his shoulders.

"Listen, papa," she murmured, searching his face; "listen.

You are tired. Go and lie down. Rest yourself. These gentlemen won't need to talk with you any longer. I can tell them what they want to know."

She shot a glance at us, and Bencolin nodded.

"Well," the old man said, hesitantly—"well—if you don't mind. It's been a great shock. A great shock. I don't know when I've been so upset…" He made a vague gesture. "Forty-two years," he continued, his voice rising, "forty-two years, and we have a name. A name means a lot to me. Yes…"

He smiled at us in an apologetic way. Then he turned and began to waver and grope his way towards the shadows of the room, his back stooped and his dusty head bobbing in the lamplight. Then he dissolved among the ghosts of antimacassars, among horsehair-stuffed chairs, and the dim pallor of a street lamp falling between thick curtains. Marie Augustin drew a deep breath.

"And now, monsieur?"

"You are still prepared to maintain that the woman in the brown hat is a myth?"

"Naturally. My father has—fancies."

"Your father, yes. There is one little point in connection with that I should like to mention. Your father spoke of his name; he is a proud man… Is the running of this waxworks a profitable business?"

She was wary now, feeling for the trap. She countered, slowly, "I see no connection."

"And yet there is. He has mentioned his poverty. I dare say you attend to the financial arrangements?"

"Yes."

Bencolin took the cigar out of his mouth. "Does he know, then, that at various banks in Paris you have on deposit sums totalling nearly a million francs?"

She did not reply. A dusky pallor crept up under her cheek bones, and her eyes grew enormous.

"Now, then," Bencolin said in his conversational tone, "have you anything to tell me?"

"Nothing." She spoke huskily, with an effort at flinging the word. "Except—you are a clever man. O, my God! but you are a clever man! I suppose you will tell him."

Bencolin shrugged. "Not necessarily. Ah! I think I hear my men."

Along the street outside swept the clangour of a bell on a Sûreté car. It ground to a stop outside and we heard the murmur of voices. Bencolin hurried out to the front door. Another car squealed in beside the first. I glanced at Chaumont's puzzled face.

"What the devil," Chaumont suddenly groaned, "is all this about? I can't understand any of it. What are we *doing*? What…" He seemed to remember that he was speaking before Marie Augustin, and subsided with a confused smile.

I turned to her. "Mademoiselle," I said, "the police are here, and they are likely to turn things upside down. If you want to retire, I am sure Bencolin will offer no objection."

She examined me gravely. With something of a shock I realized that, in the proper environment, she would be almost beautiful. If she relaxed her rigid carriage, her strong and supple body would be graceful; clothes and colour would set off her features and enhance the moody brilliance of her eyes. This I saw as a sort of spectre behind the girl in dowdy black. She saw it reflected in my face, so that for a moment we spoke together without a word being uttered. I did not know then how well that communion was to stand me in the near future, at a time of deadly danger. She nodded as though answering.

"You are a very ingenuous young man." It was the spectre speaking! A little smile twisted round the tight lips. I felt a sudden compression in my chest, as though the spectre were really taking form; our unspoken words echoed and replied. She went on: "I am inclined to like you. But I do not care to retire. I am interested in seeing what the police do."

Through the door we could see them tramping in: a sergeant in uniform, two quick-eyed men in slouch hats, the attendants with boxes and spindly camera-legs slung over their shoulders. I heard Bencolin giving directions. He came back into the room, accompanied by one of the slouch-hats.

"Inspector Durrand," he said, "is taking charge. I leave everything in his hands. You understand, Inspector, what I have told you—about the passage?"

"We will be careful," the other assented, briefly.

"And no photographs?"

"No photographs *there*. Understood."

"Now, about these things." Bencolin approached the table. On it lay the handbag with contents arranged in a line, together with the black domino mask we had seen on the floor of the passage. "You will want to look at them. As I told you, they were in the passage…"

The inspector's shrewd, clean-shaven face bent over the table. His fingers ran over the articles rapidly. He said: "The handbag belonged to the dead woman, I take it?"

"Yes. Her initials are on the clasp. I find nothing significant in the contents of the bag, except this."

Bencolin held out a small slip of paper, apparently torn hastily from the sheet of a writing-tablet. On it had been written a name and an address. The inspector whistled.

"By God!" he muttered. "Is *he* concerned in this? Ah, I see! The house next door… Shall I round him up?"

"Under no circumstances! I am going to interview him personally."

I heard a slight noise behind me. Marie Augustin had seized the back of the rocking-chair, which creaked suddenly.

"May I ask," she said in a clear voice, "whose name that is?"

"You may, mademoiselle." The inspector looked up sharply from under the brim of his hat. "The paper reads, 'Etienne Galant, 645 Avenue Montaigne. Telephone Elysée 11–73.' Is it familiar to you?"

"No."

Durrand seemed about to question her further, but Bencolin touched his arm. "The address-book contains nothing significant. Here is the key of a car, and her driver's licence. Also the car number. You might give the patrolman on this beat the number and see whether the car has been left in this neighbourhood…"

In response to Durrand's summons an *agent* came in and saluted. When he had received his instructions he hesitated.

"I have something to report, monsieur," he said, "which may bear on this matter." As both Bencolin and the inspector whirled on him, he grew flustered. "It may not be of importance, messieurs. But earlier in the evening I noticed a woman outside the door of the museum. I noticed her particularly because I passed her twice within ten minutes, and each time she was standing outside the door, as though trying to make up her mind to ring the bell. When she saw me she turned away; she seemed trying to make it appear that she was waiting for somebody…"

"The museum was closed?" demanded Bencolin.

"Yes, monsieur. I noted that. I was surprised, because ordinarily it stays open until twelve, and when I first passed it was barely twenty minutes of the hour… The woman also seemed puzzled."

"How long did she remain there?"

"I don't know, monsieur. The next time I passed it was well after twelve, and she had gone."

"Should you recognize this woman if you saw her again?"

The man frowned doubtfully. "Well—the light was very dim. But I think I should recognize her. Yes, I am almost positive."

"Good!" said Bencolin. "Accompany the rest of them back here and see whether it was the dead woman. Be careful about your identification, now! Wait! Did she seem—nervous?"

"Very nervous, monsieur."

Bencolin waved him out. He looked swiftly at Marie Augustin. "You heard or saw nobody outside here, mademoiselle?"

"Nobody!"

"The bell was not rung?"

"I have already told you it was not."

"All right, all right. Now, Inspector"—he picked up the black mask—"this was found near the bloodstains. As I reconstruct it, the girl must have been standing with her back to the brick wall of the house next door, in the passage, say about a foot and a half away from it. The murderer must have stood directly in front of her; judging by the way the blood spurted, he must have struck over her left shoulder and down beneath the shoulder blade. The direction of the wound will determine that. Now, this mask is very suggestive. You see that the elastic has been ripped out on one side, as though it had been torn off…"

"Torn off the murderer?"

Bencolin grunted. "Well, how do *you* explain it?"

Holding the white inside of the mask close under the lamp, Durrand let out an exclamation.

"The mask," he said, "was worn by a woman. Its lower edge would just touch the upper lip on a small face, and here is a red smudge of"—he scraped it with his finger nail—"yes, of lipstick. Faint, but you can see it."

Bencolin nodded. "Yes. It was worn by a woman. What else?"

"Wait! Suppose it had been worn by the dead woman?"

"I examined her carefully, Inspector. She wears no lipstick. But look further. The colour of the lipstick, you can see, is very dark. The woman was of fairly dark complexion: probably a brunette. Now examine the elastic." He snapped it out. "It is quite long, though, by the fact of an ordinary domino mask's reaching down to the upper lip, we know that the face was small. A small woman, then, wearing a mask with a very long elastic—?"

"Yes," said Durrand, nodding as the other paused interrogatively, "long and heavy hair, to be confined by that band."

Bencolin smiled and blew out a cloud of cigar smoke. "Therefore, Inspector, we get a brunette of small stature, using cosmetics freely, and wearing her hair piled up. That is all, I think, the mask can tell us. It is of a common variety, which may be bought at any shop."

"Anything else?"

"Only this." Taking an envelope from his pocket, Bencolin shook out on the table a few small bits of glass. "On the floor of the passage," he explained, "one minute particle clinging to the wall. I leave them for your consideration, Inspector; at present I have nothing to go on. I don't think you will find any footprints out there; or fingerprints, either, if I am any judge… Now I am taking Jeff and Captain Chaumont along to interview Monsieur Galant. Afterwards, if you want me, I shall be in my rooms; you can telephone at any time. For the present I have no instructions."

"I want the dead woman's address. We shall have to notify her relations that we are taking the body for an autopsy."

"Durrand," the other said, whimsically, and clapped him on the shoulder, "your common-sense bluntness is delightful. I am sure Mademoiselle Martel's father would appreciate having the news broken to him in that way. No, no. I—or Captain Chaumont here—will attend to that. But be sure to let me know about the surgeon's findings on that wound. I don't think you'll discover a weapon… Ah, here we are! Well?"

The policeman appeared again, his cap in his hands.

"I looked at the body, monsieur," he answered. "I am positive that the dead woman is not the one I saw outside the museum tonight."

Durrand and Bencolin exchanged glances. The latter asked:

"Can you give us any description of the one you saw?"

"It is hard." The man made gestures. "Nothing distinctive, you understand. I think she was well dressed. I think she was a blonde, about medium size…"

Durrand gave his hat a yank down on his head. "Great God!" he said. "How many women are there around here? We just finish getting a description of one—from the mask—and here we find a *blonde*! Anything else?"

"Why, yes, monsieur," the policeman replied, hesitating again. "I believe she wore a fur neckpiece and a little brown hat."

After a long pause, during which Chaumont put his hands to his head, Bencolin bowed politely to Mlle. Augustin.

"The myth," he said, "has come to life. I bid you good night, mademoiselle."

Bencolin, Chaumont, and I went out into the cool darkness of the street.

5

THE CLUB OF THE SILVER KEY

KNOWING BENCOLIN OF OLD, I KNEW THAT THE MERE fact of the time being past one in the morning would not prevent him from routing out any person he wanted to speak with; not out of a desire to hurry, but because night and day were the same to him. He took his sleep where he found it, when he did not forget it altogether. In any case which absorbed him, he neither noticed the hour nor allowed anybody else to notice it. So when we left the museum he said, briskly:

"If you care to accompany us, Captain, Jeff and I are on a most interesting errand. First, though, I suggest a cup of coffee. I want information. So far, Captain, you are the only one who can tell me…"

"Oh, I'll come," Chaumont assented, gloomily. "Anything to keep from going home and going to bed. That's what I can't face. I want to stay up all night." He looked round with vigour. "Lead on."

Bencolin's car was parked at the corner of the Boulevard Montmartre. Near it a late café yawned with a dingily lit window. The sidewalk tables had not yet been taken in, though the pale street was deserted and a wind rattled shrewdly at the awning. Bundled into our coats, we sat down at one of the tables. Far down the boulevard was that empty glimmer, that high nimbus which shimmers round Paris by night; distantly you could hear a singing drone of traffic, pierced by the flat quack of taxis. Dead leaves scurried in ghostly rustlings across the pavement. Nervousness had strung us all to a high pitch. When the waiter brought our glasses of hot coffee, laced with brandy, I gulped at mine greedily.

Chaumont had his coat collar turned up. He shivered.

"I'm getting tired," he said, with a sudden change of mood. "Who are we to see? This weather…"

"The man we are going to see is called Etienne Galant," Bencolin replied. "That is one of his names, anyhow. By the way, Jeff, you saw him tonight; he is the man I pointed out to you first in the night club. What did you think of him?"

I remembered. But the impression was almost lost in the welter of terrors which had swept over us since: I retained only a memory of green lights, horribly like those of the museum, playing over grotesque eyes and a crooked smile. "Etienne Galant, Avenue Montaigne." He lived on my own street, which is not occupied by those whose incomes are small. His name was known to Inspector Durrand; he seemed to have lurked over the evening, bogy fashion, from the first. I nodded.

"Who is he?"

Bencolin frowned. "Etienne Galant, Jeff, is a very, very dangerous man. Beyond that I am not prepared to say anything just yet, except that he is in some fashion connected with tonight's events." He pushed his coffee-glass back and forth on the table, his eyes a blank. "I know that both of you are impatient at this working in the dark; but I promise you that if we can find him at home you will understand a great deal about tonight. You may understand it all…"

He was silent a moment. A yellow leaf fluttered down under the bright lights of the awning, and trembled on the table. The cold wind crept round my ankles.

"There are Mademoiselle Martel's parents to be notified," Bencolin said, slowly.

"I know. I know. It's the devil. Do you think," Chaumont hesitated, "we'd better telephone…?"

"No. Better wait until morning. It's too late a story for tomorrow morning's newspapers, and they won't see it there. I know her father; I can spare you the duty, if you wish… It's incredible!" He spoke with great intensity. "Both girls of high family. Most people, yes. But those…"

"What are you hinting at?" Chaumont demanded.

"A trap," said Bencolin. "I don't know. My wits are fuddled. And yet I would stake my reputation that I have not misread the signs!… I want information. Talk, Captain!—tell me about these girls, about your *fiancée* and Claudine Martel."

"But what do you want to know?"

"Anything, everything! I'll pick out the important parts. Just talk."

Chaumont stared straight ahead. "Odette," he said, in a low, thick, tense voice, "was the loveliest…"

"Oh, damn it, I don't want that!" Bencolin so rarely lost his easy suavity, as he had lost it several times tonight, that I looked at him in surprise. He was almost biting his nails. "Spare me the lover's point of view, please. Tell me something about her. What was she like? Who were her friends?"

Faced with the necessity for a definite answer, Chaumont groped after words. He looked at the lights in the awning, at his glass, at the leaves; he seemed to be trying to call back images, and he was slightly bewildered.

"Why...why, she has the sweetest..." That, he decided, wouldn't do; and he checked himself, flushing. "She lives with her mother. Her mother's a widow. She liked the house, and the gardens, and singing—yes, she was very fond of singing! And she was afraid of spiders; she nearly had a fit when she saw them. And she reads a lot..."

He went on in bold and clumsy outline, mixing his past and present tenses, hurrying back into his memory with jumbled, pathetic eagerness. Little incidents—Odette cutting flowers in a bright garden, Odette sliding down a hayrick, laughing— emerged to show a good-humoured, naïve, and very happy girl. Behind his account of the solemn earnest love-affair, I saw the girl in the photograph: the lovely face, the cloudy dark hair, the small chin, the eyes which had looked at nothing save coloured picturebooks. Oh, yes! All monstrously earnest, these two; their plans, their letters, under the supervision of a mother who (I gathered from Chaumont's description) was quite a woman of the world.

"She liked my being a soldier," Chaumont told us, eagerly. "Though I'm not—much. After St.-Cyr I was sent out, and I saw some fighting against the Riffs; but then my family got uneasy. Pah! They had me transferred to the post at Morocco. White-flannel stuff! I'm not like that. But Odette was pleased, and so—"

"I see," Bencolin interposed, gently. "And her friends?"

"Well, she didn't go out much. She didn't like it," Chaumont asserted, with pride. "*That's* how she was! There used to be three girls they called the Inseparables, they were such good friends: Odette, and—and Claudine Martel..."

"Go on."

"And Gina Prévost. That was when they were in the convent. Nowadays they're not so close as they used to be. But—I don't know. I'm in Paris so seldom, and Odette never wrote much about where she went or whom she saw. She just—just talked. Do you see?"

"Then you don't know much about Mademoiselle Martel?"

"N-no. I never liked her much." He lifted his shoulders. "She had a quick, sarcastic way of talking, and she laughed at you. But she's dead, and Odette was fond of her. I don't know. I am so seldom here."

"I see. And this Mademoiselle Prévost, who is she?"

He was taking up his glass again, but he put it down in surprise. "Gina? Oh, just—well, a friend. She's around. She wanted to go on the stage, I understand, but her family wouldn't let her. She's good-looking, very, if you like the sort. Blonde, rather tall."

There was a silence. Bencolin drummed with his fingers on the table; once he nodded obscurely and his eyes were half closed.

"No," he said at length, "I suppose you are not the person to give us the most complete account of those two. Eh, well! If you are ready"—he tapped on his saucer with a coin to summon the waiter—"we can start."

Paris is unjustly blamed. Paris goes to bed early. The boulevards were grey and shuttered, deserted under a few mournful lights. Bencolin's big Voisin swept down into midtown, where the pale lamps of the Place de l'Opéra drowsed under electric signs; buildings were washed with bluish-grey under the sharp stars, and muffled auto horns called faintly. The trees of the Boulevard des Capucines looked ragged and sinister. We were all crowded into the front seat, where Bencolin drove in his usual detached manner, at his usual speed of fifty miles an hour, never seeming to be aware that he was driving at all. The cry of our horn caught up echoes along the rue Royale, and through an open windscreen the chill breeze against our faces smelt of wet pavements, of chestnut trees, and the turf of autumn. Threading that forest of white lamps which is the Place de la Concorde, we turned right up the Champs Elysées. The brief, violent ride flung us out of the dinginess round St.-Martin's Gate; we were in an atmosphere of sedate window-grills, of ordered trees and the decorum of the Avenue Montaigne.

Nearly every day I had passed number 645, for I lived only a few doors away. It was a high old house with a grey wall fronting the street, but those big brown-painted doors in the wall, with their polished brass knobs, never stood open. Bencolin pulled at the door-bell. Presently one of the doors was opened. I heard Bencolin exchanging swift words with somebody, and we entered, past a protesting voice, into a damp-smelling courtyard. The protesting voice, whose owner I could not see in the dark, followed us up the path. Light shone from the open door of the house. Then it was blocked by the protesting voice's owner, who was backing before us into the hallway.

"—but I tell you," said the man, "monsieur is not at home!"

"He will be," Bencolin said, pleasantly. "Stand out here, my friend; let me see if I know you."

A cut-glass globe of light depended from the ceiling, which was very lofty. It showed a very correct, very pale face, close-cut hair, and injured eyes. "Ah yes," Bencolin continued, after a moment's study. "I do know you. You are in our files. We will wait for Monsieur Galant."

The pale face squeezed its eyes almost shut. It said, "Very well, monsieur."

We were ushered into a room at the front of the house. It also was very lofty and of an ancient pattern, with gilded cornices worn almost black. The glow of a shaded lamp did not penetrate far into its depths, but I could see that the steel shutters were closed on the long windows. Though there was a bright wood fire burning, the place looked bleak; the very elaborateness of its grey-and-gilt carvings, its marble-and-gilt tables, its spindly chairs, made you feel that you would as soon try to be comfortable in a museum. Grotesquely, in one corner stood an enormous harp. Every piece of furniture was valuable, just as every piece of furniture was alien to use. I wondered what sort of man lived here.

"Sit down by the fire, messieurs," Bencolin suggested. "I do not think we shall have long to wait."

The servant had vanished. But he had left open the double-doors to the hallway, and I could see a dim glow beyond. I lowered myself gingerly on a brocaded chair near the fire, where I could look at that glow in the hall, and wonder what sort of footsteps we should hear. Somehow, I did not want to face the fire; I wanted to keep my eye on that door. But Bencolin had seated himself facing the blaze, fallen into a study, with his gaunt figure slumped and his chin in his hand. To the accompaniment of a stirring and crackling, with the occasional flaring pop of an ember, the red light washed his face weirdly. I heard Chaumont's restless footfalls up and down the hardwood floor. Rustling, brushing, a wind swished past the house, and I heard dimly the bell at the Invalides striking two…

There was no warning of it. I was watching through the gloom the dimly lit rectangle marking the doors to the hall, and a part of the outer door; I saw nobody enter the outer one, though I heard the faintest of clicks from a closing latch.

Suddenly a great white cat darted into the room. It whisked round and into the firelight, where it stopped, with a kind of inhuman squeal and snarl…

A man's shadow moved across the rectangle; a huge shadow, removing a top-hat and swinging a cloak from its shoulder. Footsteps, slow and jaunty, sounded on the hardwood.

"Good evening, Monsieur Galant," said Bencolin, without altering his position or taking his eyes from the fire. "I have been expecting you."

I rose as the man approached us, and Bencolin turned also. The newcomer was tall, very nearly as tall as Bencolin, and of a thickness of muscle which he moved with a curious fluid grace. That was your first impression of him: a grace like that of the white cat, whose unwinking yellow eyes stared up at me. In a swarthy manner he was very handsome; or he would have been handsome but for one thing. His nose was bent with an almost horrible crookedness, and it was of a slightly reddish tinge. Against the fine features, the strong line of the jaw, the high forehead, the thick black hair, the long yellow-grey eyes—against these, the crooked nose had grown like the proboscis of an animal. He smiled at all of us; it lit up his face affably, and the nose made it hideous.

But before speaking to us he leaned over and spoke to the cat. His eyes widened affectionately.

"Here, Mariette!" he said in a soft voice. "You must not spit at my guests. Here!"

His voice was cultured, with deep rollings; he could play on it, you sensed, as with the stops of an organ. Taking up the cat in his arms, folding it in the long cloak he had not yet removed, he sat down within range of the firelight. The eyelids drooped over his yellow-grey eyes, luminous, almost mesmeric. His fingers, which continued to stroke the head of the cat, were short, spatulate, and immensely strong. And the force of the man was intellectual as well as physical; you felt its power, you felt that he was coiling his muscles for a deadly spring, and you braced yourself as though to meet a charge with a knife.

"I am sorry," he said in his soft deep voice, "to have kept you waiting. It has been a long time, Monsieur Bencolin, since we have met. These are," he nodded towards us, "your associates?"

Bencolin introduced us. He was standing with his elbow on the mantelpiece, negligently. Galant turned first towards Chaumont and then towards me, nodding briefly. Afterwards he continued his scrutiny of the detective. Gradually an expression of smugness and complacence spread itself over his face like thin oil; he wrinkled the red grotesque nose and smiled.

"I saw you tonight," he went on, thoughtfully, "for the first time in several years. My friend Bencolin grows old; there is much grey in his hair. Nowadays, I could break you in pieces..."

He settled his vast shoulders under a very correct dinner jacket. His fingers tightened, playing softly with the neck of the cat, which continued to regard us with glassy yellow eyes. Suddenly he turned to me. "You are wondering, monsieur, about this." With the utmost delicacy he touched his nose. "Ah yes, you were! Ask Monsieur Bencolin about it. He is responsible."

"We fought once, with knives," Bencolin said, studying a design in the carpet. He did look old then; thin and drawn and leathery of skin, a tired Mephistopheles. "Monsieur Galant was pleased to think himself a master of the *apache's* art. I struck with the handle of the knife, instead of using its blade..."

Galant pinched his nose. "That," he said, "was twelve years ago. Since then I have perfected myself. There is no one in France who could—But we will let that go. Why are you here?" He laughed, loudly and not pleasantly. "Do you fancy that you have anything against me?"

It was, surprisingly enough, Chaumont who broke the long silence after this. He walked round a table into the firelight; he stood for a moment uncertainly, as though revolving suspicions, and then he said, with sudden vehemence:

"Look here...who the devil *are* you?"

"Well, that depends," said Galant. He was not astonished or irritated; he seemed to be musing. "In his poetic way, Monsieur Bencolin would say that I am lord of the jackals— king of the cockleshells—high priest of demonology..."

Chaumont stared at him, uncertainly still, and the other chuckled.

"Paris," he continued, "'the underworld'—what romances are committed in thy name! Monsieur Bencolin is at heart of the bourgeoisie. He has the soul of a three-franc novelist. He looks into a frowsy café, full of labourers and tourists, and he sees in these people creatures of the night, full of sin, drugs, and butchery. The underworld. Hé!—what an idea!"

Behind these words, uttered during many knowing quirks and chuckles, you could see a struggle. These men were old enemies. You could feel the hatred between them, as palpable as the heat of a fire; but also between them was a wall which Galant dared not break to fly at his foe. His words were as small vicious scratchings against that wall, like the claws of a cat...

"Captain Chaumont," said Bencolin, "wishes to know who you are. I will tell both of you a little. To begin with, you bore the title of doctor of letters. You were the only Frenchman ever to occupy a chair in English literature at Oxford."

"Well, well, that is admitted."

"But you were anti-social. You hated the world and your fellow men. Also, you found the remuneration too small for a man of really excellent family—"

"That, too, is admitted."

"Without any doubt, then," Bencolin said, thoughtfully, "we can trace this man's course by his own peculiar mentality. Here, we shall say, is a man of extreme brilliance, who has read books until his brain bursts with the weight of them; he is brooding, introspective, vicious of temper; he begins to look out upon what he considers a crooked world, wherein all moral values are hypocrisies. If a person has a reputation for honesty, that person must be the lowest of thieves. If a woman is reported virtuous, she must be a harlot. To feed this colossal hate of his—which is merely the hate of a misplaced idealist—he begins to root among the pasts of his friends, for he has the ear of what we call good society..."

All the bones in Galant's face seemed suddenly to have grown hard with wrath; when colour came into his face, it was confined to his nose, and the grotesque thing assumed a monstrous redness. But he sat motionless, his eyes open and fixed, stroking the cat softly.

"So," continued Bencolin, "he began, against this good society, a campaign. It was a sort of super-blackmail; let me call it a blackmail without honour. He had his files, his spies, his gigantic cross-indexed system, with every letter, photograph, hotel slip or its photostat copy, all carefully arranged, waiting for the proper moment. He waged war only against the highest names in the land; but he picked each small misstep out of the past, enlarged and touched it up, and then waited for his time. A woman about to be married, a candidate running for public office, a man just entering on a career of promise and honour... then he appeared. I do not think it was the money, especially. He drew fantastic sums from these people, but what he liked was to rip open reputations, smash idols, and have the power of saying: 'There, you who have achieved such eminence! This is how I can tear you down! You think you can reach the high places? *Try*!'"

Like a man hypnotized, Chaumont drew out a chair and sat down on its edge. He was staring at Galant as Bencolin's low voice went on:

"Do you understand, messieurs? It was the immense mirth of a man who shares his joke with the devil. Look at him now. He will deny what I say, but you can see the secret satisfaction in his face..."

Galant jerked up his head. It was not Bencolin's accusations which had caused this touch on an open nerve, but the fact that he knew this very expression, of hidden delight to be creeping round his mouth.

"But this was not all," Bencolin mused. "I spoke of blackmail without honour; there is such a thing. When he had bled his victim of everything, he still did not keep faith. He did not hand over the evidence after it had been paid for. He published it instead, as he had always intended to do. For his real purpose was to ruin somebody, so that the last bit of triumph could be extracted from the jest... Oh no! They could not prosecute him afterwards. He had covered himself too well; *he* never wrote to his victims, or threatened them except when the two were alone together, with no witnesses. But his reputation went round. That is why they do not receive him in the drawing-rooms any more, and why he has a bodyguard night and day."

"For what you are saying," Galant told him in a repressed voice, "I could take you into court and—"

Bencolin laughed, with a sort of tired savagery, and rapped with his knuckles on the mantelpiece. "But you won't! Don't I know, monsieur, that you are waiting to settle with me in another way?"

"Perhaps." Silkily pleasant, even yet!

"Now, why I am really here tonight," Bencolin resumed, with a slight gesture as though he were discussing a business deal, "is to inquire about the newest aspect of your business..."

"Ah!"

"Oh yes. I know about it. There has been opened, in a certain part of Paris, an institution unique of its kind. You are pleased to call it The Club of Coloured Masks. The idea, of course, is not new—there are places of the same nature— but *this* one has an elaborateness to which the others would not aspire. Membership in the club is restricted to those names in the very select Almanach de Gotha, and the dues are enormous. The names of the members are, theoretically, kept with the utmost secrecy."

Galant blinked a little. He had not suspected Bencolin knew this. But he shrugged.

"Now," he said, "I really think you are mad. What is the purpose of this club?"

"A social gathering of men and women. Women unhappy in marriage, women who are old, women looking for a thrill; men whose wives are a bore or a terror, men in search of adventure—these meet and mingle, the woman to find a man who pleases her, the man to seek out a woman who does not remind him of his wife. They cross in your great hall, which is dimly lighted and muffled with thick hangings—and they all wear masks. One may not know that the masked lady he sees, and who appeals to him, and who leads him for private speech into the corridors off your great hall—one may not know that this seductive charmer is the very dignified woman whose sedate dinner he attended the night before. They sit and drink, they listen to your hidden orchestra, then they vanish into the depths of their amours…"

"You say '*my*' great hall," Galant snapped, "*my* hidden orchestra—"

"I do. You own the place. Oh, not in your own name! It is, I believe, in the name of some woman. But you are the controlling element."

"Even so—I do not, of course, admit it—the place is perfectly legal. Why should it interest the police?"

"Why, yes, it is legal. It furnishes you with the best blackmail evidence you are ever likely to get, since the members do not know you are the proprietor. But if they insist on going there, I suppose it is their own lookout…" Bencolin bent forward. "However, I will tell you why it interests the police. In the passage leading to your club—a passage which is directly behind the waxworks known as the Musée Augustin—a woman named Claudine Martel was murdered tonight. Will you tell me, please, what you know about it?"

6

MADEMOISELLE ESTELLE

GALANT'S COUNTENANCE WAS BLURRED BEFORE MY eyes. I heard Chaumont's sudden gasp, and I saw him jump in the firelight, but his figure was like a ghost's. For I was looking at that narrow stone-flagged passage behind the museum. At its left end I saw that significant door without a knob; at the right, giving on the street, the door with the burglar-proof spring lock, which stood ajar. I remembered the push-button in the hall, which controlled soft lights there, and, lying beside bloodstains on the floor, a black mask with a torn elastic...

From a distance, as though it were booming down that very corridor, came Galant's voice.

"I can offer proof," urbanely, "that I have no connection whatever with the club you mention. If I am a member—what then? So are others. I am able to demonstrate that I was nowhere in the neighbourhood tonight."

"Do you know what this means?" cried Chaumont, who was trembling.

"Sit down, Captain!" Bencolin's voice became sharp. He

made a movement forward, as though he feared an outburst from Chaumont.

"But—if that's true—O God! you *are* crazy! He's right! You are. It can't be. It—" Looking round desperately, Chaumont caught Bencolin's eye. Then he sank down in his chair. He seemed now to be wearing uniform and holster, a puzzled soldier with sunken eyes, seated on a foolish gilt chair in a foolish overdecorated room.

A long silence. Odette Duchêne, Claudine Martel, The Club of Coloured Masks...

"Let me tell you a little more of what I know, Monsieur Galant," Bencolin was saying, "before you make any more comments. As I have pointed out, the club is apparently owned and operated by some woman; the name does not matter, for it is obviously assumed. Further: contacts with the upper world—that is to say, the securing of new members for the club—is also done by a woman. At the prefecture we do not know the name of this woman; she clearly belongs to the upper circles and approaches trustworthy people who might be interested. Let that part of it pass. You run an expensive, high-strung, dangerous *ménage* (if relatives should find out!), and I dare say your own large bodyguard is forever on hand to prevent trouble. A tragedy there, with the newspapers publishing the whole story and the members afraid to go again lest their dear ones discover—why, you are undone."

With steady fingers Galant took out a cigarette-case.

"Being myself only a member," he said, "I cannot, of course, understand all this. Nevertheless, I think you said a murder was committed in the passage *outside* the entrance. That need not involve the club."

"Ah, but it does. For, do you see, this passage is actually a part of the club-rooms. You enter it from the street through a door with a special lock, which is always fastened. Members are provided with a special key for this door. It is a silver key, stamped with the name of the member. Therefore—?" Bencolin shrugged.

"I see." Galant lighted a cigarette, still impassive, and blew out the match. He seemed again to admire the absolute steadiness of his hand. "In that case, I suppose, the newspapers will get the story, and the full account of the club."

"They will get nothing of the kind."

"I—I beg your pardon?"

"I said," Bencolin repeated, complacently, "they will get nothing of the kind. That is what I came here to tell you."

After another long pause, Galant murmured: "I do not understand you, monsieur. Therefore I admire you."

"Not a word of this whole affair will leak into the newspapers. The club will continue on its usual cheerful course. By no word will you intimate what has occurred tonight... There is another interesting feature of the club also. 'Coloured masks' is no idle term. I am informed of the signs by which members may be guided. Those who have no lover, but are merely looking at random for someone who pleases them, wear black masks. Those who are seeking out a definite person wear green. Finally, those who are there by assignation with some definite person, and will speak to no other, wear—as a hands-off signal—scarlet. The mask found in the passage tonight was black... I ask you again, by the way, what you know of the murder."

Now Galant was again in his element. He relaxed. Letting smoke drift out of his weird nose, he sat back and eyed Bencolin whimsically.

"My dear fellow, I know nothing. You tell me a crime has been committed there. It is sad. Oh, most tragic. Nevertheless,

I don't know who was murdered, or how, or why. Will you enlighten me?"

"Are you acquainted with Mademoiselle Claudine Martel?"

Galant frowned at his cigarette. Then he looked up, startled. I would have defied anybody to tell when this man was lying and when he was evading answers by telling the simple truth. Now I was at a loss; he seemed to be genuinely astonished.

"So?" he muttered. "Eh, but this is odd! Why, yes. The Martels are a very good family. I used to have some slight acquaintance with the girl. Claudine Martel!" He chuckled. "A member of the club! Well, well!"

"That's a lie," Chaumont said, swiftly and coldly. "Look here! And as for Mademoiselle Duchêne—"

I heard Bencolin swear under his breath. He interposed, "Captain, will you be so good as to keep out of this?"

"'Duchêne?'" Galant was repeating. "'Duchêne?' I never heard *that* name. Besides, it's too common. What about her?"

"She does not concern us... Let me continue with Mademoiselle Martel," said Bencolin. "She was found tonight, stabbed through the back, in the waxworks whose rear door communicates with the passage."

"In the waxworks?—Oh! Oh yes, I know that place you mean. *Tiens!* that is too bad! But I thought you said she was killed in the passage?"

"She was. Her body was later carried in, through an open door, to the museum."

"For what purpose?"

Bencolin shrugged. But there was a twinkle in his eye; he was enjoying himself. These two had a subtle way of communicating, so that you fancied Galant heard Bencolin's unspoken words. "Why, that is our solution." Aloud the detective asked:

"Are you acquainted with Monsieur Augustin or his daughter?"

"Augustin? No. I never heard... Wait; yes, of course! That is the owner of the waxworks. No, monsieur, I have not the pleasure."

A falling log dropped with a rattle in the fireplace, and a shower of sparks flickered yellow lights on Galant's face. He was all thoughtful concern—an admirable witness, choosing his words carefully. Under it lay an edge of satire. Now that it had come merely to fencing, he felt that he was in no danger. The quiet was jarred by Bencolin's laugh.

"Oh, come now!" he suggested. "Think, my friend! Don't you want to reconsider?"

"What do you mean?" Elaborate casualness!

"Why, only this. For the information about your place I have previously given, I take no credit. It was supplied me long ago by our own agents. But when I visited the waxworks tonight, certain facts were manifest."

Bencolin examined the palm of his hand, as though he were consulting notes. His face puckered, he went on:

"The street entrance to the passage, we know, is carefully guarded by a burglar-proof lock, for which special silver keys are given to members. The club wishes its outer entrance to be impregnable. But there is another entrance to this passage!— the back of the museum. Now, with all these precautions, is it reasonable to suppose that the clubowners would have neglected this back way? Is it reasonable to suppose that they would have left unnoticed a door with an ordinary spring lock, opening from the inside of the museum, through which any casual prowler could step into the passage? Of course not. Then I noticed that this museum door had a very new lock, freshly oiled and in excellent working order. Yet Monsieur

Augustin assured me, with evident sincerity, that the door was never used and that he had lost the key. His daughter's attitude, however, intrigued my interest…

"Well, well, it is rather obvious, isn't it? Monsieur Augustin's daughter, who takes care of everything for a rather doddering father, has seen a way to capitalize the Musée Augustin aside from its waxworks display. Going into the museum would make an excellent blind for those of its members who were afraid of being caught! They could go to the rear and step in without the need of a key—though, of course, they must be club members—"

"One moment!" Galant interposed, raising his hand. "This Mademoiselle Augustin could not refuse to admit everybody to the museum except club members, could she? The general public—"

Bencolin laughed again. "My friend, I am not so ingenuous as to suppose that those two entrances—*i.e.*, from the street through the bulldog-locked door, and from the back of the museum through the door that can be opened from inside—are the sole barriers to be overcome. No, no! The door into the actual club has yet to be passed. This also must be opened with the silver key, I am told, and subsequently the key must be shown to a man on guard inside. So, whichever way a member entered, he must have his key."

Galant nodded. He seemed to be examining the matter as an abstract problem.

"Some inkling of this situation in the museum," said Bencolin, "had come to me before I visited it. At the prefecture of police, my friend, we are thorough. We have a department which is in communication with the Ministry of State, and with the three leading banking institutions of France. We receive monthly lists of the citizens of Paris whose incomes or bank balances are larger than their occupations warrant. Very often, in that way, we are able to pick up evidence which will be useful—later. When, this afternoon, we recovered the body of a woman who was last seen going into the Musée Augustin (Oh yes, don't look surprised! Two murders have been committed)—when we did that, I looked over the bank balance of Mademoiselle Augustin as a matter of routine. She was credited with nearly a million francs. Incredible! Then, tonight, the source of it became plain…"

Bencolin spread out his hands. He was not watching Galant, but I was. I thought I saw again the expression of smugness, of fierce secret triumph, creeping behind Galant's eyes, as though he laughed in his brain, and as though he said, "Still you don't know…!" But Galant lazily tossed his cigarette into the fire.

"So you are convinced, then, that I *do* know this charming lady?"

"You still deny it?"

"Oh yes. I have already told you I am only a member."

"I wonder, then," Bencolin said, musingly, "why she expressed such agitation at the mention of your name."

Galant's fingers descended softly on the neck of the cat…

"There were other things, too," said the detective. "We had quite a talk, mademoiselle and I; we questioned and answered without saying what we meant, though each of us understood. Several things are clear. Her father does not know that she is using the museum for that particular purpose, and she does not want him to know. She is afraid; the old man is proud of his place, and if he knew… well, we can't speculate on *that*. Also, my friend, she definitely has seen Mademoiselle Martel before."

"What makes you think that?" Galant's voice had risen slightly.

"Oh, I am convinced of it. Yet you—you never saw Mademoiselle Martel before, I think you said? Also you do not know Mademoiselle Augustin. A tangled affair, I am afraid." He sighed.

"Look here," Galant returned, a little hoarsely, "I am getting tired of this. You break in on my house tonight. You make stupid accusations, for which you could pay in court. By God! I am tired!"

He rose slowly from his chair, spilling the cat; his big face looked ugly and dangerous.

"It is time to end this. You will go, or I will have you thrown out of the house. As for your murder, I can prove that I had nothing to do with it. I do not know at what time it was supposed to be committed—"

"I do," said Bencolin, placidly.

"Is there any reason to bluff *me?*"

"My friend, I would not take the trouble to bluff you or anybody else. I say that I know almost to the very second when the murder was committed. There is a piece of evidence which tells me."

Bencolin spoke in a level, almost indifferent voice. There was a line between his brows and he scarcely looked at Galant. "Evidence!"—so far as I knew, there was no evidence as to just when, during a period of over an hour, Claudine Martel had been stabbed. But we all knew that he was telling the truth.

"Very well, then," agreed Galant. He nodded, but his eyes were glazed. "I dined, about eight o'clock, at Prunier's in the rue Duphot. You can verify it there, and also that I left there about nine-fifteen. As I was leaving there, I met a friend—a certain Monsieur Defarge, whose address I will give you—and we stopped at the Café de la Madeleine for a drink. He left me around ten o'clock, and I got in my car and was driven to the Moulin Rouge. Since it has become a dance-hall, you can easily get corroboration from the attendants; I am well known there. I sat in one of the boxes off the dance-floor, where I stayed for the eleven-o'clock stage-show. It was over by half-past eleven. I then went in my car in the direction of the Porte St.-Martin, with the intention—you perceive that I do not conceal it—of going to the Club of Masks. When I reached the corner of the Boulevard St.-Denis, I changed my mind. That must have been… well, in the vicinity of eleven forty-five, I judge. So I went to the night club called 'The Gray Goose,' where I sat down to drink with two girls. You, monsieur, entered there not many minutes afterwards, and I dare say you saw me. Certainly I saw *you*. I trust that accounts for my movements. Now—when was the murder committed?"

"Between eleven-forty and eleven forty-five, exactly."

All Galant's wrath seemed to evaporate. His tense muscles sank back to easy grace, and he looked past Bencolin's shoulder to smooth his hair by his reflection in the mirror over the fireplace. Then he shrugged.

"I don't know how you can be so sure. But it helps me. I think the car-starter at the Moulin Rouge will tell you that it was shortly after eleven-thirty when I left. There is, I recall, an illuminated clock in a store almost immediately across the street. So, then, allowing for a ten-minute drive—it is some little distance—the parking of the car, and my arrival at 'The Gray Goose' about eleven forty-five… is it conceivable that I could have killed Mademoiselle Martel, carried her body into the waxworks, and returned to the night club, *without any blood on me*, at that time? Of course, you can question my chauffeur. But I don't suppose you will believe him."

"I thank you," said Bencolin, smoothly, "for your story. It

was not necessary. You have not been accused, or even—so far as I am concerned—suspected."

"You admit, then, the impossibility of my guilt?"

"Oh no."

Galant's lips were bunched together in an unpleasant fashion. He thrust his head forward. "Frankly, why are you here?"

"Why, merely to tell you that you need fear no ugly publicity for your club. A friendly gesture, you see."

"Now please listen to me. I am a quiet man." Galant's slight gesture indicated the bleak room. "I have only hobbies. My books. My music"—his eye travelled to the great harp in the corner—"and my little pet, Mariette here... But, my dear fellow, if any police spies are discovered in that club you speak of—"

He allowed his voice to trail away and he smiled. "So good evening, messieurs. My house has been honoured by your visit."

We left him standing motionless in the firelight, the white cat beside him. He was fingering his nose musingly as the door closed. The servant let us out into the damp-smelling garden, which was as a well under the cold starlight. When the outer gates had closed behind us, Chaumont seized the detective's arm.

"You told me to keep quiet," he said, heavily, "and I did. Now I want to know. Odette! Does this mean that *Odette* was going—there? Don't stand there like a dummy; tell me! Why, that club, it's only a kind of glorified—"

"Yes."

The light of a street lamp fell wanly through the trees on Chaumont's face. He did not speak for a long time.

"Well," he muttered at length, squinting up at the light— "well, anyway, we—we can keep it from her mother."

It was a sort of eager catching at consolation. Bencolin studied him in the dim light. He put his hand firmly on Chaumont's shoulder.

"You deserve to know the truth. Your Odette was—well, she was entirely too naïve, like yourself. Not the army, not anything else, will ever teach you a thing about life. The fact is your Odette was probably enticed there as a joke. Monsieur Galant is fond of jokes like that... Damn you, be still!" His fingers dug into the young man's shoulder and he yanked Chaumont round to face him. "No, my friend. You are *not* going back to see Galant. I will attend to that."

There was a tense silence in the rustling street while Chaumont writhed in the detective's grip.

"Had she wanted to go there," Bencolin asserted, still calmly, "she would in all likelihood have come out alive. You don't understand Monsieur Galant's sense of humour."

"You mean, then," I said, "that this Galant is responsible for these—enticements and murders."

Slowly releasing his grip, Bencolin turned; he looked suddenly bewildered and despondent.

"That's the rub, Jeff. I don't believe he is. Such a course is entirely consistent with him, but—there are too many things against it. The crimes lack smoothness; they are too clumsy; they are not like our friend's technique and they point too directly to him. Besides... oh, I could name a dozen reasons from the evidence tonight! Wait. We are going to see what he did before he came home."

He rapped the ferrule of his stick sharply against the pavement. Down the Avenue Montaigne a figure detached itself from the shadows of the trees and sauntered in our direction. Nodding to us to follow, Bencolin walked to meet him.

"Tonight," he explained, "when I was fairly certain that the waxworks and the club were related to the murder of Mademoiselle Duchêne—before even we found Mademoiselle Martel's body—I made a phone call, you may remember. I had seen Monsieur Galant in the night club, and I thought his presence was too… well, fortuitous. It is not a usual haunt of his, and he is not generally seen, this fastidious scholar, pretending drunkenness and fondling street-walkers anywhere. So I telephoned from the waxworks for a man to shadow him, provided he was still at 'The Gray Goose.' Here is the result."

We had halted in the deep shadow of a tree which retained much of its foliage. The red end of a cigarette pulsed there; then it was tossed away in a growing arc as a man stepped forward.

"In short, it looked too much as though Monsieur Galant were preparing an alibi for something, before I had the vaguest idea what that something was," said Bencolin. "Well, Pregel?"

"I found him at the night club when I arrived," answered a voice. The faint glow from the street lamps shone on a starched shirt-front, and the voice was commanding; for the Sûreté does not take chances on having its operatives recognized as operatives. "That was at twelve-twenty precisely. He waited fifteen minutes longer, and then left. I had thought at first he was drunk; that was a pretence. He left 'The Gray Goose' and walked round the corner. His car, a Hispano limousine numbered 2X–1470, was parked two blocks away. The chauffeur was waiting, and I thought there was a woman in the rear seat. At first I could not be sure. He entered the limousine. I took a taxi and followed…"

"Yes?"

"They drove to Number 28, rue Pigalle, Montmartre, a

small apartment-house. The street was full of people and I got a good look at the limousine's occupants as they left it. There *was* a woman with him, a very good-looking blonde who wore a fur-piece and a brown hat."

"The lady again," Bencolin sighed. "What then?"

"I was almost positive I recognized her, but when they had gone upstairs I showed my credentials to the *concierge* and asked who the woman was. It is the new singer at the Moulin Rouge—she is supposed to be an American—who goes under the name of Estelle."

"It may explain why Monsieur Galant is so well known at the Moulin Rouge. H'm, yes. Go on."

"He stayed upstairs about an hour. Then he came down, entered the limousine, and was driven directly to a garage farther up this street. He walked down here and entered his house…" The voice grew embarrassed; it left its monotonous tone and became hesitant. "I—er—it happens that I am a great admirer of—the lady's singing. I—I have a magazine photograph from *Paris Plaisir* here, if you wish to verify what I say."

"Ah!" said Bencolin, appreciatively. "Well done, Pregel! I never saw the lady, to my knowledge. By all means let's look at her." His voice dropped its bantering. "Messieurs, do you realize that this is probably the woman the policeman saw waiting at the door of the museum after it had closed—the mysterious blonde in the brown hat? Strike a light."

The flame of a large match spurted up, cupped in Pregel's hands. Then he held it carefully before a large coloured picture inscribed "Estelle, Grande Chanteuse Américaine du Moulin Rouge." Blue eyes, set wide apart, looked at us with a sideways quirk which was half allure and half appraisal. The full pink lips were slightly open, the head thrown a little back, with the suggestion of a smile. Her nose was straight, and her chin firm. The hair, secured with a network of pearls, was not so much yellow as that rich brown which gives off flashes of gold under lights. We were silent, looking at it in the match-flame which Pregel was shielding against the wind. Then the match went out.

"Wait a minute!" Chaumont cried, suddenly. "Strike a light again! I want to look…"

His voice was bewildered. He muttered, "It can't be—!" and checked himself as Pregel struck another match. A silence. Then Chaumont expelled his breath hard. He said, wryly:

"Monsieur, I seem fated to give you identifications tonight. Do you remember my mentioning that Odette formerly had two great friends who were called the Inseparables? Claudine Martel, and Gina Prévost—who wanted to go on the stage and her family wouldn't permit it? Well, I can't believe it, and yet it's an extraordinary resemblance. I am almost willing to swear that this 'Estelle' is Gina Prévost. Good God! Singing in the Moulin Rouge! She must be…"

We were in darkness again. After a pause Pregel spoke softly:

"Monsieur is quite right. I asked the *concierge*. Mademoiselle Estelle, as I told you, is supposed to be American, but, under threat, I got the truth from the *concierge*. She is French, and her name is Prévost." He drew a deep breath as though to say, "Another illusion gone!" Afterwards he said: "Shall I be required further tonight, Monsieur Bencolin?"

"No," said Bencolin. "I think, messieurs, we have had about enough of this for one night. You had better go home. I want to think."

He turned, his hands jammed into his pockets, and began to walk slowly in the direction of the Champs Elysées. I saw his tall figure moving through patches of shadow and star-light, chin sunk on his breast, as he would walk until dawn. Distantly, the bell at the Invalides tolled three.

7

THE SECOND MASK

GREY CLOUDS HUNG OVER PARIS THAT MORNING AFTER. It was one of those autumn days when the wind has an ugly whine, when the sun lies behind those dull clouds and tips them with a cold gleam like steel. The air itself is mouse-coloured, houses look old and sinister, and every span of the Eiffel Tower stands out chill against the sky. When I break-fasted at ten o'clock, my apartment was dismal despite the bright fire in the drawing-room. I could see its reflection on the walls, rising and shrinking, to remind me of Etienne Galant and the white cat...

Bencolin had phoned earlier. I was to meet him at the Invalides—a large order, but I knew exactly where I should find him. He was in the habit of haunting the battle-chapel which is directly behind Bonaparte's tomb. I do not know what fascination this place exercised over him, for he took not the slightest interest in any of the great churches; but in this dusky stone chapel, where the old war-flags hang dry from the rafters, I have known him to sit for hours absorbed, leaning on his cane, staring down at the dim pipes of the organ.

When I drove to the Invalides I was still thinking of Galant. The man obsessed me. While I had had no further opportunity to question Bencolin about him, it occurred to me at last why his name had been vaguely familiar. A chair in English literature at Christ Church, Oxford, yes. And his book on the Victorian novelists had won the Goncourt prize only a few years ago. No Frenchman, with the possible exception of M. Maurois, had so thoroughly understood the Anglo-Saxon mind. As I remembered the book, it had not been—as so often with Gallic writers—cheaply satirical. Hunting-field, punchbowl, tall hat, overstuffed parlours, all this robust world of ale and oysters and parasols, was set forth with a sympathetic pleasure which, as I recalled Galant, seemed amazing. More and more the figure of Galant grew distorted, as in crooked mirrors; I saw him sitting in his cold house, with his harp and his white cat, and the nose which seemed to move of its own volition, like a live thing. He smiled.

A wet wind swept across that vast dry-brown open space which marches up to the Invalides, and the gilded eagles on the Pont Alexandre looked murky. I went past the sentinels at the iron gates, up the slope to the great dark building, and into a courtyard that is always murmurous with echoes. A few people moved in the cloisters where the embalmed guns lie; my own footsteps were loud on the stones, and the whole place smelled of decayed uniforms. Here above all you felt the shadow of the Emperor's gilded dome. At the door of the chapel I paused. Inside it was dusky, except for a few pinpoint candles burning before shrines; and the organ sent a thin wave of sound rolling under the arches, rising in ghostly triumph round a dead man's battle-flags…

Bencolin was there. He stepped out to join me, his jaunty appearance momentarily neglected, for he wore an old tweed topcoat and a disreputable hat. We walked down the cloister slowly. At last he made an irritable gesture.

"Death," he said. "This atmosphere—it's like the case. I have never known an investigation recently in which it seemed so to penetrate everything I touch. I have seen horrifying things, yes, and black fear, but this terrible sombreness is worse. It's so meaningless. Ordinary young girls, such as you might meet at any tea, without enemies or grand passions or nightmares; sensible, steady-going, not even especially beautiful. And they die. That's why I think there's a worse horror than any other at the end of it..." He broke off. "Jeff, Galant's alibi checks at every point."

"You've tested it out?"

"Naturally. It's just as he says; my best agent, Francois Dillsart—you remember him in the Saligny case?—has all the testimony. The car-starter at the Moulin Rouge summoned the limousine at eleven-thirty precisely. He remembers, because Galant looked at his watch before getting in, and then towards the illuminated clock across the street; the car-starter automatically followed his glance."

"Doesn't that in itself seem suspicious?"

"Not at all. Had he been trying to form an alibi, he would definitely have called the starter's attention to it; he could hardly have risked the psychological chance that the man would notice."

"Still," I said, "a subtle man—"

Bencolin twirled his stick, staring down the dim cloister. "Turn right, Jeff. We'll go out on the other side; Madame Duchêne, Odette's mother, lives on the Boulevard des Invalides... H'm. Subtle or not, there's the clock. The traffic in Montmartre is always congested at that hour. It would easily have taken him between ten and fifteen minutes—even longer than he said—to get from the Moulin Rouge to the night club. Under those circumstances it doesn't *seem* humanly possible for him to have committed the murder. And yet I am willing to swear he came into 'The Gray Goose' for the definite purpose of establishing an alibi! Unless—"

"Oh yes," I said, wearily, for I had known this habit before. "I won't feed your vanity by asking you what... But here's something. Last night, when you were talking to Galant, I thought you were tipping your hand entirely and telling him too much. Maybe you had a purpose. But, anyway, what you didn't tell him was the very reason why we connected him with Claudine Martel. I mean his name written on a piece of paper in her handbag. When he denied having known her, you could have smashed him with that."

He looked at me with raised eyebrows. "You are very naïve indeed, Jeff, if you fancy *that*. Good God! Haven't you had enough police experience to know that people in real life do not scream and faint, as they do in the theatre, when they are faced with a piece of damaging evidence?—Besides, that piece of paper may not mean anything?"

"Rot!"

"All the same, it was not in Mademoiselle Martel's handwriting. I thought, when I first looked at it, that people do not themselves write down the full name, full address, and telephone number of a person they know very well. Had she been a friend of his, she would probably have scribbled, 'Etienne, tel. Elysée 11–73.' As it was—well, I compared the handwriting with the names written in her address-book. It was not the same."

"Then who—?"

"It was in the handwriting of Mademoiselle Gina Prévost, who calls herself Estelle... Listen, Jeff. We seem to be manoeuvring this lady into a very bad position before we have even seen her. She went out early this morning. Pregel was on the watch, and immediately paid a little informal visit to her rooms. We had previously ascertained, at the Moulin Rouge, that she did not put on her act last night. She telephoned the manager that evening that she would be unable to go on, and she left her apartment, the *concierge* says, about twenty minutes past eleven..."

"Which would allow her time to reach the front entrance of the waxworks by, say, twenty-five minutes to twelve. If she is the woman the policeman saw hanging about there—"

We had come out on the vast sweep of lawn which runs up to the front of Bonaparte's tomb. The gold dome was dull under a mottled sky. Bencolin stopped to light a cigar. Then he said:

"She *was* the woman. We have shown photographs to the policeman, and he identifies her. Oh, this morning has not been wasted!—But let me tell you the rest. Pregel, as I told you, went to her rooms. He found specimens of handwriting. He also found a silver key and a scarlet mask."

I whistled. "Then—the scarlet mask, you said, indicates one with an accepted lover at the club?"

"Yes."

"Galant's frequent visits to the Moulin Rouge... and he took her home last night; she was waiting in the car... Bencolin, when did she get into that car? Have you questioned the chauffeur?"

"She was not in the car when it left the Moulin Rouge, anyhow. No. I have not questioned the chauffeur, nor have I let Mademoiselle Prévost know we are even aware of her existence."

I stared at him as we went down the driveway.

"For the moment, Jeff," he said, "we must let Galant think we know nothing of his connection with her, or her connection with the club. If you will be patient, you will see why. Her telephone wires have been tapped, for a purpose you will learn also. And for the greater part of the day I have seen to it that she will be out of Galant's reach. I think we shall find her at the home of Madame Duchêne, where we are going now."

We said no more while we went out through the gates, round to the left, and up the Boulevard des Invalides. Mme. Duchêne, I knew, was a widow, who before the death of her husband had been conspicuous in the sedate rooms of the Faubourg St.-Germain. She lived in one of those dingy-looking houses of grey stone whose dinner-tables are served with the deftest cooking and the oldest port. A man could turn to the right here at the rue de Varenne and wind his way through the gloomy streets of the Faubourg, without ever suspecting the vistas of gardens that lie behind, or the old jewel-boxes shut up in cracked dark walls.

The door was opened by a young man who stood very stiff and nervous, appraising us. At first I took him for an Englishman: his hair was black, thick, and curtly trimmed; his face was very ruddy, with a long nose and thin lips, and his eyes pale blue. The impression was heightened by the black double-breasted suit, cut thin at the waist and full at the trousers, the handkerchief in his sleeve, and the rather weird necktie. But his carriage was too unnatural; he seemed always to be watching himself out of the corner of his eye, and to refrain from making gestures. Consequently, in those few minutes of introduction he had rather the look of a mechanical toy whose clockwork is not properly functioning. He said:

"Ah yes. You are from the police. Please come in."

He had greeted us with a somewhat patronizing look

before he recognized Bencolin. Now he became almost effusive. He had a trick of moving backwards, as though he were manoeuvring not to hit any chairs in the way.

"You are related to Madame Duchêne?" the detective asked.

"No. Oh no," said the other, deprecatingly. He smiled. "Permit me. My name is Paul Robiquet. I am an *attaché* of the French embassy in London, but just now—" A wave of his hand, which he checked instantly. "They sent for me, and I was permitted to come. I am a very old friend. I grew up with Mademoiselle Odette. Now I fear the arrangements would be too much for Madame Duchêne. The funeral, you see? Please come this way."

The hall was almost dark. Portières were drawn over a door at the right, but I could smell the thick odour of flowers, and a chill went through me. It is more difficult to overcome this childish fear of death when a human being lies placidly in a new and shining coffin than even when that human being is first struck down in blood. The last is merely horrifying or pitiful, but the first has that ordered and grisly practicality which says, "You will not see this person ever more." I had never seen Odette Duchêne, in life or death. But I could visualize her lying there, because I remembered the smile on that misty face in the photograph, and the clear, impish eyes. Every dust-mote in the old hall seemed to be impregnated with that sickening heaviness of flowers, to catch the throat.

"Yes," Bencolin was saying, conversationally, as we went into a drawing-room on the left, "I came here early last evening to inform Madame Duchêne of the—the tragedy. I did not meet her, but I conveyed the news to Captain Chaumont. Is he here now, by the way?"

"Chaumont?" the other repeated. "No. Not at present.

He was here earlier this morning, but he had to go. Won't you sit down?"

This room, too, had its blinds drawn, and no fire burnt below the great white-marble mantelpiece. But it was a room of mellowness and grace, where people had lived graceful lives. The old blue walls, the gilt-framed paintings, the soft chairs companionably worn. Here, through many years, wit had waited on the coffee, and death could not make it ugly. Above the mantelpiece there was a large portrait of Odette as a girl in her early 'teens, chin in her hands, looking out. The great dark eyes, the wistful eagerness of her mouth, illumined the lonely room; and when I caught again the thick sweetness of flowers I felt a lump in my throat.

Bencolin did not sit down. "I came to see Madame Duchêne," he said, in a low voice. "She is—well?"

"She takes it hard. You can understand," said Robiquet, clearing his throat. He was trying to keep his diplomatic calm. "The shock. It was horrible! Monsieur, have you—do you know who did this? I have known her all my life. The idea that anybody would—"

He was pressing his fingers together hard, attempting to be the level-headed young man who saw to all arrangements, but, for all his newly acquired British reserve, he could not keep the quaver out of his voice. Bencolin interposed:

"I think so, monsieur. Is anybody with Madame Duchêne now?"

"Only Gina Prévost. Chaumont phoned her this morning, and said Madame Duchêne wanted her here. That was a piece of imposition; Madame Duchêne expressed no such wish." His lip tightened. "I think I am capable of all that is necessary. Still, she *can* help, if she pulls herself together. She is almost as bad as Madame Duchêne."

"Gina Prévost?" Bencolin repeated, inquiringly, as though he heard the name for the first time.

"Oh, I forgot!... One of our old crowd, before we broke up. She was a great friend of Odette's and—" He paused, his pale eyes widening. "That reminds me. I must phone Claudine Martel. She will want to be here. Zut! What an oversight!"

Bencolin hesitated. "I take it," he murmured, "you did not talk to Captain Chaumont when he was here this morning? You did not hear—?"

"Hear? What? No, monsieur. There are developments?"

"A few. But no matter. Will you take us to Madame Duchêne?"

"I suppose it is all right for *you*," the young man admitted, eyeing us as though he were receiving people in the ambassador's anteroom. "She will want to hear. But no others. This way, please."

He led us out, towards the back of the hall, and up a carpeted staircase. Through a window on a dusky landing I could see the scarlet of maples in the yard. Robiquet paused abruptly when we were almost at the top. From above came a murmur of voices, then a few chords struck on a piano and a riffle as though the hands were dragged away. One of the voices rose in a shrill and hysterical cry...

"They're mad!" snapped the young man. "They're both mad, and Gina's being here makes it worse. Do you see, messieurs—Madame Duchêne walks about and walks about; she won't sit down; and she tortures herself by looking at Odette's things and trying to play the piano Odette played. Will you please see if you can quiet her?"

When he knocked on a door in the darkened upper hallway, there was a sudden silence. Presently an unsteady voice said, "Come in."

It was a girl's sitting-room, with three wide windows overlooking a ruined garden, and, beyond, the yellow raiment of the trees. Dull light through the windows turned the ivory furniture to grey. Swung round on a piano stool before a grey baby grand, staring at us with dry, sharp eyes, sat a little woman in black. Her black hair, which she wore loosely coiled about her head, was streaked with grey, but her face, though very pale and pinched about the eyes, was unlined. Yet there were sagging muscles in her throat. The eyes, hot and fierce, lost their sharpness gradually as she saw strangers.

"Paul," she said, quietly—"Paul, you did not tell me—we had visitors. Please come in, messieurs."

She did not apologize. She was not conscious of her careless, almost shabby dress, or her tousled hair; you saw in her a deep indifference to all surrounding things, and her poise was that of a hostess as she rose to greet us... But it was not Mme. Duchêne who attracted my attention. Standing beside her, hand still half lifted, was Gina Prévost. I should have recognized her anywhere, despite the fact that she was taller than I had imagined. Her eyelids were red and swollen and she wore no cosmetics. The pink full lips, the gold-lighted hair, the firm chin; but the lips were open, the upper partly raised in fright, and she had flung back the hair from her forehead. Now she seemed almost on the edge of a collapse.

"—My name is Bencolin," the detective was saying, "and this is my colleague, Monsieur Marle. I come to bring you the assurance that we will find the person—you are interested in."

His voice, deep and quiet, soothed the tense atmosphere of the room. I could hear the faint noise as Gina Prévost, who had been holding down one of the piano keys, released it. She moved out against the grey light of the windows with a supple, almost masculine, stride; then she hesitated.

"I have heard of you," said Mme. Duchêne, nodding. "And you, monsieur"—she looked at me—"are very welcome. This is Mademoiselle Prévost, an old friend of ours. She is staying with me today."

Gina Prévost tried to smile. The older woman continued:

"Please sit down. I shall be happy to tell you anything, anything at all, you want to know. Paul, will you put on the lights?"

Then Mlle. Prévost cried, rather breathlessly: "No! Please—No lights. I feel…"

Her voice was husky, with a caressing note which, in a song, must make one's blood beat fast. Mme. Duchêne— who, a moment before, had seemed the more brittle and high-strung of the two—looked at her with a tired smile.

"Why, of course not, Gina!"

"Don't—please!—don't look at me like that!"

Again madame smiled. She sat back against a *chaise-longue*.

"Gina has to put up with *me*, messieurs. And I am a crazy old woman." Momentarily there were wrinkles in her forehead; her eyes stared at futility. "It comes on me in gusts, like a physical pain. For a while I am quiet, and then—there! but I will try to be sensible. You see, what makes it so bad, I am responsible."

Mlle. Prévost had seated herself nervously on a divan, in shadow, and so Bencolin and I drew out chairs. Robiquet remained standing, stiffly.

"We have all known the grief of death, madame," the detective told her, as though musing. "And we always feel responsible, if only because—we did not smile often enough. I should not worry on that account."

A cheerful little enamel clock ticked in the heavy grey silence. The lines in madame's forehead deepened. She opened her mouth as for a fierce denial; she appeared to be fighting, trying to speak with her eyes.

"You don't understand," she said at last, quietly. "I was a fool. I brought Odette up wrongly. I thought I ought to keep her a child all her life, and I did, all her life..." She looked down at her hands, and after a pause she went on: "I myself—well—I have seen things. I have been hurt. I was willing to do these things; they were all right for *me*; but Odette—you wouldn't understand—you wouldn't understand—!"

She seemed very small, for all the passionate emotion behind that pale, strong face.

"My husband," she said, as though something were forcing the words from her, "shot himself—you knew that—ten years ago, when Odette was twelve. He was a fine man—he didn't deserve... he was in the Cabinet, and being—blackmailed..." She had grown incoherent, but with an effort she steadied her voice: "I resolved to devote myself to Odette. This is what I have done. I was amused at her, as though she were a little toy shepherdess. And now I haven't got anything—but her trinkets. At least I can play the piano a little; songs she liked, 'Clair de Lune',—'Auprès de ma Blonde,' 'Ce N'Est Que Votre Main,' 'Auld Lang Syne...'"

"I think, madame, you are trying to help us," Bencolin interposed, gently, "and I am sure you would help Odette if you will just answer me some questions..."

"Of course. I—I am sorry. Continue."

He waited until she sat back composedly, her chin up.

"Captain Chaumont has told me that he noticed, since his return from Africa, a change in Odette. He could not be more specific than to say that her behaviour seemed 'odd.' Have you noticed any change recently?"

She meditated. "I have thought of that. In the last two

weeks, ever since Robert—Captain Chaumont—has been back in Paris, she *has* seemed different. More moody, and nervous. Once I found her crying. But I have seen her that way before, because the slightest thing upset her, and it worried her terribly until she forgot it. Generally, she confided in me. So I did not question her. I waited, and supposed she would tell me…"

"You could assign no cause for this?"

"None whatever… Especially as—" She hesitated.

"Please go on."

"Especially as it seemed directed towards Captain Chaumont. It was just after his arrival that she changed. She was—suspicious, stiff, formal, I don't know how to put it! But entirely unlike herself."

I was looking over at Mlle. Prévost, who sat in the shadow. The lovely face had an expression of tortured doubt, and her eyes were half closed.

"Forgive me for asking this, madame," Bencolin requested, in a low voice, "but you understand that it is necessary. But— Mademoiselle Duchêne, so far as you know, had no particular interest in any man except Captain Chaumont?"

At first, anger tightened madame's nostrils; but it was followed by an expression of weary and humorous tolerance.

"None. It may have been better if she had."

"I see. You believe her death was the result of a wanton and senseless attack?"

"Naturally." Tears filmed over her eyes. "She—she was lured out of here, and…how, I don't know! That's what I can't understand! She was to have tea with Claudine Martel, a friend of hers, and Robert. Suddenly she cancelled both engagements by telephone, and a little later she ran out of the house. I was surprised, because she always comes to tell me good-bye. That—that was the last time I saw her before…"

"You did not hear these telephone conversations?"

"No. I was upstairs. I assumed, when she left the house, that she was going to tea. Robert told me later."

Bencolin inclined his head, as though he were listening to the little enamel clock. Beyond the grey windows I saw the sodden trees trembling under the wind in a flicker of scarlet maple leaves. Gina Prévost had sat back on the divan with closed eyes; the dim light washed the perfect contour of her throat, and her long eyelashes were wet. It was so quiet up here that the jangle of the door-bell from below made us all start a little.

"Lucie is in the kitchen, Paul," madame said. "Do not trouble; she will answer it… Well, monsieur?"

The bell was still pealing as we heard hurried footsteps go along the lower hall. Bencolin inquired:

"Mademoiselle Duchêne kept no diaries, no papers, that might give us a clue?"

"She started a diary every year, and never carried it past the first two weeks. No. Her papers she kept, yes; but I have been over them and there is nothing."

"Then—" Bencolin was beginning, when he stopped short. His eyes remained fixed, his hand halfway to his chin. Suddenly I felt a horrible excitement pounding in my chest. I glanced at Gina Prévost, who had seized the arm of the divan and was sitting there rigid…

Very distinctly we could hear, floating up from the hall below, the voice of the person who had rung the door-bell. It said deprecatingly:

"A thousand pardons. I wonder if I might see Madame Duchêne? My name is Etienne Galant."

8

CONFIDENCES ARE EXCHANGED OVER A COFFIN

NONE OF US MOVED OR SPOKE. THE VOICE HAD SUCH an arresting quality that, even though you heard it for the first time without seeing the speaker, you would wonder to whom it belonged. Deep, ingratiating, tenderly sympathetic. I could visualize Galant standing there in the doorway, framed against the damp leaves outside. He would have a silk hat in his hands; his shoulders, under their correct morning coat, would be slightly bent as though he were offering apologies on a platter; and the yellow-grey eyes would be full of solicitude.

My eyes travelled to the faces here. Madame's gaze was opaque, rather too set. Gina Prévost stared rather wildly at the door, as though she could not believe her ears…

"Unwell?" the voice repeated, in reply to a murmur. "That is too bad! My name will be unknown to her, but I was a very great friend of her late husband's, and I very much want to convey my deepest sympathies…" A pause, as though he were meditating. "Let me see. I believe Mademoiselle Gina Prévost is here. Ah yes. Perhaps I might speak to her instead, as a friend of the family? Thank you."

A maid's light footfalls crossed the lower hall towards the stairs. Hurriedly Gina Prévost rose.

"You—you don't want to be disturbed, Mamma Duchêne," she said, trying to smile. "Now don't disturb yourself. I will go down and see him."

She uttered the words as though she were breathing too hard. Madame remained motionless. I saw the girl's white face as she swished past us. She closed the door after her. On the instant, Bencolin whispered, swiftly:

"Madame, is there a back stairway to this house? Quick, please!"

Startled, she met his eyes, and it seemed to me that a look of comprehension passed between them.

"Why—yes. It goes down between the dining-room and kitchen, then out to the side door."

"Can you get to the front room from there?"

"Yes. The room where Odette—"

"You know where this is?" he demanded of Robiquet. "Good! Show it to Monsieur Marle here. Hurry, Jeff. You know what to do."

His fierce eyes told me to listen to that conversation at any cost. Robiquet was so bewildered that he almost stumbled, but he had caught the urge to hurry and to make no noise. We could hear Gina Prévost descending the stairs, but she was hidden in the darkened hall. Robiquet showed me a narrow flight of steps—carpeted, fortunately—and his pantomime gave me directions. A door at their foot emitted a slight creak, but I pushed through it into a dim dining-room. Beyond it, through half-opened double doors, I could see the dull white of flowers. Yes! In that front room where the casket lay, the portières were almost drawn shut over the door to the hallway. I wriggled through to this room, almost knocking over a huge basket of lilies. The closed shutters building up slits of light, the stuffy sweetness, the dove-grey coffin with its polished handles—into the quiet of this place drifted voices. They were standing in the centre of the hall. Then I realized that they were speaking in voices audible on the second floor, and adding their real communication in whispers which barely reached me as I stood behind the portières.

"—understand, monsieur—I did not catch your name—you wished to see me?"

("You must be mad! That detective is here!")

"Probably you don't remember me, mademoiselle; I had the pleasure of meeting you once at Madame De Louvac's. My name is Galant."

("I had to see you. Where is he?")

"Oh yes. You understand, monsieur, that we are all upset here—?"

("Upstairs. They're all upstairs. The maid is in the kitchen. For God's sake, go!")

I wondered how long her voice would keep that casualness; husky, indifferent, with the unconscious caress beneath it. Behind the curtain I could even hear her breathing.

"A mutual friend of ours, whom I telephoned, told me you were here, so I ventured to ask for you. I can't tell you how profoundly shocked I was to hear of Mademoiselle Duchêne's death."

("He suspects me, but he doesn't know about you. We must go somewhere to talk.")

"We—we were all shocked, monsieur."

("I can't!")

Galant sighed. "Then you will convey my deepest sympathy to madame, and tell her I shall be happy to do anything I can? Thank you. I might, perhaps, look at the poor mademoiselle?"

("They can't hear us in there.")

My heart rose up sickeningly. I heard a sort of protesting sob, a rasp as though her hand had brushed his sleeve and he had shaken it off. His voice remained gentle and tender. Standing in the centre of the room, I felt as though I had been caught against a wall. I could not understand the horror and repulsion I felt at doing what I did then. Crossing to the coffin, I slid behind a gigantic floral tribute of white carnations at its head. I was wedged against the screen before the fireplace, in imminent danger of having my foot rattle against it. The situation had about it a sort of ghastly comedy which was as much of an insult to Odette Duchêne as though mud had been flung at her dead face. A human being had lived for *this*! I put my fingers against the steel side of the casket, with some vague idea that I might reach through it to press her hand... Their footsteps approached. Then there was a long silence.

"Pretty," said Galant. "What's the matter, my dear? You're not looking at her. But weak, like her father... Listen to me. I've got to have a talk with you. You were too hysterical last night."

"Please, *won't* you go? I can't look at her. I won't see you. I promised to stay here all day, and if I go out, after you've been here, that detective may..."

"How many times have I got to tell you"—his own voice was losing a little of its whimsical tolerance—"that you aren't suspected? Look at me." A tinge of amusement, a tinge of hurt. "You love me, don't you?"

"How can you *talk* about that here?"

"Ah, well! Who killed Claudine Martel?"

"I tell you," hysterically, "I don't know!"

"Unless you did it yourself—"

"I didn't!"

"You must have been standing at the murderer's elbow when she was stabbed. Keep your voice down, dearest. Was it a man or a woman?"

He spoke with repressed eagerness. I could almost feel his eyes searching her, prowling over her face like a cat.

"I've told you, I've told you! It was dark—"

He drew a long breath. "I see the circumstances are not appropriate. Then I will ask you to be at the same place tonight, usual hour."

After a pause, she said in a sort of half-gasping, half-laughing voice, "You don't expect me to go back—to the club—?"

"You will sing at the Moulin Rouge tonight. Then you will go to our own number eighteen and you will remember who killed your dear friend. That is all. I must go now."

So long I remained twisted behind the casket, the words beating in my head, that I almost forgot to slip out and hurry upstairs before Gina Prévost should have let him out the front door. Fortunately they had not pulled the portières entirely open, and I was able to escape unobserved. This conversation—well, definitely it ruled out Galant as a possible murderer, whether it eliminated the girl or not, but all sorts of nebulous suspicions were afloat in my mind because of it. I was just entering the door of the sitting-room upstairs when I heard her begin to ascend the steps.

Mme. Duchêne and Bencolin were still in the same positions, and still impassive, though Robiquet badly concealed his curiosity as he saw me. What explanation of my departure Bencolin had given to madame I did not know; but she seemed neither excited nor curious about my absence, so I presumed the detective had found some plausible excuse. A moment later the girl entered.

She was quite calm. She had taken time to apply powder and lipstick, and to arrange the gold-lighted hair in its sweep across her forehead; now her eyes darted between Bencolin and madame, wondering what had been said.

"Ah, mademoiselle," Bencolin greeted her. "We were about to go, but perhaps you can help us. I understand you were a good friend of Mademoiselle Duchêne. Can you tell us anything about this 'change'?"

"No, monsieur, I am afraid not. I have not seen Odette in several months."

"But I understood—"

Mme. Duchêne gave her a glance of amused tolerance. "Gina," she said, "has thrown family conventions overboard. A fond uncle left her a legacy and she has cut loose from home. I—I've scarcely had time to think of it. What on earth are you doing, Gina? And that reminds me"—she looked bewildered—"how did Robert find you to telephone?"

She was in a bad position. All attention seemed focussed on her. How she must have wondered, desperately, what we all knew! Galant had just said enough to stir up all manner of fears, without any explanations. Did Bencolin connect the second murder with the first, or either with her? He had not mentioned Claudine Martel's death at all. Did he possibly suspect that she was Estelle, the American singer? All these problems must have twisted through her mind in a horrible kaleidoscope, so that you had to admire her poise. She sat down carelessly; the wide-set blue eyes were expressionless now.

"You mustn't ask too many questions, Mamma Duchêne," she said. "I'm just—enjoying myself. And I'm studying for the stage, so I've got to keep my headquarters a secret."

Bencolin nodded. "Of course. Well, I don't think we shall

bother you any longer. Rest assured, madame, that you will have news shortly. If you are ready, Jeff—?"

We left them among the dull shadows of the room. I could see that Bencolin was eager to be gone, and that Mme. Duchêne, despite her politeness, wanted to be left alone. But in the last few minutes I had noticed a decided change in Robiquet; he fidgeted with his tie, he cleared his throat, he kept a nervous eye on madame, as though he were wondering whether to speak. When we were tramping down the hall he laid his hand on Bencolin's arm.

"Monsieur," he said, "I—er—Will you step into the library for a moment? I mean the drawing-room. The library is where... That is, I have just thought of something..."

Once inside, he peered up and down the hall. Then he resumed:

"You were speaking up there of a—what shall I say?—a difference in Odette's behaviour of late?"

"Yes?"

"Why, you see," deprecatingly, "nobody had mentioned it to me. I arrived only last night. But I am in regular correspondence with a friend of hers, a certain Mademoiselle Martel, who keeps me informed. Yes. And—"

He was no fool, for all his mannerisms and assumption of dignity. That pale eye had caught the expression on Bencolin's face, and he said, sharply:

"What's the matter, monsieur?"

"Nothing. You are well acquainted with Mademoiselle Martel?"

"I will be frank. At one time," he acknowledged, as though conferring a favour, "I had considered asking her to be my wife. But she has no conception of a diplomatist's duties. None! Nor does she understand the conduct that would be necessary as my wife… Men, of course"—a wave of his hand, judicially—"are entitled to a little—ah—amusement, *hein*? But Cæsar's wife; you know the quotation. Yes, certainly. I detect in her a certain hardness. Unlike Odette! Odette would listen when you talked. She thought a great deal of my career… But I am wandering."

He brought himself up with a jerk. Drawing out a violently coloured handkerchief, he mopped his ruddy face, and seemed to find difficulty in approaching the subject he had opened.

"What, precisely, are you trying to say, monsieur?" asked Bencolin. For the first time that day he smiled.

"We, all," Robiquet began again, "used to be much amused at Odette's—ah—domestic qualities. Her refusal to go out with anybody but Robert Chaumont, and so on. That is to say, we pretended to be. For myself, I admired it. *There* would be a wife! Had I not grown up with her, I myself…" He waved his hand. "But I remember, when we would be playing tennis at the Touring Club, a group of us, they would try to get Odette on a party. Everybody would laugh when she refused, and Claudine Martel would say, 'Ah, her captain in Africa!'— and she would picture him twisting his big moustaches and waving his sword at the Riffs."

"Yes?"

"You asked upstairs, a while ago, whether she had been interested in anybody else. The answer is, definitely, *no*. But"—Robiquet lowered his voice, his pale eyes looking very intent—"by a recent letter I received from Claudine, I understand that *Chaumont* has been—playing round, and Odette knew it. There! Understand me, I say nothing against him. It is only natural for a young man, if he is careful about it—"

I glanced at Bencolin. This piece of information, worded

in Robiquet's mealy-mouthed fashion, was very difficult to believe. It did not sound at all like Chaumont. Studying Robiquet's ruddy, sharp-nosed face, imagining the delicate steps he took in furtherance of his career ("It is only natural for a young man, *if he is careful about it*—" Thus spoke his small, cautious soul), I doubted this information. It was petty, and it was mean. But obviously Robiquet believed it. Bencolin, to my surprise, manifested the greatest interest.

"'Playing about'?" he repeated. "With whom, monsieur?"

"That Claudine did not say. She mentioned it in passing, and said, rather mysteriously, not to be surprised if Odette had her fling yet."

"No person even hinted at?"

"None."

"You take this, then, to be responsible for her altered attitude towards him?"

"Well—not having seen Odette in some time, I, of course, didn't know of any altered attitude until you mentioned it upstairs. But it made me remember."

"Do you by any chance have the letter with you?"

"Why—why"—his hand went automatically to his inside breast pocket—"I may have, at that! I received it not long before I left London. A moment, please."

He began to sort over letters which he drew from this pocket, muttering to himself. Then he frowned, put them back, and reached for his hip. He had caught the eagerness in Bencolin's tone, and his new prominence as a witness of possible importance made him even more flustered. It was just as well. On this small matter of feeling our eyes fixed on him, of searching in a hurried and fumbling fashion for the letter, rested a whole series of events by which we were to be led to the solution of the case. From his hip pocket he drew a wallet and some more papers, but his hand slipped on the back of his coat. Out spilled an envelope, an empty cigarette-package, and an object which tinkled on the hardwood floor and lay there gleaming in the low lights from beneath the blinds...

It was a small silver key.

For a moment I felt again that constriction in the chest. But Robiquet treated it casually, not even noticing us. He was reaching down to pick up the wallet, muttering an exclamation of annoyance, when Bencolin stepped swiftly past him.

"Allow me, monsieur," he said, and picked up the key.

I also had taken a few steps forward, involuntarily. I saw the key in Bencolin's palm as he held it out. It was rather larger than the sort which generally fits a spring lock. It bore in finely engraved characters the name "Paul Desmoulins Robiquet," and the number 19.

"Thank you," Robiquet murmured, absently. "No, I don't seem to have the letter here. I can get it if you like..."

He looked up, startled, his hand still outstretched to take the key. Bencolin was holding it there just beyond him.

"Forgive me for seeming to pry into your private affairs, monsieur," the detective said, "but I assure you I have good reason. I am much more interested in this key than in the letter... Where did you get it?"

Still staring at his level eyes, Robiquet became first nervous, and then very much alarmed. He swallowed hard.

"Why, it can't possibly interest you, monsieur! It—it is only something private. A club I belong to. I have not been there in a long time, but I brought that key along from London in case, during my stay, I should want to—"

"The Club of Coloured Masks, in the Boulevard de Sebastopol?"

Now Robiquet became downright panicky. "You know

about it? Please, monsieur, this must not become known! If my friends—my superiors in the service—knew I belonged to that club, my *career*—!" His voice was rising.

"My dear young man, it is quite all right with me. I shall never mention it." Bencolin smiled genially. "As you yourself have expressed it, 'young men'..." He shrugged. "I am only interested because certain other events, not concerning you in the least, have intrigued my curiosity."

"I still think," Robiquet returned, stiffly, "it is my own affair."

"May I ask how long you have been a member?"

"About—about two years. I have been there only half a dozen times in my life! In my profession it is necessary to be discreet."

"Ah yes. And what is the significance of this number, nineteen, on the key?"

Robiquet froze. He set his lips in a hard line. With repressed fury he said: "Monsieur, you have admitted that the matter does not concern you. It is secret! Private. Not for strangers. And I refuse to tell you anything. I see by your emblem that you are a Mason. Would you divulge, if I asked you, the—?"

Bencolin laughed. "Well, well," he interrupted, deprecatingly, "I think even you will have to admit, monsieur, that it is hardly the same thing. Knowing the purpose of *this* club, I can't help being amused." Then he grew serious. "You are determined not to answer my questions?"

"I am afraid you must excuse me."

A pause. "I am sorry, my friend," mused Bencolin, shaking his head. "Because a murder was committed there last night. Inasmuch as we do not know the names of any of the members, and this is the first key that has come into our possession, it might be necessary to take you to the prefecture of police for questioning. The newspapers... It would be sad."

"A—a *murder!*" cried Robiquet, in a kind of yelp.

"Think, my friend!" I knew that Bencolin was with difficulty repressing a grin, but he lowered his voice and made it thrilling and portentous. "Think what a story it would be for the newspapers. Think of your career. Prominent young diplomat held for questioning in a murder committed in a house of assignations! Think of the awful consternation in London, the turmoil in Parliament, the feelings of your own family, the—"

"But I didn't do anything! I—You're not going to take *me* to—"

Bencolin pursed his lips dubiously. "Well," he admitted, "as I told you, the whole thing need never be mentioned. I don't think you had anything to do with the murder. But you must speak out, my friend."

"O my God! I'll tell you anything!"

It took some time to soothe him down. After he had mopped his face several times, and made Bencolin swear the most appalling oaths that he need not appear, Bencolin repeated the question about the number 19.

"Why, you see, monsieur," Robiquet explained, "there are exactly fifty men and fifty women in the club. The men all have—rooms, do you see? some large, some small, according to the dues they pay. That is mine. Nobody can use another's room…" His very natural curiosity bubbled up under his fear. "Who," he asked, hesitantly—"who was murdered?"

"Oh, that doesn't matter…" Bencolin stopped short. I was trying to attract his attention, for I remembered the conversation between Gina Prévost and Galant, wherein the latter had said, 'You will go to our own number eighteen.' So I said, casually:

"Eighteen is the sign of the white cat."

This cryptic utterance seemed to puzzle Robiquet, but Bencolin nodded.

"You say you have been a member for two years. Who introduced you?"

"Introduced me? Oh! Well, no harm in telling *that*. It was young Julien D'Arbalay, the one who drove his own racing-cars, you know? Great for the ladies, Julien was—"

"Was?"

"He was killed in America last year. His car overturned at Sheepshead Bay, and—"

"Damnation! No lead there." Bencolin snapped his fingers in irritation. "How many of your friends—in your own set, I mean—are members?"

"Monsieur, believe me, I don't know! You don't understand. People are masked! And with the mask off, I never saw a single woman I knew. But I have walked in the big hall, where it is so dark you could scarcely recognize people if they wore no masks, and I have wondered who of my friends, even of my family, might be there! I swear it gives you shivers!"

Again the detective eyed him with that cold, publicity-threatening glance, but Robiquet met his gaze steadily. He was fighting to be believed, clenching his hands with earnestness; and it seemed to me, at least, that he was telling the truth.

"You never even saw a person whose identity you suspected?"

"I have been there so few times! I have heard, though"—he looked round cautiously—"that there is a sort of inner circle where the members are well known to one another, and that there is a woman who makes a regular business of getting new members. But I don't know who she is."

Another silence, while Bencolin tapped the key against his palm.

"Imagine!" Robiquet said, suddenly. "Imagine going there masked, and meeting a girl, and—and finding she was the girl you were engaged to. Oh, it's too dangerous for me! Never again! And murder..."

"Very well. Now, monsieur, I will tell you what the price of my silence to the newspapers is to be. You shall lend me this key—"

"Keep it! A murder!"

"—for a few days. Then I shall return it. I suppose the news of your return to France will be among the—er—social notes of the papers?"

"Why, I suppose so. But why?"

"Good! Very good! H'm. Number nineteen: is that across from or beside number eighteen?"

Robiquet reflected. "I never paid attention, believe me! But it's beside it, I think. Yes!" He made an elaborate pantomime to himself, as though to get the location straight. "Beside it, I remember."

"Windows?"

"Yes. All the rooms look out on a sort of airshaft. But please—!"

"Better and better!" Bencolin put the key in his pocket and buttoned up his coat. Again he fixed a stern eye on Robiquet. "Now I don't need to warn you not to breathe a word of what you've told us to anybody. Is that clear?"

"*I?*" demanded the young man, incredulously. "I speak about it? Ha! What do you take me for? But you swear to me you will keep your promise?"

"I swear!" said the detective. "And now, my friend, a thousand thanks. Look at this afternoon's papers if you want to see who was killed. Good day!"

9

THE HOUSE OF THE DOMINOES

OUT IN THE STREET THE WIND HAD TURNED NOTICEABLY colder and the whole sky was murkily shot with black. Bencolin turned up the collar of his coat, grinning sideways at me.

"We have left a very much worried young man," he commented. "I hated to do that, but this key…invaluable, Jeff, invaluable! For the first time we have luck. What I wanted to do we could have arranged without the aid of the key, but now it is a million times more simple." He strode along with fierce energy, chuckling to himself. "Now you are going to tell me that Galant has made an appointment, after the Moulin Rouge show, with Mademoiselle Prévost. Aren't you?"

"I see you caught my hint."

"Caught your hint? My dear fellow, I've been preparing for it all day! He tried to steal a march on me by coming to that house; but I anticipated that. Now she'll be afraid to see him for the rest of the day. He found out from the *concierge* at her place where she had gone. The *concierge* was instructed to tell him. Ho! We want him to have a long interview with her—tonight, where we can hear it." He laughed in his deep, almost soundless fashion and slapped me on the shoulder. "The old man's wits still work, in spite of what Galant said…."

"That was why you had her come to Madame Duchêne's?"

"Yes. And why I so carefully told Galant last night that we were not going to expose his club. Because he'll meet her *there*, Jeff. Do you see why it has been inevitable? More than that, do you see the sequence of events, likewise inevitable, which lead up to it?"

"I do not."

"Well I'll give you an outline at lunch. But first tell me exactly what they said to each other."

I told him, omitting, so far as I could remember, scarcely a word. At the end of it he slapped his hands together triumphantly.

"Better than I had hoped for, Jeff. Ah, but we're being dealt the right cards! Galant thinks that Mademoiselle Prévost knows who the murderer is, and he is determined to find out. He couldn't find out last night, but in the right rendezvous—it exactly squares with my theory."

"But why this interest in law and order on Galant's part?"

"Law and order? Use your wits! It's blackmail. With the hold of a murder charge over somebody, Galant would add the tidiest threat of all to his collection of blackmail material. I've suspected this…."

"Wait a minute," I said. "Granted even a suspicion that Galant might meet this girl somewhere—though how you came to believe that, God knows!—granted that, why pick on the club? I should think that would be the last place he would go, knowing you suspect it."

"On the contrary, Jeff, I thought it would be the very first place. Think a moment! Galant has no idea we suspect Gina Prévost, or any other woman, of being tangled up in this;

he said so himself, from what you tell me. Undoubtedly he strongly suspects that he is being shadowed by my men. (A shadow has been put on his trail, as a matter of fact, with orders to make himself as conspicuous as possible.) Now, if he meets Gina Prévost anywhere—at her apartment, or his house, or any public theatre or dance-place, we are almost bound to see her! We then commence to ask ourselves, he will reason, Who is the mysterious blonde lady? We investigate, we find who she is, we discover she was near the scene of the murder... and Galant has betrayed both of them! On the other hand, the club is safe. There are only a hundred keys, the lock is practically burglar-proof, and the police cannot get in to spy. Moreover, in an establishment of that sort they could both go in at different times, and police spying on the outside door would never in the world connect them with each other... Do you see?"

"Then," I said, "you deliberately played into his hands and told him all you knew about the club, so that he would bring about a meeting between himself and this girl?"

"A meeting which I could overhear!—or one of my operatives could overhear, anyhow. Yes."

"But why such an elaborate plan?"

He scowled. "Because, Jeff, Galant is an elaborate criminal. Question him, grill him, torture him even, and you would learn just what he wanted you to know, not a word more. We're dealing with superlatively nimble wits, and our only hope is to outmanoeuvre him. I knew he would meet that girl again, before I even knew who the girl was."

"Meet her 'again,'" I said, gloomily. "Yes. Granted you knew he had met her the first time."

"Oh, that was clear! You shall hear it in good time. Now, thanks to our friend Robiquet, we have overcome our difficulties easily. The stronghold could be entered, but this key makes it child's play. We have the room next to his, a window giving on an airshaft... Jeff, he'll have to possess magical powers if he divines it. Do you know," he asked, abruptly, "what was the most significant point in his conversation with Gina Prévost?"

"Her knowing, very probably, who committed the murder."

"Not at all. I could have told you that. It was the statement of hers, '*It was dark.*' Remember it! Now for a little visit to the rue de Varenne before lunch. We are going to see Mademoiselle Martel's parents."

We had stopped at the corner of that winding street, which runs through the heart of the Faubourg St.-Germain. I hesitated, and said:

"Look here. These scenes with hysterical parents...they make you squirm. If we're to go through anything like that one a while ago, I'd prefer to be absent."

Slowly he shook his head, staring at a lamp-bracket in one dark-stained wall. "Not with these people. Do you know them, Jeff?"

"Heard the name, that's all."

"The Comte de Martel is the oldest, most unyielding stock of France. 'Family honour,' with them, is an almost morbid thing. But, for all that, the old man is a fierce republican; don't, by the way, make the mistake of addressing him by his title. They come of a line of soldiers, and he is prouder of his rank of colonel than anything else. He lost an arm in the war. His wife is a little old woman, almost completely deaf. They live in a gigantic house, and they spend their time playing dominoes."

"Dominoes?"

"Hour after hour," said Bencolin, nodding sombrely.

"The old man was a great gambler in his youth. Not so much gambler as what you call 'plunger'; the kind who doesn't reason, but bets huge sums on an even chance at anything. Dominoes—he must get a sardonic pleasure in that!" Still the detective hesitated. "This has got to be handled carefully. When they learn where their daughter was murdered... Well, Jeff, this 'family honour,' obsession is devilish difficult."

"Has Chaumont told them?"

"I most fervently hope so. And I hope he was careful not to mention the club. I think, though, that they would consider the waxworks almost as bad. However—"

Vast spaces are hidden from Paris. The gardens of the Faubourg St.-Germain come with the suddenness of an illusion when these tall old walls open their gates. You would swear that the avenues of trees stretch away for miles, that pools are enchanted and flower-beds spectral, and that no such spacious countryside can exist in the very centre of Paris traffic. Here are stone houses, gabled and turreted, on phantom estates. In summer, when all the flower hues flame against green, and the trees sparkle with sunlight, these houses still seem proud and forlorn and ghostly. But in autumn their gables against a grey-white sky make you feel you have strayed into a countryside which is a thousand leagues from Paris or reality, and which exists only in time. A light in a window startles you. On these gravel walks at twilight you might meet an unlighted coach, with footmen and four white horses, and you would realize, in the wind and thunder of its passing, that the passengers had been dead two hundred years.

I do not exaggerate. When the outer gates of the Martel estate were opened by an old man in a *concierge*'s lodge, and we walked up a gravel drive sprouting with weeds, Paris had entirely ceased to exist. Automobiles were not yet invented.

The lawn looked gutted with the brown patterns of dead flower-beds, mingling with yellow where leaves were plastered in soggy patches under the trees. From the back of the house, which was mournful in iron scrollwork, we heard a rustle, the play and creak of a chain, and then the terrific barking of a dog. It yelped and boomed through the damp twilight in these gardens; it had its echo down rustling vistas behind. As though in reply, a light shone out from a window on the ground floor.

"I hope the brute's not loose," said Bencolin. "They call him Tempest. He's the most vicious—Hallo!"

He stopped short. From under a copse of chestnut trees at our right a figure had darted out. It ran with a horrible hopping motion, as though it were not human. You could see the rags of an overcoat fluttering from its back as it disappeared into another clump of trees; then only the wind rasped through the gardens and the dog's barking suddenly died.

"We're being watched, Jeff," said Bencolin, after a pause. "Shakes you up, eh? It did me. That's one of Galant's men, on your life. The dog scared him out."

I shivered. Swishing, the wind lifted in one vast upheaval through the trees, and all the gardens seethed to its turmoil. A heavy drop of rain spattered on the leaves, then another. We hurried up to the house, past a line of old hitching-posts, into the shelter of the porch. This porch, apparently, was an addition from the last century, for iron link-brackets were still in the walls. It must have been a gloomy enough place for a young girl like Claudine Martel. Behind a sheathing of dead vines I saw a few wicker chairs covered with bright chintz, and the breeze was fluttering the pages of a magazine which lay open on a padded swing.

The front doors were already being opened at our approach.

"Come in, messieurs," said a deferential voice. "Colonel de Martel has been expecting you."

A manservant led us into a dim hall, very spacious, panelled in black walnut. It was not shabby, but it needed an airing; it smelled of old wood, of dusty hangings, of brass-polish and waxed floors. Again I caught that scent of clothes and hair, as at the waxworks; but these, I could not help feeling, were the clothes and hair of dead people; and the walls, dark red satin above their panels, exhaled an indefinable reek of decay. We were ushered into a library at the back of the house.

At a mahogany table, on which burnt a shaded lamp, sat Colonel de Martel. At the rear of the room, above tall bookcases, there were diamond-paned windows of blue and white glass. You could see the silver rain thickening, and pale flickers of light were on the face of the woman who sat motionless, her hands clasped, in the shadow of the bookshelves. About them both was an atmosphere of stiff waiting, of tears that would never be shed, and of doom. The rustle of the shower deepened, echoing. The old man rose.

"Come in, messieurs," he said in a deep, monotonous voice. "This is my wife."

He was of medium height, very stocky, but bearing himself with the utmost rigidity. His face, rather sallow of complexion, would have been handsome had it not been so fleshy. The light was reflected on his big bald skull; his eyes, sunken under thick brows, had a sort of grim bright glaze. I saw a play of muscles tightening the mouth under a large moustache, sandy-white in colour and drooping at the corners, and I saw the folds of his chin flatten over a high collar with a narrow band of cravat. His dark clothes, though somewhat old-fashioned in cut, were of the finest cloth, and there was an opal stud in his shirt. Now he was bowing towards the shadow.

"Good day!" sang the woman's voice, high and shrill like that of many deaf people. The eyes in her faded, bony face searched us; her hair was completely white. "Good day! Bring chairs for the gentlemen, André!"

Not before the servant had brought them out and we were seated near the table did the Comte de Martel sit down himself. I saw on the table a set of dominoes. They had been built up like blocks for a sort of toy house, and I had a sudden vision of him sitting there for long hours with a steady hand, patiently building them up, patiently taking them down, like a solemn child. But now he sat looking at us grimly and fixedly, fingering a piece of blue paper like a part of a telegram.

"We have heard, monsieur," he said at length.

The atmosphere was getting on my nerves. I saw the woman nodding her head in the background, straining to catch each word; and it seemed to me that shattering forces were gathering round this house, to tear it down.

"That is good, Colonel Martel," said Bencolin. "We are relieved of an unpleasant duty. I speak to you frankly: there now remains only to get all the information we can about your daughter..."

The other nodded deliberately. For the first time I noticed that he was fingering that paper with only one hand; his left arm was missing and the sleeve was tucked into his pocket. It was a queer touch, indefinably tragic, to this quiet room under the rain.

"I like your straightforwardness, monsieur," he assented. "You will not find either madame or myself weak-kneed at this time. When may we—have her back?"

Again I shivered, regarding those glazed bright eyes. Bencolin replied:

"Very soon. You know where Mademoiselle Martel was found?"

"In a certain waxworks, I believe"—the rumbling voice rose mercilessly—"stabbed through the back. Speak out. My wife cannot hear you."

"Is she really *dead*?" sang the woman, suddenly. The cry jabbed through all of us. M. Martel turned cold eyes, slowly, to regard her. A big grandfather clock ticked in the immense silence; seeing his look, madame subsided with blinking eyes, her face pinched eagerly still.

"Our hope is," Bencolin went on, "that her parents can throw some light on her death. When was she last seen alive?"

"I have tried to think of that. I am afraid"—this time the merciless voice was directed against himself—"I am afraid I have not kept good account of my daughter. All that I left to her mother. A son, now—! But Claudine and I were almost as strangers. She was active, gay; a different generation." He pressed his hand hard to a spot just over his eyes, staring at the past. "The last time I saw her was at dinner yesterday evening. On the same day, once a month, I always go to the home of the Marquis de Cerannes to play cards. It is a ritual we have observed for nearly forty years. I went last night about nine o'clock. At that time, I know, she was still in the house, for I heard her moving about in her room."

"Do you know whether she had intended to go out?"

"I do not, monsieur. As I have said," his mouth tightened again, "I did not follow her doings. I left my instructions with her mother as to what Claudine should do, and I rarely observed. This—is—the—result."

Watching madame, I saw a bright, rather pitiful expression come into her face. An old-school father and a doting, rather simple-minded mother. From what I had been able to deduce earlier, Claudine Martel was not at all like Odette. She would be able to get away unsuspected with almost anything. I saw that the same thought was in Bencolin's mind, for he inquired:

"You were never in the habit of waiting up for her, I take it?"

"Monsieur," the old man said, coldly, "in our family we have never thought it necessary."

"Did she entertain her friends here frequently?"

"I was compelled to forbid it. Their noise was unsuited to our home and I feared it might disturb the neighbours. She was permitted, of course, to invite her own friends to our receptions. She declined. I discovered that she wished to serve our guests with what are called 'cocktails'..." A faint, contemptuous smile twisted the thick muscles of his jaw. "I informed her that the Martel wine-cellar was unsurpassed in France, and that I did not feel called on to insult my old friends. It was the only time we ever had words. She asked me, in an almost screaming voice, whether I had ever been young. Young!"

"To return, monsieur. You say you saw your daughter at dinner. Did her behaviour seem as usual, or should you have said there was anything on her mind?"

M. de Martel fingered one end of his long moustache, his eyes narrowed.

"I have thought of that since. I noticed it. She was—upset."

"She wouldn't eat!" shrilled his wife, so abruptly that Bencolin turned to stare at her. The colonel had spoken in a low voice, and both of us wondered how she had heard.

"She is reading your lips, monsieur," our host explained. "You need not shout... That is true. Claudine scarcely ate at all."

"Should you say that her behaviour was due to excitement, or fright, or precisely what?"

"I do not know. Both, perhaps."

"She wasn't well!" cried madame. Her sharp face, which once must have been beautiful, turned from side to side, and her faded eyes looked at us appealingly. "She hadn't been well. And the night before that I heard her crying in the middle of the night. Sobbing!"

Every time that queer, high voice, hovering on the edge of tears, trembled from the shadows under the rain-splattered windows, I felt an impulse to grip the edge of my chair. I could see that her husband was fighting to keep his self-control; his mouth was pulled down and the lids fluttered over harsh eyes.

"I heard her! And I got up, and went into her room the way I did when she was a baby, and she was crying in bed." After a gulp the woman went on: "And she didn't snap at me. She was nice to me. And I said, 'What's the matter, dear? Let me help you.' And she said, 'You can't help me, mother; nobody can help me!' She was that way all the next day, and last night she went out…"

Fearing an outburst, Colonel Martel had turned to regard her again; his one big fist was clenched and his empty left sleeve trembled. Bencolin took care to fashion his words carefully with his lips when he addressed her:

"She told you what was troubling her, madame?"

"No. No. She refused."

"Had you any idea?"

"Eh?" A blank look. "Trouble her? What *would* trouble a poor little child? No."

Her voice had become a whimper. The booming and decisive tones of her husband took up the gap.

"A little more information, monsieur, I learned from speaking to her and to André, our butler. In the neighbourhood of nine-thirty o'clock, Claudine received a telephone message.

Shortly after that she seems to have left the house. She did not tell her mother where she was going, but promised to return by eleven."

"A message from a man or a woman?"

"They do not know."

"Was any part of the conversation overheard?"

"Not by my wife, naturally. But I questioned André closely on that point. The only words he overheard were these: 'But I didn't even know he was back in France!'"

"'I didn't even know he was back in France,'" the detective repeated. "You have no idea to whom these words referred?"

"None. Claudine had many friends."

"She took a car?"

"She took the car," asserted the other, "without my permission. It was returned to us this morning by a man from the police; I understand it had been left close to the waxworks where she was found. Now, monsieur!"

His fist pounded slowly on the table, shaking the edifice of dominoes. His eyes had a dry glitter as they fixed Bencolin.

"Now, monsieur!" he said again. "The case is in your hands. Can you tell me why my daughter, why a Martel, should be found dead in a waxworks, in that dingy neighbourhood? That is what I want most to know."

"It is a formidable problem, Colonel Martel. At the present moment I am not sure. You say she had never been there before?"

"I do not know. In any event"—he made a heavy gesture—"it is clearly the work of some thug or sneak-thief. I want him brought to justice. Do you hear, monsieur? If necessary, I will offer a reward large enough to—"

"I hardly think that will be necessary. But it brings me to the chief question I wanted to ask. When you say 'the work of a thug' you perhaps know that your daughter was not robbed—robbed, I mean, in the ordinary sense. Her money was untouched. What the murderer took was some object which hung on a slender gold chain round her neck. Do you know what it was?"

"Round her neck?" The old man shook his head, frowning and biting at his moustache. "I can't even imagine. It was certainly none of the Martel jewels. I keep them locked up, and they are worn by my wife only on formal occasions. Some trinket, perhaps; it could scarcely be anything of value. I never noticed…"

He glanced over inquiringly at his wife.

"No!" she cried. "Why, that's impossible! She never wore anything like a necklace or a locket; she said it was old-fashioned. I'm sure! I would *know*, monsieur!"

Every lead seemed to end in a blind alley, every clue produced nothing. We were silent for a long time, while the rustle of the rain grew to an uproar and the windows blurred to darkness. But, instead of disappointing Bencolin, this last piece of information appeared to stimulate him. He had an air of repressed exultation; the light of the lamp made long triangles of shadow under his cheek bones and showed a gleam of teeth in a smile between small moustache and pointed beard. But his long eyes were still sombre as they moved from M. de Martel to his wife. With a whir of weights the grandfather clock began to chime twelve. Each hoarse note beat with a slow finality, as of the grave, and intensified the nervous tension. M. de Martel looked at his wrist, frowned, and then glanced up at the clock in a polite intimation that it was growing late.

"I do not think," Bencolin observed, "that we need question you any further. The solution does not lie here. Any attempt to go into Mademoiselle Martel's affairs farther than we have done will, I think, be futile. I thank you, madame, and you, monsieur, for your help. Rest assured that I will keep you informed of our progress."

Our host rose as we did. For the first time I noticed how the interview had shaken him; his stocky body was still rigid, but his eyes were blank and baffled with despair. He stood there in his fine clothes and linen, as for a gala day, the lamp-light shining on his bald head...

We went out of the old house into the rain, leaving a deaf woman and a man with one arm.

10

DEATH IN SILHOUETTE

"ROOM OF THE JUGE D'INSTRUCTION. BENCOLIN SPEAKING. Connect with central office, medical bureau."

A buzz of wires, a prolonged clicking. "Medical bureau, desk."

"*Juge d'instruction*. Report autopsy of Odette Duchêne, file A-forty-two, homicide."

"File A-forty-two, reported on by commissaire, first *arrondissement*, two p.m. October nineteenth, nineteen hundred and thirty, to central office. Body of woman, found in river at foot of Pont au Change. Correct?"

"Correct."

"Compound fracture of skull, caused by fall from height of not less than twenty feet. Immediate cause of death, stab-wound in third intercostal space, piercing heart, from knife one inch wide by seven inches long. Minor bruises and lacerations. Cuts about head, face, neck, and hands, caused by broken glass. Dead, when found, about eighteen hours."

"That's all… Central office, department four."

"Central office, department four." A sing-song voice.

"*Juge d'instruction.* Who is in charge of case A-forty-two, homicide?"

"A-forty-two. Inspector Lutrelle."

"If he is in the building, let me speak to him."

The bleak autumn dusk was already setting in. I had not been able to see Bencolin until then; he had been summoned back to his office on routine business shortly before lunch, and it was past four o'clock when I arrived at his office in the Palais de Justice. Even then I did not find him in the great bare room with the green-shaded lights, where he conducts his examinations. He has a private room of his own at the very top of the vast building, a sort of den shut off from its buzz and clamour, but connected by a battery of telephones with every department of the Sûreté, and with the *prefecture* of police several blocks away.

The Ile de la Cité, which really is an island shaped like a narrow ship, stretches for nearly a mile in the Seine; at the rear end, broadening out, is the Cathedral of Notre-Dame, and at the front—tapering out in the fashion of a bowsprit—is a drowsy park bravely called The Square of Gallant Green. Between these two, jutting up over the bustle of the New Bridge, rise the buildings of justice. The windows of Bencolin's room are high up under the roof; they look down on the New Bridge, past this tapering point, and up the dark river. From here you have an illusion of keeping watch over all Paris. It is an eerie place, with its brown walls, its easy-chairs, its grisly relics in glass cases, its framed photographs, and an old rug worn threadbare by the ceaseless pacing of Bencolin.

We sat in the dark, except for dim lights over bookcases in an alcove. Their yellow illumination was faint behind Bencolin, silhouetting his head as he sat beside the windows with a telephone in his hand. My chair was across from his, beside the windows, also, and I wore a headpiece from an extension to the phone. I heard the clicking and buzzing, the ghostly voices which spoke from all parts of the building, and my hands were on all the filaments which stretched from this room, responsive to the slightest pull, wound invisibly about every house in Paris.

There was silence after his last request. I saw his long fingers tap impatiently on the chair arm, and my eyes wandered out the windows. They rattled dimly, for a cold wind was sweeping down the river. The glass was still blurred with rain, which snapped there in little whips. I could see the smudgy lamps on the New Bridge, far below; it was thick with pedestrians, traffic whistles, the lights and rumble of busses. Then, out farther, there were a few gleams on the tapering point, reflected brokenly in the river. But the rest was lost. Cold lamps, a row of them on each bank of the river, moved away, grew blurred, and then were dimmed in rain.

"Inspector Lutrelle speaking," sang a voice in my ear. We were far from that prospect in the cold. We were shut in behind glass, with great machinery in motion; with a scent of thick cigar smoke, and a frayed rug where those pacing footfalls followed killers.

"Lutrelle? Bencolin. What have you on the Duchêne killing?"

"Routine, so far. I went round to see her mother this afternoon, and was told you had been there. Had a talk with Durrand. He's in charge of the Martel affair, isn't he?"

"Yes."

"He says you believe the two are connected with the Mask Club in the Boulevard de Sebastopol. I wanted to crash in there, but he told me you'd issued orders to lay off. Is that right?"

"For the present."

The voice said, querulously: "Well, if those are instructions, all right. I don't see the idea, though. Here's the lead. The body was picked up against the foot of the Pont au Change, against one of the piles of the bridge. The current is swift, and that hadn't been allowed for. It was probably thrown in just about *there*, where it got wedged in. And that bridge is right at the end of the Boulevard de Sebastopol. It could have been brought down from the club in a direct line."

"Anybody notice anything suspicious?"

"No. We've questioned in that neighbourhood. That's the devil of it."

"Laboratory reports?"

"Laboratory can't tell a thing. She was in the water too long, and it destroyed indications as to the clothes. There's one more lead, if you insist on keeping away from the club..."

"The glass cuts in her face, eh? The glass is probably of an unusual type—opaque, certainly, and probably coloured—and you found pieces of it. Oh yes, Inspector. She either jumped or was thrown out a window, and windows of that club would in all likelihood have—"

Over the wire there was a smothered exclamation of annoyance. "Yes," the voice admitted grudgingly, "there were slivers in some of the cuts. It's dark red and very expensive. So you saw that, eh? We're questioning all the glaziers within a mile of the Porte St.-Martin. If they got that window repaired... Any instructions?"

"None for the present. Keep after it, but, understand! No inquiries of any kind at the Mask Club until I give you permission."

The voice grunted and rang off. Bencolin put down his telephone, shifting his fingers nervously up and down the arms of the chair. We were silent, listening to the distant hum of the building and the spurting rain.

"So," I said, "the Duchêne girl was killed at the club. That seems to establish it. But Claudine Martel… Bencolin, was she killed because she knew too much about the first death?"

He turned his head slowly. "What makes you think so?"

"Well, her behaviour at home on the night of Duchêne's disappearance. You know—the crying, the agitation, and telling her mother 'You can't help me. Nobody can help me.' She seems ordinarily to have been a very self-possessed young lady… Do you think they were both members?"

He leaned over slightly to draw closer to him a tabouret on which stood a decanter of brandy and a box of cigars. The light from the alcove behind lay along the side of his face, hollowing the cheek bone, and glowed scarlet through the liquid in the decanter.

"Well, we can make a shrewd guess. Odette Duchêne, I think, was not a member. The Martel girl, however, clearly *was*."

"Why 'clearly'?"

"Oh, there are any number of indications. First, because she certainly was known to Mademoiselle Augustin, and well known; Mademoiselle Augustin had her freshly in mind, though she may not have known the name. Claudine Martel must have been in the habit of going to the club through the waxworks, by which we may infer she was a constant visitor…"

"One moment! Suppose her face was known to Mademoiselle Augustin, and fresh in the lady's mind, because she had seen Claudine Martel *dead*?"

Pouring out a glass of brandy, he regarded me thoughtfully.

"I see, Jeff. You are trying to tangle up our waxworks

proprietress in a guilty knowledge of the murder?—Well, it is possible from several angles. We will discuss that point later. But, as to Mademoiselle Martel's being a member of the club, there was (secondly) the black mask we found in the passage beside her body. It obviously belonged to her."

I sat up straight and said: "What the devil! I distinctly heard you tell Inspector Durrand, and prove it by the mask, that it belonged to another woman!"

"Yes," he said, chuckling—"yes, I was forced to deceive you both in order to deceive the inspector. I was afraid for a moment he would see the ghastly and glaring flaw in my reasoning—"

"But why?"

"Deceive him?… Because, Jeff, Inspector Durrand is too much a man of action to be discreet. He believes that she was lured to the club, an innocent girl, and murdered during a brutal attack; that is what I want everybody to believe. If Durrand had known she was a member, he would instantly have called on her parents—her friends—everybody, and he would have told them all that fact. Result: they would either have flown into a terrific rage and kicked us all out of the house, or else slammed the door in our faces to begin with. In any event, we should have received no help or information whatever… As you may have noticed, I have not told either family that these deaths were connected, or that either girl had any connection with the club."

I shook my head. "It's a damned intricate game."

"It has to be! Otherwise, we shall get nowhere. A public scandal of this club, now, would blast our whole hope of getting at the truth. But about the mask: Here was the weak point in the argument I put forth to the inspector. If you remember, the woman whose appearance I deduced from the indications could have been nobody else but the dead girl! Small, dark complexion, brown hair worn long: why, it fitted perfectly, and there was the mask to prove it. But by sleight-of-hand reasoning I convinced Durrand—"

"There was lipstick on the mask. You pointed out that the dead woman wore none."

This time his chuckle became a roar of laughter. "And yet you yourself picked up the lipstick she was carrying in her bag! Why, Jeff, surely you realize that her wearing no lipstick at the time of her death does *not* mean she never wore the mask… I grieve to think how easily Durrand swallowed it. On the contrary, all it means is that she *had* definitely worn the mask in the past, but did not have it on then."

"The torn elastic?"

"Torn, my friend, by the murderer in his or her frantic search through her handbag. You see? She took the mask with her in her handbag when she left home that night. In all probability, the old-fashioned severity of the Martels prevented her from applying lipstick before she left; and then she forgot it. Definitely she was coming to the club. The final point to prove she was a member… Well, let us discuss the whole thing."

He sat back, his finger tips together, and stared out of the window.

"From the beginning, we know that the 'lady in the brown hat,' Gina Prévost, has been somehow concerned with the disappearance of Odette Duchêne. Old Augustin saw her, you remember, following the Duchêne girl down the stairs of the waxworks that afternoon, and mistook her for a ghost. We may also say that Claudine Martel was also concerned with this disappearance, for, considering her membership in the club also, and the facts we have heard about her behaviour on that night, there can be no other interpretation. I do not say that these two are necessarily implicated in the murder. On the contrary, I think I have an idea of how they *are* implicated. But they are afraid, Jeff—horribly afraid they *may be* implicated. So they arrange for a meeting, Gina Prévost and Claudine Martel, and on that night Claudine Martel is murdered.

"At twenty-five minutes to twelve, then, we have Mademoiselle Prévost waiting in front of the waxworks, where she is seen by the policeman. She is not only upset, but indecisive. Unquestionably she has arranged to meet her friend either (a) in the waxworks itself or (b) in the passage, for girls of that type would scarcely wait *outside* the passage door giving on the Boulevard de Sebastopol—it's not a pleasant neighbourhood to loiter in doorways, you know. But what happens? Something has gone wrong, Jeff, and we do not need to look far in search of it. She reaches the museum at eleven thirty-five, *but the museum is closed.*

"Sheer chance has upset things. Sheer chance caused me to telephone Monsieur Augustin for an appointment, and sheer chance made him lock up his waxworks half an hour before its usual closing-time. On her arrival, Mademoiselle Prévost finds the gates shut and the museum dark. It has never happened before, and she does not know what to do. She hesitates. Undoubtedly she has accustomed herself to go in by way of the museum, and so she hesitates to enter by the door giving on the Boulevard de Sebastopol.

"Claudine Martel has arrived before her. Whether or not she arrived also after the museum was closed, or whether she is accustomed to using the Boulevard de Sebastopol entrance, this we do not know. In any case, she clearly entered by the boulevard door…"

"Why so?"

"She had no ticket, Jeff!" Bencolin leaned forward and slapped the arm of his chair impatiently. "Surely you know that (if only for appearance's sake) each member of the club must buy a ticket for the waxworks when entering. Those blue tickets! You must keep them constantly in mind! But there was no museum ticket among her effects. Surely we can't be so mad as to suppose that the murderer might have stolen it, for why should he? He left her in the museum; he certainly tried to make no mystery of her presence there."

"I see. Go on."

"Therefore, we have Mademoiselle Martel going in one door, and her friend waiting on the street before the waxworks. While each waits, and each wonders where the other is, we come to the significant points.

"The first significant point is this. Once inside that passage, there are three ways by which the murderer could have approached his victim. First, there is the door with the Bulldog lock, opening on the street. Second, there is the door into the actual club itself, in the rear of the brick wall. Third, there is the door from the museum. Now this last door is significant; it has a spring lock, and can be opened only from *inside* the museum. It is used, but by people going one way only—*viz.*, into the club. They never leave that way; they have no keys. And why? Because the club keeps late hours. After twelve, when the museum closes, they couldn't go tramping out through the waxworks, unbolting and unbarring that huge front door, and making it necessary for Mademoiselle Augustin to get up and lock it again every time somebody left! That in itself would be impractical, to say nothing of the fact that it must surely be discovered by old Augustin, and stopped. You yourself have seen how anxious his daughter was to conceal it from him… No, no, Jeff! A person could enter by way of the museum; but that spring lock was always caught on the museum side, and the key thrown away; the exit was the boulevard door.

"Now, then. In determining which way the murderer approached his victim, we have these three doors. The murderer, you see, *could* have come by one of the first two—from the street or from inside the club. But," said Bencolin, emphasizing each word by a tap on the chair arm—"but if he came in either of those ways *he could not possibly have carried the body into the waxworks.* Do you see? The museum door being locked on the inside, he could not have opened it from the passage. Therefore, my friend, we see that the murderer must have crept upon her from inside the museum, by opening that door from the inside…"

I whistled. "You mean," I said, "that when old Augustin locked up the museum at eleven-thirty, he locked the murderer in?"

"Yes. Locked him in—in the dark. Now, clearly, anybody who wanted to get out when Augustin closed up, could have gotten out; it was no accident. The killer waited there deliberately, knowing that Mademoiselle Martel would enter the passage. It did not matter which way she came—museum or street door—he would have her. And he could hide himself very nicely in that cubbyhole behind the dummy wall where the satyr stands."

As he paused to light a cigar, eagerly, his hands trembling as he saw the recital unfold, my first ominous thought came back.

"Bencolin," I said, "might it necessarily have been somebody from outside who was locked in the museum?"

"What do you mean?" The match flame lit briefly the

gleam of his eyes. He was touchy when you questioned any point of his reconstruction, and he spoke irritably.

"The Augustin woman was alone in the museum. There is that queer affair of her turning on the lights on the staircase—you remember? She *said* she thought somebody was moving about in the museum... By the way," I said, remembering suddenly, "how the devil did you know she had? You asked her about it, and she admitted it, but there was no indication..."

"Oh yes, there was!" he corrected, recovering a little of his good humour. "Jeff, precisely what are you trying to tell me? That Marie Augustin committed the murder?"

"Well...no, not exactly. There isn't the shadow of a motive. And I can't see why she would have stabbed the girl and then taken the trouble to lug the body in and dump it right in her own museum, where it pointed directly to her. But her presence alone there—and the lights—"

He gestured with the red end of his cigar. I could sense his satirical grin.

"You are insistent on those lights. Let me explain actually what happened," suggested Bencolin. He leaned forward again, his voice becoming grave. "First, we have Mademoiselle Martel in the passage. Second, we have the murderer in the cubbyhole. Third, we have Mademoiselle Prévost waiting outside the museum... What has happened in the meantime? The Augustin woman is, as you say, alone in their living-quarters. Imagine it! She glances out the window giving on the street. In the light of the street lamp she sees—as the policeman saw—the face of Gina Prévost, and she sees Gina Prévost pacing up and down nervously. Now, whatever her faults, Mademoiselle Augustin is a conscientious young lady; she earns her money from whoever pays it. And she knows what the other wants. To refuse entrance may mean the loss of a lucrative position. So she switches on the lights...the central ones, you recall, and those on the staircase which leads to the door into the passage...so that the visitor's way may be illuminated. Then she unbolts the big front entrance of the museum.

"And Mademoiselle Prévost is gone! It is nearly twenty minutes to twelve and Prévost has decided to go in by the other way. The street is deserted. Marie Augustin is puzzled, doubtful, and suddenly a bit suspicious. Was this (she might wonder) by any chance a trap of some kind? I can see this resolute young lady peering up and down the rue St.-Appoline, thinking. Then she bolts the door again. She walks into the museum, I fancy, as a matter of habit; she stares round in that green gloom...

"In the meantime, what has happened in the passage behind? The murderer has been waiting, since eleven-thirty, in the cubbyhole between the dummy stone wall and the museum door into the passage. At eleven-thirty the lights have been turned out in the museum. The killer is in complete darkness. Shortly afterwards he hears the door to the Boulevard de Sebastopol being unlocked. It opens, and the figure of a woman is outlined, very dimly, against the vague lights from the boulevard outside..."

In that high room under the rain, I saw the scene take form. Our darkened room; the dull yellow bar of light from the alcove, with Bencolin's Satanic face bent forward and his hand half lifted against it; the scurry of rain on the windows, and the thin mutter of traffic—all this dissolved into the damp passageway he pictured. The boulevard door was opening, throwing a spangled glimmer like moonlight. A woman stood there. Bencolin's low voice quickened:

"It is Claudine Martel. She is coming into the passage,

where she is to wait (let us say) for Gina Prévost. She is silhouetted there, but too dimly. The murderer does not know—he cannot know, since he came by way of the museum—that this is his victim, Mademoiselle Martel. He thinks it is she. But he must make sure, and it is too dark to be sure.

"He must have undergone some horrible moments of indecision while he hears her pacing up and down the passage in the dark. He hears her footsteps on stone, the click of her heels, but he cannot see her. *She* paces here, Mademoiselle Prévost paces outside the waxworks, and there are three hearts beating heavily; all because the museum has been closed at eleven-thirty and the lights turned out... Jeff, if Claudine Martel had illuminated the passage by pressing that light-button at the entrance! If she had done that, the whole tale would have been different. But she didn't. This we must know from that vital statement of Mademoiselle Prévost, which you heard, *'It was dark.'*

"Note now how the time must synchronize with each act, in order to get the situation as we found it, and see what inevitably followed:

"It is precisely eleven-forty. Gina Prévost determines to enter the passage by way of the boulevard door. So she leaves the front of the waxworks, and turns up into the Boulevard de Sebastopol. Immediately afterwards, Mademoiselle Augustin turns on the lights inside the museum, and, in doing so, she switches on that green light which is in the corner of the staircase beside the satyr. As I pointed out to you, with the dummy wall and the museum door into the passage both open, the green light would shine faintly into the passage beyond... just enough for a person to be recognized at close range...

"Seeing the light, Claudine Martel whirls round. It falls green on her face as she stares, and she sees before her the silhouette of the murderer. As she retreats a step towards the brick wall, he hesitates no longer. She has not even time to scream before he pulls her against him and drives the knife into her back…

"And this, Jeff, occurs at the very instant when Gina Prévost unlocks the boulevard door with her silver key and opens it!"

He paused, his voice tense, and the cigar had gone out in his fingers. My blood pounded at the suggestion of that scene: the dull green glow, the murderer's thrust, just as the lock clicked to the turn of the silver key, and another woman's figure loomed in the passage. How the murderer's heart must have turned over in a sick wrench when he saw it!

A long silence, eerie with portent, like small fingers stroking the nerves, and the ceaseless gurgling splash of the rain…

"Jeff," the detective continued, slowly, "what went on in that passage we can only guess. Thus far we have been able to reconstruct with tolerable certainty, but the sequel—? The light was so dim that the murderer could have recognized his victim only at close quarters. Therefore it is not reasonable to say that Gina Prévost, being some distance away, could have recognized either murderer or victim. Clearly, however, judging by her talk with Galant, she must have known at least who the victim was.

"It is inconceivable that she ran down to investigate. She must have seen the gleam of the knife, the blood, the fall of the body; she knew it was murder, she saw a killer turning his face towards her, and she would not likely have a wish to see much more…

"She screamed and ran, leaving the door open. Therefore we must believe that Claudine Martel, with the dagger buried under her shoulder-blade, must have cried out some words. Gina Prévost recognized the voice and knew that it was her friend who had been stabbed. If we assume this, we must assume something more than a cry or a scream; Gina Prévost could scarcely have known, from a mere outcry, whose voice it was. Words, Jeff; several words!" He paused, and then his low voice rolled through the gloom: "We may say, then, that with death clouding her brain, Claudine Martel cried out, echoing along those hollow walls, the name of her murderer."

Bencolin's telephone rang stridently. He picked it up.

"Allo!" I heard his voice from a distance, and a buzzing. "*Who?* Madame Duchêne and Monsieur Robiquet?... H'm. Well, all right. Send them up."

11

SOME CHARMING HABITS
OF RED-NOSE

Bencolin's words I scarcely heard. I knew he was speaking on the telephone, but I heard him as one hears a radio programme when absorbed in a book. More than any person I know, he has in his choice of words the power to *suggest*. A few phrases clang in the mind like bells, and then go reverberating with multitudinous echoes through every corner of that brain, so that spectres are roused. The white-washed passage, with the green light falling into it, seemed now more ghastly than ever before. The sudden spring of the murderer from his cubbyhole in the dark took on a suggestion of the thoughtless, inexorable savagery of an animal. I could feel the shock of horror, like a blow under the heart, which Claudine Martel must have experienced when the thing, he or she, leapt. And, more terrifying than even the rest was the thought of the dying girl crying the name of her murderer to the senseless walls…

"Madame Duchêne and Monsieur Robiquet." For the first time I recalled the words. Bencolin had switched on the hanging light over his desk; its yellow pool threw into shadow all the room save the vast flat-topped desk, which was littered to confusion with papers. He sat down in a padded chair behind it, a slouching image with heavy-lidded eyes, face shadowed and lined harshly, and the greying black hair which was parted in the middle and twirled up like horns. One hand lay on the desk, idly. Beside it, as he stared at the door, I saw glittering on the blotter a small silver key.

An attendant ushered in Mme. Duchêne and Robiquet; Bencolin rose to greet them, and indicated chairs beside his desk. Despite bad weather, the woman was exquisitely turned out—sealskin and pearls, her face almost youthful under the wings of a tight black hat. The pouches under her eyes might have been shadows, like her pinched look: she hardly seemed the bedraggled and sharp-featured woman we had seen that morning. Her eyes, I now perceived, were not black; they were of a misty dark grey. With one gloved hand she tapped on the desk a copy of a newspaper, and, as she tapped, her wet face became grey with something like despair...

"Monsieur Bencolin," she said in her dry voice, "I have taken the liberty of coming to you. Certain insinuations were dropped to me by an inspector of police who called this afternoon. I did not understand them. I should have forgotten them entirely, but...I saw this." Again she tapped the paper. "I asked Paul to bring me here."

"Of course," said Robiquet, nervously. He was bundled into a thick overcoat, and I saw that he was glancing at the silver key.

"The pleasure is mine, madame," said Bencolin.

She made a gesture, as of brushing politeness aside. "Will you speak to me frankly?"

"About what, madame?"

"About my daughter's—death. And Claudine Martel's," breathlessly. "You did not tell me about *that* this morning."

"But why should I, madame? You surely had enough on your mind, and any other painful—"

"Please, *please* don't try to evade me! I must know. I am sure they are related. This matter of Claudine's being found in a waxworks, that is police subterfuge, is it not?"

Bencolin studied her, his fingers at his temple. He did not reply.

"Because, you see," she went on, with an effort, "I myself was once a member of that Club of Masks. Oh, years ago! Fifteen years. It is not a new institution, though I suppose," bitterly, "it is under new management since my time. I know where it is located. The waxworks—no, I might never have suspected the waxworks at all. But I sometimes suspected that Claudine went there, to the club. And when I learned of her death—and thought of Odette's death…"

She moistened her lips with her tongue. The greyness had settled with leathery fixity on her face. She continued to tap the newspaper spasmodically…

"All of a sudden, monsieur, it rushed over me. I *knew*. Mothers do. I have felt something wrong. Odette was concerned. Wasn't she?"

"I do not know, madame. If so—innocently."

A blankness had come into her eyes. She murmured: "'Unto'… What is it?… 'Unto the third and fourth generation.' I have never been religious. But I believe in God now. Oh yes. And His wrath. On me."

She had begun to tremble. Robiquet was so pale that his face resembled wax; he dug his chin into his coat collar and said, in a muffled voice:

"Aunt Beatrice, I told you—you shouldn't have come out. It's useless. The gentlemen are doing all they can. And—"

"Then, this morning," she rushed on, "when you sent your

friend down to listen to Gina talking to that man, I should have known. Of course. Gina is concerned. Her behaviour! Her horrible behaviour. My little Odette. They were all concerned in it…"

"Madame, surely you are overwrought," the detective observed, gently. "The mere formality of a man calling at that house, and Mademoiselle Prévost's seeing him…"

"Now I will tell you something. I got a shock then, and it made me think. It was the voice of that man."

"Yes?" prompted Bencolin. His fingers began to tap softly on the desk.

"As I say, it started me thinking. I have heard it before."

"Ah! You are acquainted with this Monsieur Galant?"

"I have never seen him. But I have heard his voice four times."

Robiquet stared, hypnotized, at the gleaming silver key, as madame went on steadily:

"The second time was ten years ago. I was upstairs, and Odette—she was a little girl—was with me, learning how to do fancy-work. My husband was reading down in the library; I could smell the smoke of his cigar. The door-bell rang, the maid admitted a visitor, and I heard a *voice* in the hall. It was pleasant. My husband received him. I could hear them talking, though not what was said. But several times the visitor laughed. Later the maid let him out… I remember that his shoes creaked and he was still laughing. A few hours after that I noticed powder fumes instead of cigar smoke, and I went downstairs. My husband used a silencer on his pistol when he shot himself, because—because he didn't want to wake Odette…

"Then I remembered when I had heard that voice for the *first* time. In the Club of Masks, where I had been—oh, before

I was married, I swear it! I heard it from a masked man, who was laughing. That must have been twenty-three or -four years ago. I remembered it only because the man had a hole cut in the mask for his nose, which was a horrible red thing, all twisted; and to see him was like a nightmare; so I never forgot it, or the voice…"

She bowed her head.

"And the third time, madame?" said Bencolin.

"The third time," she replied, swallowing, "was less than six months ago, in early summer. It was at the home of Gina Prévost's parents, at Neuilly. It was in the garden. Towards evening. There was a yellow sky, and I could see a summer-house down at the end of the garden walk, dark against it. I heard somebody's voice talking inside the summer-house. It had a spell in it, as though the man were making love; but all the high trees seemed to get cold, and the sun turned dark, because I recognized it. I ran away. Ran, I tell you! But I saw Gina Prévost come out of the summer-house, smiling to herself. *Then* I said to myself I was mistaken, and hysterical…

"But today, when I heard it again, all this rushed back over me. And I knew. Don't deny it! My little Odette… I didn't pay any attention to your glib explanations. When I read this paper, about Claudine…!"

She glared at him. He remained motionless, his elbow on the chair arm and his fingers at his temple, watching her out of bright unwinking eyes. Presently, when the emotional tension had spent itself, she said:

"You have nothing to tell me?" eagerly.

"Nothing, madame."

Another silence. I heard somebody's watch tick.

"Oh… I see," she said. "I—h-had hoped you would deny it, monsieur. Somehow, I still hoped. But I see now." Smiling faintly, she shrugged her shoulders, snapped at clasps of her handbag in an aimless manner, and glanced round with something of wildness. "Do you know, monsieur, I read in the paper that Claudine had been found in the arms of a wax figure called the Satyr of the Seine. That is the way this man had impressed me. I don't know about the Seine...but a satyr, a ghoulish..."

Robiquet interposed hurriedly. He said: "Aunt Beatrice, we had better go. We are taking up monsieur's time. We can do no good here."

They both rose as the woman did. She continued aimlessly to smile. Bencolin took her hand as she extended it; he made a brief bow which had a queer ancient courtliness about it.

"I fear I can give you no comfort, madame," he murmured. "But this at least I promise you"—he raised his voice slightly and pressed her hand—"that before many hours are out I will have this man where I want him. And then, I swear, he will not trouble you, or anyone else, ever again!—Good afternoon, and...take courage."

His head was still bowed when the door closed after them. The light shone on the thick grey patches in his hair. He walked slowly behind his desk again and sat down.

"I grow old, Jeff," he observed, suddenly. "Not very many years ago I would have permitted myself a secret smile at that woman."

"Smile? Good God!"

"And I would be saved from hating all human beings, as Galant does, only because I could laugh at them. That has always been the essential difference between us."

"You're comparing yourself to that—?"

"Yes. He saw a world mismanaged, and loathed it; he thought, by striking into poor squashy faces, that he was battering down a little of an iron world. And what about me, Jeff? I continued to chuckle, like a broken street-organ, and I turned the crank, like the blind man, and I threw my thin little dissonances against the passion and pity and heart-break that jostled me in the street.—Pass me that brandy, like a good fellow, and let me talk foolishness for a minute! I get little enough chance to do it. Yes. So I laughed, because I feared people, feared their opinions or their scorn..."

"Permit me," I said, "to laugh myself at that idea."

"Oh yes, I did! So, because they might take me for less than I was, I tried to be more than I am; like many others. Only my brain was strong, and, damn me! I forced myself to become more than I am. There walked Henri Bencolin— feared, respected, admired (oh yes!)—and behind him now begins to appear a brittle ghost, wondering about it."

"Wondering what?"

"Wondering, Jeff, why they ever took as a wise man that fiendish idiot who said, 'Know thyself.' To examine one's own mind and heart, and explore them fully, is a poisonous doctrine; it drives men crazy. The man who thinks too much about himself is padding his own cell. For the brain is a greater liar than any man; it lies to its own possessor. Introspection is the origin of fear, and fear builds these walls of hate or mirth, and makes me dreaded; and I am paid back, many times over, by dreading myself... Never mind."

It was a curious mood. He had rattled off his words in jumbled fashion. I did not understand, but I knew that of late these fits of black depression had been more frequent. He seemed to be casting about for something to take his mind off it, and he picked up the silver key. With a bewildering change of mood he fired a new statement at me.

"Jeff, I've told you that we are going to plant somebody,

tonight, in the Mask Club, to get the conversation between Galant and Gina Prévost. Do you think you could do it?"

"I?"

"Why not? Will you do it?"

"Why," I said, "as a matter of fact, there's nothing I'd like better. But of all the trained men you have here, why bank on my abilities?"

He looked at me whimsically. "Oh, I don't know. For one thing, because you're the same height and build as Robiquet, and you'll have to use his key and pass inspection, under a mask, when you enter. For another—maybe to see how you, who haven't my fluctuating moods and don't seem to be given to nerves, will act under fire. It will be dangerous, I warn you."

"That's the real reason, isn't it?"

"I suppose so. What do you say?"

"With the greatest pleasure," I said, exultantly. A chance to examine that club, the strong drink which is adventure, and the bright eyes of danger… He saw my expression, and regarded me sourly.

"Now attend me! This is no lark, damn you!"

I sobered appropriately. His agile brain had already darted off along a new vista of speculation.

"I'll give you instructions… First, though, I want to tell you what you may have to expect. Gina Prévost may or may not know who the murderer is; you heard my theory, but it's only a theory. There is nothing in our evidence to support it. But if she does know, Galant will in all likelihood worm it from her much more easily than the whole department of police could do. If we can get a dictograph record…"

"Bencolin," I said, "who *is* the murderer?"

It was a direct challenge, on a point which was the sorest of all with his vanity; and I knew that, if he were as puzzled as I fancied, he would tell me; but I also knew that it would anger him beyond measure.

He answered, slowly: "I don't know. I have no idea." After a pause, "I suppose that's what has been so rasping my nerves."

"And hence the philosophizing?"

He shrugged. "Probably. Now let me tell you about the sequel to the murder, which I *can* imagine. There is the irritating part. I can outline the whole scene of the crime, what led up to it and what followed it. But the face of the killer remains a blank. See here…"

He hitched his chair round, took another drink, and approached the subject as though he were burrowing under a wall.

"We have carried the story of the murder up to the time when the assassin strikes and Gina Prévost runs away from the passage. From the first time I looked into that passage, I knew that—despite old Augustin's tale of turning off all the lights at eleven-thirty—somebody had turned them on (briefly, at least) in the museum. The bloodstains on the wall, the rifled purse on the floor, all lay in a direct line with the museum door. Light, however dim, had come from there, so that the killer could see his victim and see to loot her purse. So I asked Mademoiselle Augustin, and she admitted having put the lights on for five minutes.

"Now this can lead us to a significant deduction. The killer rifled her purse. What did he want? Not money; it was left untouched. Certainly nothing in the nature of *writing*, like a letter or card—"

"Why not?"

"I think you have agreed, have you not, that the light was so very dim that one could with difficulty recognize a face?" he demanded. "Then how, among all that jumble of envelopes and written matter in her handbag, could he have picked out what he wanted? He couldn't read a word there. But he didn't take the bag or its contents into the museum-landing by the satyr, where the light was fairly good; he tossed them all down… No, no! It was some *object*, Jeff, which he could recognize even in half darkness. Before determining what this was, and whether or not he found it, let me ask you a question. Why did he carry the body into the museum?"

"Apparently to hide the fact that she had been murdered in the passage. To throw suspicion away from the Club of Masks."

Bencolin looked at me with raised eyebrows. Then he sighed.

"My dear fellow," he said, sadly, "sometimes you are so profoundly brilliant that… Ah, well. He carried the body in to make it appear that she had been murdered in the museum, eh? And, in doing so, he left a big handbag lying slap in the middle of the passage, its contents scattered all over the floor? He left wide open the door to the museum, for everybody to notice? He—"

"Oh, shut up! He might have had to leave in a hurry, and forgotten."

"And yet still he had time to put the body in the satyr's arms, arrange the drapery over it, and do everything else up to a nicety… Again, no. It won't do. He didn't care where the body was found. He took it into the museum for a very definite purpose, and his putting it in the satyr's arms was an afterthought. Think! What did you notice about the body?"

"Good God! The broken gold chain round her neck."

"Yes. That was the object: the thing she carried on that chain. Do you see now? He thought it would be in her handbag; so he rifled the handbag, and found it wasn't there… It must, he reasoned, be about her person somewhere. Very likely the pockets. But in that very dim light he couldn't see the pockets of her coat, he didn't know *where* she might be carrying it. So—?"

I bowed. "All right! He dragged her in to the museum-landing, where the light was fairly good."

"There is another reason. He knew that Gina Prévost (not knowing who it was, of course) had looked in and saw him stab the girl. He had seen her dash out—for all he knew, to scream for a policeman. He couldn't stand there all night, exposed. Somebody had switched on the museum lights; *that* way was dangerous, but it was less dangerous than remaining in the passage, for he could simply drag the girl into the museum and lock the door behind him. In a pinch, he could always hide. And he wasn't willing to run out the boulevard door until he had found what he searched for.

"So he went into the landing beside the satyr. A second more, and he has found the gold chain, and—the object."

"I suppose you will now proceed to tell me what it was?"

He sat back in his chair and stared up thoughtfully at the lights.

"I'm not sure, of course. But there are suggestive points. For one thing, even aside from Madame Martel's assuring us that Claudine never wore pendants or anything of that nature, what she carried on that chain was not a light locket, or even a charm such as men carry on their watchchains. As I pointed out to you, that chain was strong. It had been snapped in two—demonstrating that the object was also strong, and not made with a flimsy link to hold it on. It was probably one of these."

From the table he took up the silver key. I looked at the round hole in its thumb-grip; I looked back to Bencolin and nodded...

"Claudine Martel's own key," he amplified, tossing Robiquet's on the desk. "It is (I admit) sheer conjecture, but in the absence of any more tenable hypothesis, I suggest the key. Why did the murderer want it? Why did he run appalling risks of discovery in order to wrench it off?... Anyhow, his story is soon complete. He found the key. The idea occurred to him of putting the body in the satyr's arms. He does so, and what happens? As though by a kind of ghastly curtain-fall, the lights go out; Mademoiselle Augustin is satisfied that nothing is amiss in the museum. Not more than five minutes have elapsed since he stabbed his victim. He opens the museum door, slips into the passage, and escapes by way of the boulevard. And he must be damnably puzzled as to why that girl, that intruder who saw him at work, has not summoned the police!"

"Well, if your theory is correct, why didn't she?"

"Because she feared a police investigation, and what it might lead to in Odette Duchêne's case. She wanted to be tangled up in *no* suspicious events centring round the club, or even to explain her presence there. What she actually did do will be apparent to you..."

"I can guess at it," I admitted. (I couldn't quite guess it, actually, but another matter thrust itself forward, and I dismissed Gina Prévost to hurry on with it.) "However, there's one thing in your line of campaign which seems inconsistent. You say you believed from the first that the murderer had gone into the museum that night before it closed?"

"Yes."

"And went in by the front door, ticket and all?"

"Yes."

"Then why the devil didn't you ask the Augustin woman— she was on guard at the door all evening—who had visited the museum that night? There couldn't have been many people; there never are. She must have seen the murderer go in!"

"Because she wouldn't have told us, and it would have served merely as a warning to the murderer. See here!" He tapped with the key on his desk, emphasizing each word. "I suspect that the killer is a member of that club. Now the good Mademoiselle Augustin is very anxious to protect, not an assassin, but all members of the organization. Failure to protect them from *any inquiry* might mean the destruction of her very lucrative business. Suppose that one, two, even half a dozen club members had gone in by way of the museum that night, do you imagine we should have got a description of them?"

"I suppose not," I acknowledged.

"Eh, well! And, knowing we were looking for one of them, she might—I say she *might*—pass a warning, unobtrusively, to all members who might have gone through last night. How many times must I tell you, Jeff, that our salvation rests on having everybody believe, the police included, that this crime is a mere wanton robbery or rape? Don't you remember?—I fostered this idea in Mademoiselle Augustin's mind by saying, carelessly, that Mademoiselle Martel had probably never been in the museum in her life. She breathed more easily afterwards... In God's name, consider that in those club members we are dealing with some of the greatest names in France! We don't want scandal. We can't 'sweat' the truth out of people, as your American forth-rightness might like... And here is another point. I am convinced that in some fashion Mademoiselle Augustin plays an important part in this affair. As yet I don't see how. And yet—there are hidden fires there, I am willing to swear! Somehow I think we shall find her bulking large in our thoughts before the case is finished, even though she sits placidly selling tickets. If her father knew..."

He was relighting the cigar, which had several times gone out that afternoon; now his hand jerked in midair and stopped. It stayed motionless until the flame grew large and toppled. But he did not notice. His eyes had taken on a frozen, startled stare.

In a whisper, as though to test incredible words, he repeated: "Selling tickets... If her father..."

His lips moved soundlessly. With a spasmodic motion he rose to his feet, rumpling his hair, staring ahead.

"What's the matter? What—?" I demanded, and paused as he made a fierce gesture. But still he did not see me. He took a few steps up and down, in and out of the shadows. Once he let out an incredulous bleat of laughter, but he checked himself. I heard him mutter, "Alibi... That's the alibi," and again: "I wonder who the jeweller is? We've got to find the jeweller..."

"*Look here!*"

"Ah yes! But," he argued, turning and addressing me with an appearance of easy good sense, "If you had one, it would be inevitable. You have got to consider the wall. What else could you use, that would do it?"

"How about bromo-seltzer?" I suggested. "''Twas brillig, and the slithy toves did gyre and gimble in the wabe.' Go to hell, will you?"

I sat down sullenly. His black mood was gone. He rubbed his hands together jubilantly. Then he picked up his glass and held it high.

"Observe a ceremony," he urged, "and join me. I drink to the most sportsman-like killer I have ever met. I drink to the only murderer in my whole experience who ever deliberately walked up and presented me with clues."

12

HOW I VENTURED INTO THE CLUB OF MASKS

THE BOULEVARD DE CLICHY, MONTMARTRE.

Lights spangled in broken reflections on wet pavements. A whiz of car lamps, a whir and honk of taxis, tangled into a noise like the brawl of a vast street-fight, and the murmur of a crowd which slides past with a kind of irregular shuffling. Orchestras blare out against radios. Saucers jar and clink on marble-topped tables, in cafés whose windows are dirty, and their *clientèle* dirtier still; but the grimy windows are dazzling with lights. Floors smell of sawdust, there are many mirrors, the beer is watered, and whiskers flourish. Out of the din, hawkers cry silk neckties at five francs, under wild gas-flares. Visiting young ladies in white wraps and pearls step carefully over the swift water of gutters. Street-walkers, graven of face, with motionless black eyes, sit before glasses of coffee, and seem to be pondering. Forlornly, a consumptive hand-organ gurgles tinkling music. Pedlars, hoarse from talking, will exhibit cardboard thingummies which crow like a rooster when you pull the string, or paper skeletons which dance the can-can when you put a match behind them. Electric signs, red and yellow, flash away with their monotonous gaiety; and the scarlet wheel of the Moulin Rouge revolves on the night sky.

The Boulevard de Clichy, Montmartre. Pivot and pulse of night life, centre of all the tiny streets on which famous night clubs cling to the hill. Rue Pigalle, rue Fontaine, rue Blanche, rue de Clichy, all revolve on a glowing hub, and startled visitors are tilted into them down cobble-stoned ways. Your brain whirls with the bang of jazz. You are drunk, or you mean to get drunk. You have a woman, or you will have one shortly. Certainly unthinking people will tell you that Paris at night has lost its lure. In Berlin, in Rome, in New York (they will say), great, shining temples of hilarity have made Paris haunts seem cheap and dingy. As though efficiency were the object in drinking, or making love, or humanly acting the fool. God save you, merry gentlemen! if this is your object, you will never enjoy the grinning, slipshod way in which Paris does things. This childish mystery, this roar, this damp smell of fresh trees and old sawdust, this do-as-you-please easiness, this splattering of coloured lights, will never turn your head: but memories will be lost to your old age.

I looked soberly on the Boulevard de Clichy that night. And yet it had got into my blood with a reckless beat. The feel of the silver key in the pocket of my white waistcoat, and the mask tucked under the waistcoat also, brought into it a cold tingle of adventure.

At the last moment Bencolin's plan had been altered. He had got from the fire commissioner the blueprint (they must be on file for every place of the sort) showing the room arrangement in the Club of Masks. It had only one entrance. Its rooms, without outside windows except for a few blind ones, were ranged round a quadrangle forming an open court.

In the centre of the quadrangle, like a separate house, rose an immense structure whose domed roof was of glass. This was the great promenade hall, connected with the main body by two passages—one at the front, going to the lounge, and one at the rear, connecting with the manager's office. For the sake of clearness, I append a plan of the first floor.

It will be observed that all the private rooms on the first floor open, by a single door and window, on the narrow court where the great hall rises. Also, that these rooms are reached by four doors, one at each corner of the great hall—so that the possessors of these rooms may go to them without returning to the lounge. However, those having rooms on the two floors above must reach them by a staircase in the lounge, which is indicated in the plan by a black square beside the bar. Now a look at the plan of the floor above this will show that room 18, where Galant was to meet Gina Prévost, is directly above the one numbered 2 in the drawing; and Robiquet's room, 19, above the one numbered 3.

Originally it had been Bencolin's idea to plant a dictograph in room 18. But the plan alone, to say nothing of what information we had been able to receive, would make this attempt too dangerous. Wires would have to be run from the window up over the roof. Considering that the club attendants would be doubly on guard, that there were no outside windows, and that any suspicious movement in the court could not fail to be observed, this design had to be abandoned. Bencolin fumed. He had not suspected such enormous obstacles, and it was too late now to undermine the club personnel.

In the end it had been determined that I should go, and that I should in some fashion contrive to be hidden in room 18 when the two arrived. It was a ticklish job, for the whole place was unknown territory. If I were caught, it would be like being caught inside a well. I could not in any fashion communicate with the outside. Nor could I be armed. Due to the temperamental qualities of jealous wives of husbands who might, being masked, find entrance, we understood that guests were given a polite scrutiny by a number of suave bruisers in evening clothes at the door.

Had I reflected, I should have known myself for a damned fool. But the prospect was too alluring. Besides, it was too early for that thick, half-pleasant hammering to begin in the chest at the approach of danger. The clocks had hardly struck ten when I sauntered along the Boulevard de Clichy towards the Moulin Rouge. Mlle. Prévost's act, we had ascertained, went on at eleven o'clock, and lasted until at least eleven-fifteen; considering encores, it would likely mean five minutes more. Afterwards she would have to change her clothes before departing for the club. Therefore, if I went to the Moulin Rouge I should be able to hear at least a few minutes of her turn and leave in plenty of time to anticipate them in number 18. On her tapped telephone wires we had heard that she would appear on the usual bill; a slip in time was impossible.

So I went up the red-carpeted stairs of the Moulin Rouge under brilliant lights; I bought my ticket, surrendered coat and top-hat to the *vestiare*, and wandered towards the blare of jazz. The place is no longer a theatre, though the red-curtained stage glitters with miniature revues. It is chiefly waxed dance-floor and gaudy decorations, with spotlights from the gallery tearing blue and white holes in a mist of tobacco smoke. Now it shrieked and pounded to the contortions of a jazz-band, dominated by cymbals, bass-drum slam, and hideous brassy wails like the howling of cats. It is, I believe, designated as hot. Just why, I have never been able to understand, unless it is to be deduced from the sweating ecstasy of the players. But then an appreciation of this artistry has been denied me entirely; so I can only report that the rafters trembled, the floor shook to pounding feet, dust tickled the spotlights, every bottle rattled in the bar, a whirl of cries pulsed up from the jigging dancers; and I sat down in a *loge* beside the dance-floor and ordered a bottle of champagne.

The hands of my watch crawled. It grew hotter, more crowded and smoky. Cries became squeals; an Argentine band set the dancers jerking with the stamp of the tango; more ladies of the evening slid off their stools at the bar and drifted past the *loges* with a tentative eye roving. With every tick of the watch, I was drawing closer to the time for leaving... Then, when the lights dimmed and the chatter died to a hum, they announced Estelle. Just before the place became dark, I noticed a man sitting in one of the boxes far across the dance-floor. It was Captain Chaumont. He sat motionless, his elbows on the rail, staring at the stage...

In a darkness thick with heat and the smell of powder, a white spotlight found Estelle standing against scarlet curtains. She wore white, with a headdress of pearls. I was too far away to catch the expression of her face, but I envisioned the blue-eyed girl with the haunted face, pink lips, and husky voice, whose voluptuous figure had that afternoon subtly warmed the house on the Boulevard des Invalides. And even now you could feel the moist brilliance of her eyes moving over the audience. The contact between them was vital, sultry, intense, making the throat dry. It had something of the crackle of electricity; it spread out across the hall in warm streams, leaving, in the electrical silence, only a dim, vast creaking, an enormous murmur as of strained breaths, which was the hall's reply. The violins had wandered into a dreaming melody, deepening and throbbing...

The girl could sing! That caress of her voice could touch your every nerve; it woke old sorrows; it made you remember pain and pity and compassion. She sang with the abandon of Mistinguett, the smouldering carelessness of Meller, dropping words as contemptuously as ashes flicked off a cigarette. But in billing her as an American singer they were stark mad. Hers were the love-songs of old Paris, whose rhythms suggest brooding as much as love. They suggest bruises and the gutter; cellars, ecstasy, and the cold rain. Grief cries out in the cunning violins and the sudden break of the husky voice. Grief jabs the heart like a dull knife, just failing to pierce. As the last soaring note shivered and dropped, and Gina Prévost's tense body relaxed in a shudder, I almost knocked over my chair in rising. I wanted to get out under cover of the applause which smashed in furious gusts across the hall hysterically; and I found that my hands were trembling. I thrust some banknotes at a waiter, pushing my way out in the dark. Still I could hear the roar beating those rafters, the waves of handclapping which spurted up, died, and spurted again. In a daze I retrieved hat and coat.

I wondered how Chaumont had taken it. I wondered, too, how much of her own terror cried out in her songs; whether her knees shook now, as she faced the acclaim limply. There were depths to this woman which you would not have suspected from this morning; you could go mad over the bitter lure of her eyes, or the sulkiness of her full fleshy mouth. "O mystical rose of the mire—!" A blast of cold air struck me as I went down to the street, and I saw dimly the car-starter raising a white-gloved hand for a taxi. Across the memory of her struck Bencolin's words: "Take a taxi there, as Galant did, and time yourself when you go to the club." Galant's alibi...

Mechanically I raised my eyes to look across the street. I

saw a dingy jeweller's shop, in whose window was the illuminated face of a clock whose hands pointed to five minutes
past eleven. I got into the cab, said, "To the Porte St.-Martin,
quickly," and compared my own watch with the clock as the
taxi door slammed. Five minutes past.

"Quickly," one syllable spoken to a Parisian taxi-driver, is a
potent word. In the very stoop of the man's shoulders, in the
terrific jerk with which we shot backwards and then wheeled
to plunge wild-bumping down the rue Fontaine, I knew what
to expect. I was lifted and hurled from one side to the other as
the shop-fronts whirled past. But the real adventure drummed
in my pulses now. The taxi windows rattled wildly, the springs
jolted and banged, and I struck up a French drinking-song in
which the driver shortly joined. When at last we spun round
into the Boulevard Poissonnière, I looked at my watch again.
Nine minutes, even at this pace, and a good twelve before we
reached the Porte St.-Martin. Oh yes, Galant's alibi checked.
It checked, if anything, too well.

My throat grew a little dry as I walked down the Boulevard
de Sebastopol, and my legs had a curious lightness. Beyond
the flare of lights at the corner, the boulevard was murky.
There were a few loungers at the dim-lit entrance to a cinema,
and they all seemed to be watching me. Here was the door,
in deep shadow. I did not suppose there would be anybody
lurking there, but I braced myself lest I should bump into
someone. It was not until I fished in my pocket for the silver
key that I realized my fingers were a trifle unsteady. I inserted
the key, which opened the door easily and without a sound.

The damp stuffiness of the passage blew over me. It was
absolutely dark, but the whole place seemed to smell of
murder. Green-lit ghosts would not be standing there halfway down, one with a knife in its hand and its head turned

sideways, and yet it was not pleasant to fancy them. Not a sound, either. I wondered if old Augustin were pottering about in his museum. Now, then. Were guests in the habit of turning on the passage lights, those concealed ones worked from the switch beside the door, as they entered? Probably, because you could see nothing whatever when the door had clicked shut behind. They could be extinguished, in all likelihood, from another switch inside the club itself. I pressed the button.

The moonlight glow from among the rafters showed the stone-flagged floor. In one place, just opposite the museum door, it had been significantly scrubbed, and the clean splotch stood out even more suggestive than the bloodstain. Damn it! there ought to *be* noise! My own footfalls echoed as I walked towards the rear, fastening on my mask. The mask set the seal on it all. Instinctively I glanced at the museum door, which was closed. My imagination moved out through the green grottos of the place, to that garish entrance with the "A" set in electric lights in the roof. It would be almost deserted. But Mlle. Augustin would be still seated in the little glass booth there, dressed sombrely in black, with the roll of blue tickets at her elbow and the money-till under her hands—those strong, white, capable hands. Very probably a crowd of the morbid had thronged the museum that day, and she was tired. What was she thinking behind her inscrutable eyes? What…?

Somebody was trying the knob of the museum door. I had been staring at it as I walked down the passage; but now, for the first time, I saw in dim light that the knob was being softly turned, backwards and forwards.

Nothing is quite so fraught with terror at night as the thin creak of a knob in silence. For a watch-tick I wondered whether to wait. No; it was ridiculous to suppose that this might be the murderer. Some club member, merely... Well, then, why didn't the person open the door? Why stand there softly working the handle, as though indecisive? But I could not wait. There must be no suspicion. Settling my mask firmly, I went on towards the other door at the right of the passage.

When I put my key into the other lock, sudden images shot through my head. Images of evil and danger, of being shut into a doorless box with Galant's red nose and the soft cat's purr of his voice. Too late now! I was pushing open the door.

At the same moment I opened it, the corridor light was extinguished behind me; it must work automatically. I was in the foyer of the club. I tried to look unconcerned beneath my mask, and to remember exactly the downstairs plan... It was a spacious hall, some twenty feet high, with blue-veined marble pillars set in a floor of blue-and-gold mosaic tiles. The light, emanating in pale wreaths from the tops of the pillars, left the lower part of the hall in twilight. At the left side I saw a cloakroom, and far at the right an arched door-way ornamented with Cupids in a heavy Edwardian style. That (I remembered from the plan) led to the lounge. From beyond it drifted a rustle as of many people on deep rugs, a hint of laughter, and the subdued murmur of an orchestra. The air was thick, powder-scented. And the very atmosphere of this luxury hidden behind blank walls, in a dingy street, dulled one's reason while it conjured up exotic images in the brain like bright poisonous orchids. To the nerves it lent stimulation—abandon, a tingle of danger as at a mad dance and a contraction at the heart as you visualized...

I started. Figures, gigantic in the dim light, were bearing down on me, making scarcely a sound on the glittering mosaic floor. Guards! I had to pass scrutiny now, from these people who appeared from nowhere. "Your key, monsieur?" said a voice. They wore correct evening clothes, and white masks. But uniformly there was a bulge under the left armpit where the holster was buckled. (They were squat .44s, Bencolin had told me, and they were all equipped with silencers.) I felt their eyes on me: lurking men, with a suggestion of a crouch even when they stood up straight, and their eyes had a sliding motion behind the holes in the mask. The idea of silencers on the pistols lent them an even more ugly quality. Removing coat and hat into the hands of the cloakroom attendant—who contrived, imperceptibly, to be sure I bore no weapon—I held out my key. One murmured, "Nineteen," a book was consulted, and I had a heart-pounding instant while all the eyes were fixed on me with snake-like glassiness. Then the ring of white-masks dissolved. The men melted into shadows. But I heard the low leather creak of a holster as I sauntered towards the lounge, and I still felt eyes.

I was inside, with the hands of my watch pointing to eleven-eighteen.

The lounge was another long hall, rather narrow, and even more dimly lighted. It was hung in black velvet. Its only illumination came in scarlet glowing from the mouth and eyes of bronze figures shaped like satyrs, and holding nymphs in their arms. They were life-size, these figures; they reminded me of the satyr in the waxworks, and the scarlet light from their eyes and mouths trembled with changing weirdness on the black hangings. About ten feet down, on my left, I saw great glass doors—these, I knew, led to the covered passage communicating with the big hall in the court. I caught the scent of hothouse flowers; the passage was banked with them. As in the room of Odette's coffin...

The murmur of the orchestra, through these doors, grew to a lure of deep strings. I could hear a buzz from inside, and somebody laughed breathlessly. Arm in arm, a man and a woman—both wearing black masks—drifted from the lounge through the passage. They looked hypnotized in the red-and-black swinging shadows, and the woman's lips were fixed in a faint smile. She looked old; he looked young and nervous. Another couple sat in a corner with cocktail glasses. Now suddenly the orchestra changed its tempo; it pounded with the fleshy beat of a tango, dragging the rise and fall of accordions, and the invisible crowd seemed to breathe with something of its murmur and hysteria. Then, in the gloom, I saw another figure.

It stood motionless, with arms folded, at the foot of the black-marble staircase far down at the end of the hall. Towering above it, one of the bronze satyrs flickered scarlet light on the newel-post; it lit the bulge of heavy shoulders and a face in a red mask. But the nose of the mask had been cut away, to show a ridged and discoloured nose, and the man was smiling…

"Your number, monsieur?" breathed a voice in my ear.

I swallowed hard. It seemed to me that Galant, standing down there by the staircase, had singled me out for suspicion. Still he did not move, but he appeared to grow larger. Turning, I saw at my elbow a woman in a white mask—it appeared to be the badge of attendants—and a low-cut black gown. She wore a heady perfume; and, as the tango beat and fell with muted strings, I found myself looking into a pair of long-lashed hazel eyes.

"Nineteen," I said.

My voice seemed startlingly loud, and I wondered whether Galant might have heard it, even at the distance. But then, I remembered, during Bencolin's interview with him I had not uttered a single word. If, on the other hand, he knew the real Robiquet... The woman was moving to one side, where she pulled open the curtain of a small alcove. Inside was an illuminated board, with small numbered buttons. She pushed one, and dropped the curtain again.

"The door of monsieur's room is opened," she told me. (Was it alarm, suspicion, scrutiny in her look?)

"Thank you," I said carelessly.

"Will monsieur have something to drink?" As I stepped forward, she had slid in front of me with smiling obsequiousness. "I will bring it to monsieur in the main hall."

"Why—yes. A champagne cocktail, please."

"Thank you, monsieur."

She moved away towards the bar. Danger? It looked uncomfortably like an attempt to lead me. But I should have had to look into the main hall for a few minutes, at least. I took a cigarette out of my case, lighting it with elaborate care, and watched her from the corner of my eye. She was approaching Galant now on her way to the bar. She paused an instant, turned her head, and spoke a few words...

Hard bands had tightened across my chest. Deliberately steadying my hand, I put the cigarette-case back in my pocket and sauntered towards the glass doors. The red-breathing satyrs had all acquired a sardonic leer. The music of the tango had taken on a fiercer drum-beat. And then, grouped behind Galant, lurking in shadow, I saw other figures.

Apaches.

Galant's bodyguard, without a doubt. Not the old *apache*, who was half a music-hall song, but the new post-war breed from St. Denis. Born in starvation. Never, unlike the American gangster, protected by the police or any underworld lord; sharpened always to a murderous hardness because he has never known easy money. He is undersized and cold, his eyes are vacant, and he is as deadly as a tarantula. You will see him at the sporting centres, at Paris gates, at the markets, playing dominoes in bars. His clothes are loud and shabby; he speaks seldom; he wears, instead of a collar, a neck-cloth loosely tucked, and that—beware of it—is where he carries his knife... Three of him were sitting now in an alcove near Galant. They were scrubbed, but they had a look of decay. I could see the glowing ends of their cigarettes in gloom. Their sallowness was hidden behind white masks, but not the pale, imbecilic, snakish beadiness of their eyes. No eye is so terrifying as the brainless one.

I had to go through with it. I had to saunter idly down the flower-lined passage. Straight ahead it ran for some distance, without lights. Down at the end I could hear the subdued noise under the orchestra; it had an echo, as though the main hall were vast, and I could see goblin masks swimming in a dusk, black and green and scarlet masks, of people who were trying for an hour to forget their homes... I glanced at my watch. Good God! Twenty-five minutes past eleven. I couldn't go in there for my drink. Gina Prévost might arrive at any moment. But there was Galant standing at the foot of the staircase. Did he suspect? If so, I was caught. There was no way out. I put my hand against the flowers at one side of the passage, halfway down its darkness, visualizing the white masks. In the boom of drums echoed a warning.

Somebody touched my shoulder from behind...

13

GINA PRÉVOST IS STUBBORN

I MUST HAVE SHAKEN TO THAT TOUCH. TO THIS DAY I do not know how I kept from betraying myself, and if the voice had not spoken, I might have done so.

"Monsieur's champagne cocktail," said a voice, reproachfully.

Relief choked me. I could see the girl dimly, holding a tray. But what now? I couldn't tell her to take it in there; time was becoming too precious. On the other hand, to go upstairs now alone would look insane, particularly with Galant standing at the very foot of the steps on guard against police spies. And then the girl spoke again.

"Monsieur," she murmured, "I have received instructions to tell you. Number nineteen. I fear there has been a slight accident…"

"Accident?"

"Yes, monsieur," humbly. "Monsieur's room has not been used for many months. Only a day or more ago, a cleaning-woman—oh, so careless!—smashed the window there. I am so terribly, terribly sorry! Will it inconvenience monsieur? It has not been repaired…"

Again I found myself steadied. This, then, was why she had taken so much trouble. This was why she had spoken to Galant. Was there any other reason? *Wait!* Odette Duchêne, found dead with glass cuts about the face, fallen from a window. Murdered inside the club; murdered, it might be, in that very room…

"That is bad," I said gruffly. "H'm. And I know the rules about other rooms. Well, never mind. Give me the drink. I'll go up and look at it now."

What ho! Things were looking up. I downed the cocktail at a gulp, brushed past her severely, and strode up to the lounge. My pulses were pounding with excitement, but I toned my hurry to a walk. What ho again, Galant, and to hell with you! I walked straight up to him, compressing my mouth with dignity like a hotel guest who finds cockroaches in his room; then, at the last moment, I seemed to change my mind and ascended the stairs in an outraged way. He was still impassive, and his plug-uglies continued to smoke in the alcove…

Steady now! I was upstairs safely, but I had to find my way along the dim and thick-carpeted halls. Number 19 would be around at the far side. I hoped there were no attendants up here, to notice any indecision; I hoped, above all, that the doors were numbered. Wait! Another snag. We had supposed that none of the room doors were locked. It now seemed that you had to push one of those buttons downstairs in order to release the catch. On the other hand, if they pressed the button as soon as you got there, to avoid embarrassment later, Galant's door might now be unlocked. The door and window of the ground-floor private rooms were both in the same wall; but up here, according to the plan, each room had two windows looking out on the court, with the door in the wall opposite. Here it was. Eighteen. For a moment I could hardly bring myself to try the knob. But the door was open. I slid into Galant's room and closed it behind me.

It was dark. But I could see a glimmer of light through one window, whose leaves were open. Heavy draperies there trembled in a cold wind. The noise of the orchestra floated up faintly. Where the devil was the light-switch? No, hold on!—it wouldn't do to risk a light up here. There might be watchers in the court who knew Galant was still downstairs. But I had to find a place to hide. Clever lad! Walk straight into a devilish dangerous situation like this, volunteer to get evidence without even knowing whether there might be a place of concealment. I strained my eyes in the gloom; but the lashes would catch uncomfortably in the eyeholes of the mask, and my vision was hampered. Lifting it up on my forehead, I hurried over to the open window and peered out. The glass was opaque and dark red. (Dark red glass-slivers found in Odette Duchêne's face, and a smashed window in the room next to this.) I breathed deeply, the cold air grateful on my hot face, and looked out. Once free of that strangling heat downstairs, you could at least think sanely... All around, in a vast oblong, dark walls rose against the starlight, their windows glimmering. It was a good twenty-foot drop from this window to the stone court below. Eight or nine feet away from the walls rose the domed glass roof of the main hall. It rose somewhat higher than the window where I stood, so I was unable to see the court except immediately below. But at my right now, I knew, must be the passage from the lounge, and, far down to the left, the passage leading to what were fantastically called the manager's quarters. From my position, the glass roof was too high for me to see down into the main hall; I saw only dim light through grimy panes, and heard the orchestra playing.

Then the moon came out. Its bluish pallor slid across the roof-tops, silvering them, and then probed into the narrow court below. The air chilled my breast through a soggy shirt-front, for I saw there a motionless figure in a white mask, staring up at this window. The mask looked blue and hideous. I heard faintly the throb of traffic from the boulevards...

They were watching. I jerked back from the window, and looked round rather wildly. Moonlight lay in a broad bar across the carpet; it touched heavy chairs of carven oak, and a Chinese screen, woven in silver filigree, shook glimmering patterns mockingly. Still I could make out no distinct out-line; but, with white-mask standing down there in the court, gloating on the windows, there could be no light. I took a step forward, to blunder into a chair. It would be madness to get behind that screen—the first place anybody would look. Then the orchestra stopped playing. Absolute stillness fell like pinioning arms, but for a wind creaking on the windows; it added a last sinister closing of doors to this prison. Was the whole damned thing a trap?

A lock clicked, and across the floor shot a narrow line of light. *O God! here they come!*

There was only one thing to do. The Chinese screen was not more than two feet from the window; I dodged behind it, with a cold feeling of suffocation and dizziness. Silence. I stood there listening to the bump of my heart...

"My dear Gina," said the voice of Galant, "I was just begin-ning to wonder what had happened to you. A moment till I get the lights on."

Footsteps on the thick rug. The scrape of a lamp chain. A barred circle of brightness sprang up on the ceiling. It hardly smudged the darkness; my screen was still entirely in shadow. Then—he still did not know? The tone of his voice was lazy, soothing, undisturbed. Wait! More footfalls, coming in my direction. His elbow knocked against the screen...

"We'll just close this window," he remarked. Then, lovingly: "Here, Mariette! Here girl! Curl up here!"

So he had the cat along with him. I heard a sort of snuffling; then the casement leaves of the window closed with a scrape and bang, and I heard the heavy catch twisted into place. Then I saw a small vertical brightness extend from the top to the bottom of my screen, at the joining of two panels. By putting my eye to it I had a view of a small segment of the room.

Gina Prévost sat with her back to me on a cushioned lounge, leaning back as though unutterably tired. The lamplight lay on her brown-gold hair, and on the black fur of an evening wrap. Two tulip glasses stood on the lamp table, and beyond them a tripod holding a champagne-cooler with the gilt foil of a bottle gleaming over it. (I could not imagine by what miracle I had failed to knock the whole thing over when I crossed the room in the dark.) Then Galant moved into my line of vision. His mask was off. On the big face was again that expression of complacency like thin oil. He touched his nose, as seemed to be a habit with him; his yellow-green eyes were full of solicitude, but his mouth seemed pleased. For a moment he stood studying her.

"You look unwell, my dear," he murmured.

"Is it surprising?" Her voice was cold, rather monotonous; she seemed to be holding herself in. She lifted her hand with a cigarette, and a deep gust of smoke was blown across the light.

"There's a friend of yours here tonight, my dear."

"Oh?"

"I think you will be interested," deprecatingly. "Young Robiquet."

She did not comment. He studied her again, his eyelids flickering slightly, as though he examined a safe door which would not open to the usual combination. He went on:

"We told him that one of his windows had been broken—by a cleaning-woman. The bloodstains, of course, have been cleaned up."

A pause. Then she crushed out her cigarette, slowly, on an ash-tray.

"Etienne"—a veiled note of command—"Etienne, pour me a glass of champagne. And then sit down here beside me."

He opened the bottle and poured out two glasses. All the time he was watching her, with an ugly look as though wondering what it meant. As he sat down beside her, she turned. I saw the full lovely face, the moist pink lips, and the sudden steady blankness of her look at him...

"Etienne, I am going to the police."

"Ah!—About what?"

"About Odette Duchêne's death... It came to me this afternoon. I have never had a genuine emotion in my life. No, don't interrupt! Did I ever say I loved you? I look at you now"—she surveyed him in a rather puzzled way, and it was like a lash—"and all I see is an unpleasant-looking man with a red nose." All of a sudden she laughed. "That *I* ever felt anything! All I ever knew was how to sing. I poured so much of emotion into that, do you hear, I was so strung up always, I conceived of everything in terms of grand passion—I was a neurotic, grabbing fool—and so..." She made a gesture, spilling the champagne.

"What are you driving at?"

"And last night! Last night I saw my fearless gentleman. I went to the club to meet Claudine, and I walked into the passage when the murderer stabbed her... And then, Etienne?"

"*Well?*" His voice was rising, dangerous and hoarse.

"I was sick with fright. What else? I ran out of that club, up the boulevard—and met you coming out of your car. You were safety, support, and I threw myself at you when I could hardly stand… And what does my Titan of strength do when he hears?" She leaned forward, smiling fixedly. "He puts me into his car and tells me to wait for him. Is he going back to the club and see what happened? Is he going to shield me?—No, Etienne. He runs straight to a convenient night club, where he can sit down openly and establish an alibi for *himself* in case anybody questions him! And he stays there while I am lying insensible in the back of his car."

I had disliked Galant before that. But I had not felt the surge of murderous rage which overcame me when I heard this. I had no longer any fear of discovery. To smash that nose into a deeper red pulp against his face… There would be sheer pleasure. Evil which possesses courage you can respect, like Richard Humpback's; but this—! His hard face was swelling as he turned it to her.

"What else have you to say?" he asked, with an effort.

"Don't," she said.

Her breast was heaving, and a glassiness had crept into her eyes when she saw his big hand move up along the back of the lounge.

"Don't do it, Etienne. Let me tell you something. Just before I left the theatre tonight I sent a *pneumatique* to a man named Bencolin…"

The enormous hand clenched, and sinews of muscle stood out on the wrist. I could not see his face, except for the working of the jaw muscles, but I felt an explosion swell and darken here…

"It contained certain information, Etienne. Just how much

I won't tell you. But if anything happens to me, you'll go to the guillotine."

A silence. Then she said, huskily:

"Why, when I look back at what I thought—there was in life... And today I saw Odette in her coffin, and remembered—and how I ragged her about being so homelike, and thought she was a damned little fool who ought to get a good waking up, and *hated* her for getting pleasure out of little things... and then the expression of her face!"

Very thoughtfully Galant nodded. His hand had relaxed.

"And so, my dear, you will tell the police. What will you tell them?"

"The truth. It was an accident."

"I see. Mademoiselle Odette died by an accident. And your other friend, Claudine, was that an accident also?"

"You know it wasn't. You know it was deliberate murder."

"Come, we are getting along! At least you admit *that*."

Something in his voice roused her from her drugged torpor. Again, her face turned; I saw the taut nostrils. She knew that he was holding threats gently, as a man shakes a whip before lashing out with it.

"Now, darling," he went on, "suppose you tell me. How did this 'accident' occur?"

"As though—as though you didn't know! Oh, damn you! *what* have you got—!"

"I was not in the room at the time, as I think you will admit. This is all I can safely say: You and your good friend Mademoiselle Martel loathed the excellent Odette... Please, please, my dear, don't use your devastating stage contempt on me; the look is too dramatic. Neither of you could understand why she should want a husband and babies, and a dull cottage at Neuilly or a duller army post in the colonies. So you arranged a little reception for her here."

"There wasn't anything in it! I tell you I'm willing to go to the police…"

He drained his glass of champagne, and then leaned over to pat her hand. She moved it away, but she was trembling.

"The moving spirit, I am willing to admit," he said, with a magnanimous gesture, "was Mademoiselle Martel. You were unable to get your friend Odette here on any pretext *except one*, which was for Mademoiselle Martel to tell her, and repeat it so frequently that she grew hysterical, a certain lie—namely, my dear, that Captain Chaumont came frequently to this club. Does she doubt it? A shrug. She may look for herself… What a good joke it would be! What a taste of the real life she should get! Bring her here, ply her with wine, introduce her to some gallant later in the evening… She wouldn't come here at night? The afternoon would do as well, for much champagne could be administered before night…"

Gina Prévost had pressed her hands over her eyes.

"Now, I was unacquainted with the precise nature of your plans, my dear," Galant resumed. "As to the last, I am only guessing. But your behaviour tells me much. However," he shrugged, "I approved the idea. I allowed you to bring her, without a key, past the guards. *But what went on in that room*—by the way, you used M. Robiquet's room, because you knew he was in London and could not possibly be there—*what went on in that room, I do not know.*"

"I told you, didn't I?"

"Please relax, my dear Gina; you are exciting yourself. Did you?"

"I don't know what your game is. I'm afraid of you… It *was* an accident; you know it. At least, it was Claudine's fault.

Odette got hysterical when we—we put her off about seeing Robert Chaumont—"

"And then?"

"And Claudine had been drinking, and all of a sudden she flared out. She told Odette not to worry: we'd get her a man as good as Chaumont. It was awful! I only intended a joke. I just wanted to see how she'd take it. But Claudine always hated her, and Claudine turned into a fury. I saw that the thing was getting past us, and I was scared. And Claudine said, 'I'll shake some sense into you, you little snivelling hypocrite,' and—"

She swallowed hard, looking at him wildly. "Claudine dashed towards her. Odette jumped up across the bed to run from her, and she tripped, and—O Christ!—when I saw that glass break, and Odette's face…! We heard her hit the court down there…"

There was a terrible, gasping silence. I turned away from the screen, feeling rather sick.

"I didn't mean—I didn't mean—!" the girl whispered. "But *you* knew. You came up and promised to take her away. You said she was dead, and that you would handle it, or we'd both go to the guillotine. Didn't you?"

"So," Galant said, meditatively, "she died by an accident, did she? She died from falling out the window, of a fractured skull?… My dear, have you seen the newspapers?"

"What do you mean?"

He rose, and stood looking down at her. "Sooner or later the fall might have killed her. But as to what else went on up here!—Why, you can see in the newspapers that the real cause of death was a stab through the heart. Eh?"

The soft swing of his hand continued, curling back for the crack of the whip. His lips were pursed and smugness again spread round his eyes.

"The knife with which she was stabbed," he said, "was not found. And no wonder: It belongs to you, I believe. If the police look, they can find it hidden in your dressing-room at the Moulin Rouge… Now I hope, my dear, you did not give too much information to Monsieur Bencolin?"

14

KNIVES!

CROUCHED THERE IN THE GLOOM, I DROPPED MY EYES again, and my brain was muddled with the crazy words which banged and echoed there. Then Galant laughed. His laughter had suddenly become high and giggling and obscene, jarring the nerves.

"Don't believe *me*, my dear," he urged. "Read the papers."

A silence. I did not dare put my eye to the crack again, lest I should betray myself by fumbling and tipping it over.

She said in a low, incredulous voice: "You—did—that…"

"Now please listen to me. I feared that exactly this might happen, from the moment your good Odette fell. I feared you might lose your nerve, or get an attack of conscience, and go to the police to explain your 'accident.' Mademoiselle Martel, I thought (and wisely), was less unstable. You might ruin us all. However, if you were bound to silence…"

"You stabbed Odette yourself."

"Well, well, I may have hastened her death. She wouldn't have lived more than a few hours, anyway." He was enjoying himself and I heard a clink as he poured out more champagne.

"Attend me, darling! Did you fancy I would rush her to the hospital, and betray everything? No, no! The police are too eager to hang something on me as it is. Better to finish her in the courtyard. Which—between ourselves—I did. You recall, you did not see her after she fell?"

I looked out again. She sat rigid, her face away from me. Galant was frowning musingly at his glass as he swirled round its contents. Behind his complacence you could feel the cold rage. I knew instinctively that he would never forgive her for one thing, above all—for striking at his vanity. He raised veiled eyes, clear cat-yellow now.

"The knife I used is—distinctive. And the crookedness of the blade left a distinctive mark. Somehow it found its way into your dressing-room. You wouldn't find it easily. But the police could… You damned little fool," he said, trying to hold back a rush of rage, "they'll blame you for both murders!— that is, if I give them the tip. You put your neck right under the guillotine last night when Claudine Martel was killed! Don't you realize that? And yet you have the nerve, the impudence, the damned cringing conceit, to—"

For a moment I thought he would fling the glass at her. Then with an effort he composed his swollen face, seeming a bit alarmed at his own fury.

"Ah, well, my dear…won't do, will it, to get upset? No. Listen, please. I took her down, after dark, and dropped her into the river from my own car. There is no shred of proof to connect me with it. But you!"

"And Claudine—?"

"Gina, I don't know who killed Claudine. But you are going to tell me."

This time he did not sit down on the lounge beside her. He drew up a chair opposite, where the lamplight painted his nose in grotesque shades. He slapped his knees, and out from the shadow bounded the white cat to climb up. For a time he was silent, stroking its fur, smiling obscurely at the champagne-glass.

"Now, my dear, if your emotions are quieted, let me continue. I will tell you precisely what I want of you. In planting this evidence against you I was only covering myself in case I came under *any* suspicion. I must never come under any suspicion, Gina dear; they must never be able to prove one single thing against me… Now, at the end of a long and useful career, I am going to leave Paris."

"Leave—Paris?"

He chuckled. "In short, my dear, to retire. Why not? I am a fairly wealthy man, and I was never greedy of money. For a while I did not want to depart before I had settled matters with a certain man, your friend Bencolin," he touched his nose, "who gave me this. It has been my ambition to keep it as—a spur. And then my success with the ladies (oh yes, my dear; with yourself also) has been due, curiously enough, in no small degree to this disfigurement. Why is it? A blotch on a handsome face invariably attracts them." He shrugged. "But as for my good friend Bencolin… Well, my dear, that *prudence* which you seem not to like (ah, but it's saved my hide, darling, when others are at Devil's Island), that *prudence*"—he had a loathsome, chuckling way of accentuating the word—"tells me to keep away from conflict with him."

Galant took a delight in building up intricate sentences now. Each time he said "prudence" he would smile, and glance sideways at her.

"So I am going. To England, I think. I have always fancied the life of a country gentleman. I shall write fine books by a river, in a garden full of laurels. And my nose shall be reshaped by the surgeon, and I shall become handsome again, and, alas! no woman will look at me."

"In God's name, what are you trying to say?"

"As you may know," he continued, comfortably, "I own a large—a *very* large—interest in this establishment. Yes. Now, I have a partner, whose identity you would probably not suspect. Of course you have seen that I have no connection with this 'manager's office'? Prudence again! It is run by my partner... Well, my dear, I have sold out."

"How does it concern me? *Please*—!"

"Patience." He waved his hand gently. Then his voice changed. It became alive with a kind of weak hatred. "I want you to know this because it concerns your whole silly, rotten tribe! Do you know what I mean? I have owned this place for a number of years. I know every member; his and her innermost affairs; every scandal, every crookedness... Ah, well. And did I use this information for what you call blackmail? Only a little. I had a bigger purpose. To publish it, Gina. To publish it, with a purely altruistic purpose. To show"—his voice rose horribly—"to show what a lot of thieving, crawling maggots masquerade as human beings, and—"

The man was mad. Staring at his face through the crack, I could not doubt it. Brooding? Solitude? Snubs? An idealist unhinged, a sensitive man and brilliant man beating at a cage in his own brain? His yellow eyes seemed to be fixed exactly on my own, burning with a light behind the eyeballs, and for a moment I fancied he had seen me. The cat let out a squeal as he pinched its neck, and streaked down from his lap. That seemed to rouse him. He recovered himself, and was looking at the girl now. She had shrunk back on the lounge...

"I entertained you," he said, slowly, "for a year. I could get you back now, if I wanted you. Because I had travelled, and because I had read, and because I knew fine phrases, you were caught. You learned a glory your poor brainless head wouldn't have dreamed of; you learned it in a cheap secondhand way. I put Catullus in a primer for you. I dragged down Petrarch to your understanding; and De Musset, and Coleridge, and all the lords of the purple dusk. Do you hear? I taught you what songs to sing, and how to sing them; I set the '*Donec gratus eram tibi*' to music, and put it into better French than Ronsard's for you to act out. Great emotions, pale loves, fidelity; and now we both know what a damned sham it is, don't we? And you know what I think of—people."

He drew a deep breath.

"Down in my safe," he said, resuming his sardonic manner, "there are a number of manuscripts. Sealed in envelopes, ready to be sent out to every newspaper in Paris. They are the stories of the—the People, the true stories. And they are to go out soon, after I depart." He grinned. "They ought to pay me for it. It will be the news of the decade, if they dare to use it. And they'll use enough…"

"You're mad," she said, flatly. "My God! I don't know what to say to you. I knew what you were. But I didn't think you were stark—"

"I regret, of course," he told her, "that it will blow this club sky-high and nobody will dare come near it. But I am no longer interested in it financially, and I fear that will have to be my partner's lookout… Now, my dear, let us be practical. There could be much news about *you* in that packet. On the other hand, your name need not figure at all—Gina the spotless!—if…"

She whirled towards him. She had recovered her cool manner.

"I thought, Etienne," she said, "that sooner or later it would be something like this."

"...if you tell me who killed Claudine Martel."

"A nice recital, Etienne." The husky voice became tantalizing. "Do you really think I would tell you? And, Etienne, my dear, why do you want to know? If you are going to become a respectable country gentleman—"

"Because I think I know."

"Well?"

"Remember that delicious word *prudence*. I was always cautious, my dear. Sometime in the future I may need money. And the parents of the person who I think committed the murder are not only proud, but immensely rich. Now tell me..."

She was taking a cigarette from her handbag, coolly, and I could imagine her raised eyebrows. His big hand shot out. "Confirm my belief, dear Gina, that the murderer is Captain Robert Chaumont."

My knees grew weak, and I saw Galant's face as in a distorted mirror. Chaumont! *Chaumont!* The name could not conceivably have surprised her as much as it surprised me. But I heard her give a little gasp. During the long silence, the orchestra downstairs began to play again. I heard it muffled by the windows, faintly.

"Etienne," she said, laughing in a choked way, "now I am convinced you are mad. What on earth—*why*—?"

"Surely you must be aware, Gina," he pointed out, "knowing what you do, that this is a crime of vengeance? Vengeance for Odette Duchêne. Vengeance on the young lady who caused her to fall to her death. Who would be the most likely person to inflict that vengeance?—Come, now! Am I right?"

Already it had grown very hot in here. I strained against

the crack in the screen, my brain lit by flashes and glimpses out of the past, where Chaumont's queer behaviour stood out. I was afraid Gina Prévost would whisper something, and I should not catch it; for the orchestra had swelled into another tango which pounded dimly against the windows. Galant stood before her, looking down…

Then, almost at my feet, I became aware of a *snarl*. It ripped out on the quiet. Something with fur shot brushing past my legs and whirled. Its cry rose again, inhumanly, and I saw yellow eyes.

The cat…

All motion was frozen in my body. I could not take my eye from that crack; I had first become stiff, and then limp as jelly. Galant straightened up. He stared straight across at the screen. Mariette, the cat, ran back and forth, still snarling.

"There's—somebody—behind—that screen," Galant said. His voice was unnaturally loud.

Another pause. The room seemed to have acquired sinister creakings. Gina Prévost did not move, but her hand was lifted towards her mouth with the cigarette, and it trembled. "There's—somebody—behind—that screen"; it still echoed, dull and hollow. On Galant's face the lamplight lay in a spangled pattern; his eyes grew large in a dead cold stare, and the lips were drawn back slowly from his teeth.

His hand suddenly flew to the inside of his coat.

"*It's a damned police spy!*"

"Don't move," I said. I did not recognize my own voice. I had spoken instinctively, and the words snapped. "Don't move, or I'll drop you. You're in the light."

Ghastly seconds hammered in my ears. Bluff him! Bluff him, or I was through. He stared at the shadows around me, which might have concealed a pistol. His big body strained as against bonds. Now his eyes were growing crimson round the irises, with a rush of blood which filled the big veins on his forehead. Slowly his upper lip raised, to show two big front teeth. Indecision held him strangled and furious…

"Up above your head!" I shouted. "High above it! Don't call out. Hurry!"

His lips writhed to spit out a word of defiance, but prudence intervened. For a second one hand trembled under the table. Then both of them were slowly raised.

"Turn around!"

He said, "You can't get out of here, you know."

I had come to that stage where the whole affair seemed pure, crazy exhilaration. My career might have only a few more instants to go; but in the meantime I felt like laughing, and pulses danced up and down my chest. So I stepped out from behind the screen. The grey room with its gilt panels and blue-upholstered furniture emerged in sharp colours; even the shadows had a hard outline, and I remember noting that the panels were painted to depict the loves of Aphrodite. Galant stood with his back to me and his hands raised. On the lounge Gina Prévost sat bending forward; she darted a glance at me, and in the same moment I remembered that my mask was still up on my forehead I saw that her eyes held encouragement and triumph. She made a gesture in the air. She laughed, and the long ashes of her cigarette spilled, for she saw that I had no weapon…

I joined in her laughter. The only thing to do was to take Galant from behind and risk a rough-and-tumble before he could call out or get his hand on a weapon. I caught up a heavy chair. Galant spoke suddenly *in English*:

"Don't worry, Gina. They'll be here in a second. I pressed a button under that table… Good boys!"

The door into the hall was flung open. I stopped, with a shock at my heart. A yellow glare of light in the hallway showed white-masks, with Galant's upraised arms silhouetted against them. I saw heads above neck-cloths—heads which seemed to rise from their necks, slowly, with a weaving motion like snakes, and glassy eyes in the lamplight. There were five of those heads.

"All right, boys," Galant said, in a low delighted voice. "Watch him; he's got a gun. Quietly, now! No noise…"

He had sprung round to face me, and his nose was like a horrible red caterpillar wriggling up his face. His shoulders were humped, his arms swung loosely, and he grinned. The blood-drum beat in my ears. The heads began to move forward, blotting the light and throwing long-necked shadows across its path. Their feet made a swishing noise on the rug. Gina Prévost was still laughing, her fists clenched. With the heavy chair in my hands, I backed towards the window…

Still that *swishing*, as though the white-masks moved on their bellies. Galant's grin grew wider. The figures loomed up still more gigantic, manicured hands stealing towards the inside pocket. Through Gina Prévost's giggling shrill laughter rose her words: "He'll beat you yet, Etienne! He'll beat—"

"He's got no gun. Get him!"

Against the yellow light, beady-eyed figures leapt in a surge. I swung the heavy chair and drove it against the window. The crash of glass blasted, an explosion; woodwork cracked and the lock was ripped out. Dragging back the chair, I whirled and flung it at the headmost figure. There was a gleam in the light, and a thud as a knife banged into the casement above my head. I saw it quiver there as I gripped the sill, shielded my face with an arm against broken glass, and toppled out into emptiness.

Cold air, a rushing grey blur. Then, blotting them out, bone-cracking hammers driven against my ankles. I staggered against brickwork and fell on my knees, overcome with a ghastly nausea. Get up! Get up! But for the moment only pain, legs that would not hold, and blindness…

I was trapped. They could cover the house; I couldn't get out. Sooner or later, like the inexorable closing in that circle of masks, they would have me in a corner. All right, damn them! give them a race! Little fun. Groggy; must have hit my head. I started to run, limping, along the court. The main hall! There were doors here somewhere to the main hall. If I ran in there, among guests, they couldn't get me just yet. Run! Where's the door? Something in my eyes; must be blood… White-mask ahead!

He was coming for me, bent low. His shoes made a spatter on the bricks as he ran. Pain was flooded out in cold fury. I drew my breath through lungs that felt stabbed; but I was no longer conscious of anything except that I hated all white-masks, I hated all *apache* sneers and knives that slammed into your back. In the dimness I saw that he wore a chequered suit. His pale bony jaw was drawn up, and his hand flicked to his neck-cloth as he leaped…

The knife whirled out and up, his thumb on the blade. My left fist went straight and low into his wind, and my right came up ten inches, full with the weight of arm and shoulder, to the point of his jaw. His breath spurted and died in a gurgle. I heard him go down on the bricks with a sodden flatness like bones breaking. Then I was running again. There were feet behind me. Sticky wetness had thickened in my eyes. Here was a lighted door. He must have been guarding it. I reached for the knob, for now there seemed to be nothing but a warm glutinous wetness on my forehead, my eyes and nose. I tried to dash it away, but it only thickened, and my head was ringing with explosions which struck off violet sparks. The absurd thought came to me that I mustn't be sick right in the middle of these luxurious surroundings. *Thud-thud, thud-thud*—coming closer, filling the whole court with a roar. I wrenched open some knob, fell ahead, and slammed a door behind me. Going to go under in a second...

Some corridor. There was music somewhere; I was safe—I must be near the main hall. The enormous pounding of my heart split the very ear-drums. I couldn't go any farther, because I couldn't see at all. Shaking, I crumpled against some wall. The whole floor swung backwards and forwards under my feet, and my legs were like rubber. I groped for my hip pocket, found a handkerchief, and fiercely swabbed my eyes...

The minute a little light flickered in, I straightened up. More blood was pouring down—my God! how was there so much blood in the human body?—and my very shirt-front was a mess. But there had come to me in one flash where I was. I saw *behind* me a covered passage, without flowers; I heard behind me a murmur and the music of an orchestra. Ahead were the lights of a big room. Somebody (I could see that dimly) stood in my path, and the light made a small bright circle round the muzzle of a pistol. I had run straight into the manager's office, straight into a trap, at the rear... *Thud-thud, thud-thud*, muffled now, but still closing in...

Desperately I jammed the handkerchief across my eyes, swabbed it at my forehead, and tried to straighten up. Rush the pistol ahead? Yes; might as well go down taking a crack at somebody.

Into my dim sight swam a figure I could not understand. The figure with the weapon was a woman. A woman in a flame-coloured dress. She stood in the middle of a room hung with rugs. Her dark eyes were steady and wide open. I heard a dim tumult behind me; I heard somebody hammering at a door, which I must instinctively have locked behind me. This woman!—it flashed over me now—Galant's partner, the new owner of the club... The surge of hope, the sudden realization of a way out, steadied my buzzing wits. My sight seemed to clear, and new breath rushed cold into my lungs. I took a step forward.

"Don't move!" said the woman. I recognized that voice...

"I do not think," I said, steadily—"I do not think you will betray me, Mademoiselle Augustin."

15

OUR SYBARITE SCRUB-LADY

EVEN THEN I COULD NOT HELP MARVELLING AT THE change in her. Seeing Marie Augustin at a distance, I should not have recognized her at all. The girl in dowdy black, with the shiny face and dull hair; and then this vivid woman! I was conscious only of the flame-coloured gown, and of her white, glossy shoulders about it. I found myself speaking to the gown, speaking swiftly. The gown; the ticket-booth at the waxworks, as though I faced her there and desperately sought admittance without money...

"There's no time to argue!" I said. "They'll be here in a moment. You're going to hide me. I—I—"

Just behind me was a door with a glass panel, through which I could see the dark passage to the great hall; and now I thought I could see white-masks pushing their way through this hall as well as hammering on the court door to the passage... To my astonishment, Marie Augustin came sweeping forwards. She drew a dark velvet curtain over the glass panel, and shot the bolt in the door.

She had not asked why. I had a good reason, though. I mumbled:

"There's information… I can give you information about Galant. He's going to sell you and wreck the club…and…"

Now I had discovered the cut in my forehead. My head must have smashed partly against the brick wall when I dropped. Pressing the handkerchief over it, I discovered that Marie Augustin was standing beside me, staring up into my face. It was impossible to see her distinctly. It seemed impossible to talk. She still covered my heart with that bright ring from the gun-muzzle. There was a sharp rattling knock on the glass; a hand twisted the knob. Marie Augustin spoke.

"This way," she said.

Somebody was leading me by the hand. When I have tried to recall that scene later, I have only hazy flashes, like the recollection of a drunken man. Soft carpets and bright light. Fierce hammering on glass behind me, and voices upraised. Then a black, gleaming door opened somewhere, and darkness. I seemed to be pushed down on something soft.

When next I opened my eyes, I knew I had lost consciousness for some time. (It was, as a matter of fact, less than ten minutes.) My face felt gratefully cold, wet, and free from stickiness; but light was painful to the eyeballs and an edifice of stone had been erected on my forehead. My hand, moving up, found bandages.

I was half reclining on a *chaise-longue*. At its foot Marie Augustin sat quietly, fingering the weapon, looking at me. In some fantastic way pursuit seemed (momentarily, at least) baffled. I lay quietly, trying to accustom my eyes to the light; so I studied her. The same long face. The same black-brown eyes and hair. But now she was almost beautiful. I remembered that fancy I had had last night in the waxworks: how, removed from ticket-booths and horsehair sofas, this girl would take on a hard grace and poise. Her hair was parted, drawn back behind the ears, and glossy under the lights; her shoulders were old ivory; I found I was looking at changing, luminous eyes which had lost their hard snapping…

"Why did you do it?" I said.

She started. Again that sense of a secret communion. She tightened her lips, and replied in a monotonous voice:

"It ought to be stitched up. I've used sticking-plaster and bandages."

"Why did you do it?"

Her finger tightened round the trigger of the pistol. "For the moment, I grant you, I told them you were not here. That—that was *my* office, and they believed me. Let me remind you, though, that they are still looking for you and that I have you under my thumb. A word from me…" The eyes grew hard again. "I told you I liked you. But if I discover you are here for the purpose of hurting this place, or trying to wreck it…"

She paused. She seemed to be gifted with an endless patience.

"Now, then, monsieur. If you can account for your presence in any legitimate way, I shall be pleased to believe you. If not, I can always press the bell for my attendants. Meantime…"

I tried to sit up, discovered that my head throbbed painfully, and relaxed again. I looked round at a large room, a woman's room, decorated in black and gold Japanese lacquer, over which bronze lamps threw a subdued light. Black-velvet curtains were drawn at the windows, and the air was heavy with wistaria incense. Following the direction of my glance, she said:

"We are in my own private room, adjoining the office. They cannot get in—unless I summon them. Now, then, monsieur!"

"Your old style of speech, Mademoiselle Augustin," I said, gently, "does not fit your new rôle. And in your new rôle you are beautiful."

She spoke harshly: "Please do not think that flattery—"

"Let me assure you I think nothing of the kind. If I wanted to win your regard, I should insult you; you would like me better. Wouldn't you? On the contrary, I have the whip hand over *you*."

I regarded her casually, trying to seem disinterested. She saw me fumbling in my pocket after cigarettes, and with an almost curt nod indicated a lacquer box on a tabouret at my elbow.

"Explain what you mean, monsieur."

"I can save you from bankruptcy. That would please you more than anything in the world, wouldn't it?"

Colour burnt under her brilliant eyes. "Be careful!" she snapped.

"But wouldn't it?" I asked, feigning surprise.

"Why do you—why does everybody—assume that I care for nothing but—!" She checked herself on the edge of an outburst. She went on calmly: "You have surprised a secret, monsieur. You see me as I have always wanted to be. But please don't try to evade. What do you mean?"

I lit a cigarette deliberately. "First off, mademoiselle, we must assume certain things. We must agree that you were formerly part owner, and are now full owner, of the Club of Masks."

"Why must we assume that?"

"Mademoiselle, please! It's perfectly legal, you know… It was an inspiration, brought about by a clout on the head after having heard certain things from Monsieur Galant. Then, too, that bank balance of a million francs! It could hardly have come from being mere—shall we say, gatekeeper?"

The last was a chance shot, which had just then occurred to me. But I suddenly realized it must be the truth, and that I had been blind for not perceiving it before. A million francs, I should have known, *was* too huge a sum to have amassed only from providing a second entrance.

"Therefore...I think I can provide you with proof that Galant intends to betray you. If I do, can you get me out of here?"

"Ah! So you still *are* dependent on me!" she said, with satisfaction.

I nodded. She glanced at the revolver; on an impulse, she dropped it beside her chair. Then she came over and sat down beside me on the *chaise-longue*, looking down into my face. My eyes must have shown that I felt her nearness, that I took in her lips and eyes with an expression which had nothing to do with bankruptcy. Yes, she felt that regard, and she was not displeased. She had lost her snappish austerity. She breathed a little more heavily, and her half-closed eyes glittered. I continued to smoke placidly...

"Why are you here?" she demanded.

"To get evidence in a murder case. That is all."

"And—did you get it?"

"Yes."

"I hope you found, then, that it did not implicate *me*?"

"It did not implicate you in the least, Mademoiselle Augustin. And it need not at all implicate the club, either."

She clenched her hands. "The club! The club! Is that all you can say? Do you think that everything with me is a matter of business? Listen. Do you know why this place has been the dream of my life?"

The hard mouth drooped a little. She pounded slowly on the cushions; she stared past my shoulder, and said, in a tense voice:

"There is only one complete joy. That is leading two lives—the drudge and—and the princess. Contrasting them and tasting them each day. I have done that. Each day is a new dream. I sit out in my glass booth by day; I wear cotton stockings, and fight with the butcher, and scrape for a sou. I scream abuse at the street children, hand tickets into grimy paws, cook cabbage over a wood stove, and mend my father's shirts. I do all this faithfully: I delight in scrubbing the floor…"

Then Mlle. Augustin shrugged. "Because at night I can feel ten thousand times more fully the pleasures of—this. *Bien!* the day is finished. I close up. I see my father to bed. And then I come back here. Each time it is like walking into the Arabian Nights."

Her low voice trailed away. She crossed her arms over her breast and pressed hard; she seemed to be breathing deeply, like one under an anaesthetic, and to be carried away by it. She seemed also to be savouring the incense, the texture of the satin gown, the deep and gleaming opulence of the room— and her dark-red slipper brushed up and down, slowly, the deep rug. Her head was half thrown back, the eyes gleaming and heavy-lidded…

I crushed out my cigarette. I half rose.

And then suddenly, at my movement, the dreaming vanished. A queer little smile twisted her lips.

"But I play with my emotions," she said, "a long time— before taking them. Lie down. Rest your head."

I applauded, making no sound, and bowed. Again we spoke to each other without words. None the less I said: "But it would be picturesque. With the bodyguard searching for me out there with knives…"

"Now that we begin to understand each other, will you tell me what you meant about 'saving' me?"

"Yes. I'm delighted to do the damned prudent lad an ill turn. As a matter of fact, I am going to tell you everything I heard tonight."

"Is it wise?"

"No. If you have a guilty knowledge of either murder—"

She shook me by the shoulder. "I swear to you that all I know about—about either of them is what I read in the papers! And if you hadn't told me last night that the two were connected, I shouldn't have known it."

"Yet, my dear girl, you lied last night. You said you had seen Odette Duchêne leave the waxworks."

"That was because of my father. And that was *all*! Your friend Monsieur Bencolin knows as much... I tell you I simply supposed she had gone out by the other door, into the boulevard."

I blew smoke rings at the ceiling. Once you drove this young lady into a corner, you could keep her there. I pointed out:

"But, being one of the owners here, you must have known she wasn't a member of the club. How, then, did you account for her 'leaving by the other door'?"

"In time," she mused, studying me, "you may be very nearly as good at questioning as Monsieur Bencolin. Oh, a long time... But listen. There are exceptions. If Monsieur Galant gives orders—they can go in. I can definitely prove that I was in the booth all day. I know nothing! Do you believe it?"

I risked everything. I told her all I had heard that night. For, if she believed my story about Galant's intent to wreck the club, then I had an ally of the most powerful sort.

"... So," I concluded, "if there's a safe in the office, and you know the combination, you might just open it and see whether or not these messages to the newspapers have been prepared."

She sat quietly while I was talking, but now her face had again assumed that rigidity of last night. She looked dangerous.

"Wait here," she snapped.

She left the room by a door at the far end, locking it after her. I lay back on the cushions. Heigho! Everything was topsy-turvy. They were searching the club for me, and here I sat cosily in their midst, with comfortable cushions under me and cigarettes within reach. The situation was almost perfect. No luckier words had ever been spoken than those of Galant when he told of his last joke. If Marie Augustin really found the evidence in the safe, then I fancied I should hear whatever she happened to know about these murders.

She returned in less than five minutes. Closing the door with a snap, she stood with her back to it. Her eyes were dull with anger, and I saw that she had papers in her hands. As though she made a sudden decision, she went to one of the braziers of hammered gold in which the incense was smoking, removed the plate of incense, and threw the papers into it. Then she struck a match.

A flame licked up out of the gold bowl. Against the black-and-gilt background, ornamented with hieroglyphics and storks, she looked like a priestess. Only when the fire had died did she straighten up from staring at it.

She said, "I am ready to go to Monsieur Bencolin and swear that I saw my friend Galant stab the Duchêne girl."

"And did you?"

"No." A dull, vindictive monosyllable. She walked over slowly; I had again the fancy of a grim-faced priestess. Every muscle in her body seemed to be tight. "But," she added, "I guarantee to make a good story of it."

"I don't know that it will be necessary. And—this sudden dropping of caution? You keep insisting that you fear your father will…"

"Not any longer. He knows."

I swung my legs off the *chaise-longue*, sat up, and looked at her. The room swam a bit; little hammers began to pound at the base of my eyes, and my head seemed to be rising towards the ceiling in long spiralling motions.

"He knows," she repeated. "There's an end to concealment. I can figure in the papers as well as anybody. And—I think I shall enjoy it."

"Who told him?"

"I think he has suspected some time. But I have him"—she pressed her finger and thumb together contemptuously— "like that. Besides, I am going to see Galant in a condemned cell if it costs everything."

The suppressed fury in her voice made me wonder whether there had ever been anything between these two. But I kept silent while she went on: "Then I end my career as a slavey. I will travel. I will have jewels, and rooms in a hotel overlooking the sea, and—and gentlemen, like yourself, to pay me compliments. And there will be one of them, like yourself, whom I can't rule… But first," she amended, smiling dangerously, "I will settle things."

"You mean," I said, "you are willing to help the police with *everything* you know?"

"Yes. I will swear I saw Galant—"

"And I tell you again it won't be necessary to perjure yourself! With the evidence of Mademoiselle Prévost and myself, we have him. You can help us much more," I insisted, trying to hold her gaze, "by telling the truth."

"About what?"

"By telling everything you know for a fact. Bencolin is convinced that you saw the murderer of Claudine Martel."

Her eyes opened wide. "So you still don't believe me! I insist—"

"Oh, not knowing it was the murderer, necessarily! But he believes that the murderer walked into the waxworks last night before your father closed up; that he was hidden there. Moreover, that the murderer was a member of the club, whom you knew. Do you know how you can help us most? Simply by telling what club members came in that way last night."

She stared at me uncomprehendingly, her eyebrows rising. Then she laughed; she sat down with a swashbuckling air, and shook me by the shoulder.

"Do you mean," she cried—"do you mean that the great Bencolin—the infallible, the great lord of logic—do you mean that he has been so thoroughly fooled? *Tiens!* this is too good!"

"Stop laughing! What do you mean—fooled?"

I twisted her round to face me. Her eyes, still hard and mocking, ran over my face.

"Just that! If the murderer was a member of the club, he didn't come in that night through the waxworks. I saw everybody who did come in all day, and, my dear boy, there were no members among them. *Tiens!* but your face is funny! Did you think he was always right? Why, I could have told you all this long ago."

I hardly heard her laughter. A whole edifice of theory, spires and towers and pinnacles, had been reared on that assumption; now, suddenly, the blocks seemed to come down with a roar. In an instant, if this were true, the whole of it became wreckage.

"Listen," she said, disengaging her shoulder, "I think I

should make a better detective than any of you. And I can tell you—"

"Wait! The murderer couldn't have come any way except in through that waxworks! The whole arrangement of doors…"

Again she laughed. "My dear boy, I am not saying the murderer didn't come that way. Through the waxworks, I grant you. But you are wrong in looking for a member of the club. And now I can tell you two things."

"Well?"

She put her hands on her lips, breathing deeply. Her face was flushed with triumph, and the lids drooped over her eyes.

"This much, then, which the whole Paris force doesn't seem to have uncovered," she told me. "First—I know where the weapon is hidden."

"*What!*"

"And second," she went on, imperturbably, "I know that the crime was almost certainly committed by a woman."

16

A DEAD MAN PUSHES OPEN A WINDOW

This thing was getting to be too much for me. I felt as a certain celebrated wanderer in a topsy-turvy land must have felt when the whole court of justice dissolved and rained down in a shower of playing-cards. Nonsense sounded like sense, and sense sounded like nonsense.

"Ah, well," I said, resignedly, after a long pause—"ah, well!..."

She inquired with the utmost politeness: "It surprises you?"

"Damn you! Are you joking?"

"Not in the least," she assured me, patting her hair. "After that detective's cheap tricks last night, I am sorry I could not have told him first. However, I shall reserve that pleasure."

"Now, first of all," I said desperately—"first of all, you say you have found the weapon?"

"I know where it is, yes. I haven't disturbed it. Tell me—by the way, what *is* your name?—" She broke off sweetly.

"Stop stalling. My name is Marle. What were you saying?"

"Tell me, didn't the police search every inch of the

waxworks, and the passage, and everywhere else, without finding it?"

"Yes, yes, go on! Your triumph is delicious. I know, but—"

"But they failed, Monsieur Marle, because they neglected an ancient rule. The knife was right in front of them all the time; so they didn't see it. Now, did you go down into the Gallery of Horrors?"

"Yes. Just before I discovered the body."

"Did you notice that masterly tableau just at the foot of the stairs? I mean the stabbing of Marat. Marat lies halfway out of his bathtub, the knife in his chest, blood streaming from it. Well, my dear boy"—she reached out and quizzically flickered a finger across my lips—"some of that blood was real."

"You mean—?"

"I mean," she said, composedly, "that the killer went down into that room. She removed the knife from the wax chest of Marat. When Papa built that figure, he used the longest, sharpest, deadliest knife he could find; wax never dulled its edge, it was sheathed from dirt and rust, and it could easily be pulled out. When the killer had finished with her work, she replaced it in Marat's chest. The police looked at it last night, and hundreds of people have looked at it today, but nobody noticed."

I saw again that grisly tableau in the cellar, as I had seen it the night before, and remarked its hideous realism. And then I remembered another thing, which caused me very heartily to curse myself. It was right there—there, in front of Marat—that I had heard something *dripping*. Later I had attributed it to the figure of the satyr, where the body was; but with the slightest grain of sense I should have realized I could not have heard blood drip from such a distance. It came from the Marat tableau all the time...

"Well," I demanded, "how did *you* notice it?"

"Ah! So I am again to be under suspicion? (Give me a cigarette, will you?) No, no; I could not avoid noticing. Monsieur Marle, I have lived in that waxworks all my life. If a single button is out of place on any of the figures, I know it…"

"Yes?"

"When I looked through this morning, I saw a dozen small changes. Marat's writing-board had been pushed a quarter of an inch to the left. Somebody had brushed past Charlotte Corday's skirt and ruffled a fold. Most of all—the dagger was not quite buried to the hilt in his wax chest, and a few spots beside the tub were not painted blood."

"Did you touch it?"

She lifted a whimsical eyebrow. "Oh no! I waited for the police to discover it. I imagined I should wait a long time."

"There may be fingerprints everywhere…"

"Possibly," she replied, with indifference. She waited for me to light the cigarette she had taken from the lacquer box. Then she said: "I am not greatly interested in Mademoiselle Martel's murder. But I didn't think you would overlook the leads that it must have been a woman—a woman who was not a member of the club."

"Why?"

"The killer was after something which she wore on a gold chain round her neck." She looked at me sharply. "Isn't that clear?"

"We have already decided that it was the silver key."

"Our opinions," she murmured, "coincide. I am happy to have thought of the same thing as the great Bencolin. Good!— Well, my dear boy, why did the killer want that key, except to get into the club? How did you yourself get here tonight?"

"Borrowed a key from a member."

"Yes. You borrowed a *man's* key, which could be examined and checked at the door. Well, what on earth good would Mademoiselle Martel's key have done the murderer *if the murderer had been a man?* I am beginning to think he is stupid, that Bencolin!... A woman took it. A woman who must have looked at least a little like Mademoiselle Martel herself, so that she could get in."

She leaned back, stretching her arms above her head.

"Now," I suggested, smiling, "if you can produce a reason why the murderer wanted to get into the club...?"

"I am afraid that would be a little too much."

"Or if I could find out whether a woman, presenting Mademoiselle Martel's key, got past the guards last night..."

She said, dryly, "I don't suppose you would care to go out and ask them, would you?"

"*You* could."

"Listen, my dear boy." She exhaled smoke savagely. "I don't care who killed Claudine Martel. I wouldn't walk a step out of my way to help you on that, because, whoever else it was, it couldn't have been Galant. So much I gather from what you've told me. All I want to do is get *him*—do you understand?"

"One involves the other."

Her eyes narrowed. "How so?"

"He's accessory after the fact, isn't he?—both he and the Prévost woman? And she's willing to turn state's evidence."

She smoked for a time in silence, and then nodded.

"Good. That goes. Now, then, what's the plan of campaign?"

"The first thing is whether you can get me out of here. Can you?"

She shrugged. "Something, my friend, has got to be done. They'll have finished looking in all the other rooms for you before very many minutes, and then..." Drawing a finger across her throat, she studied me. "I could, of course, call in my own attendants, gather the guests round, and march you out in full view. Dare Galant to do anything about it. It might mean trouble…"

I saw her narrowed eyes fixed on me speculatively again. I shook my head.

"That won't do. Galant would be warned. He might not start a fight, but he'd be sure to get away before the police could be summoned."

She said, tensely: "Good child! I like you better. Then have you nerve enough to try to get out the front door in disguise? I'll go with you. You could pass as my—lover."

"It would be a pleasure," I said, "even to adopt the pose."

She tried not to notice that. She set her lips stonily.

"It will be dangerous. If you are caught…"

Again the whole heady excitement of juggling dynamite took possession of me. I said, truthfully: "Believe me, mademoiselle, I have had more pure fun here tonight than in the last six years of my life. The adventure should end in glory… Have you got a drink?"

"Be sensible!… *Bien!* You will have to leave your own coat and hat here. I can get you others. You must take off that bandage, and pull the hat down over the sticking-plaster; I don't think it will bleed. Your shirt is a mess also; you must cover it up. Have you a mask?"

"I lost it somewhere. In the court, I think."

"I'll get you one that will cover your whole face. Finally, there's this. They'll guard the door well, and they'll probably ask everybody to exhibit his key on leaving. And they must have realized by now the key you are using. I'll get another. Wait while I look around. In the meantime there is Napoleon brandy in that cabinet by the dressing-table."

She hurried out the door again. But this time she did not lock it. I got up. Pain darted up from the back of my skull and flowed in dizzy waves across my eyes, and my legs still felt light. But the exhilaration of the whole night steadied me. I leaned against the edge of the *chaise-longue* until the floor stopped wobbling and the room swam round again into focus. Then I picked my way over to the cabinet she had indicated.

The brandy was a Napoleon cognac, 1811, in a basket of silver filigree. Remembering how I had drunk brandy the night before, under this girl's stern and domestic eye, the whole fantasy became gloriously funny. I tossed down a huge drink, and felt its warmth crawl along my veins. That was better. I poured another. Then I caught sight of myself in a mirror over the dressing-table… Gad! what a spectre! Like the result of a week's spree, pallor and all; bandage round my head, shirt a red-splattered ruin, and—so! That rat's knife had ripped the sleeve of my coat halfway up. He came fairly close, after all. I toasted the image in the mirror, gulping down a second big one. Steady! The image blurred a little. Brandy must have a queer effect when you felt like this…

I did a sort of eccentric dance-step, quite involuntarily, and surprised myself by bursting into laughter. The gilded storks and peacocks on the wall panels acquired a friendly expression. I noted the smoke of incense curling past the bronze bowls which held the lights, and the reek of the place had become intolerably hot.

Presently Marie Augustin came in. She had a soft black hat, rather too large, which she must have stolen from some guest, and a long cloak. When the arrangements had been made, we stood under the gilt cabinet, ready to put on our masks. She had turned out all the lights except the ornate silver one, shaped like a pagoda, which burnt on top of the cabinet…

The absence of light intensified the silence of this room. Now, faintly, I could hear the deep murmur of the orchestra from beyond the walls. Her face looked up, old ivory in the glow of the silver lamp. Her eyebrows were thin arches, her lips painted dark red...

"And," she was saying, "if we get past the outer door, what then?"

"Down into the waxworks. I must look at that knife," I said, all the while conscious that I was not thinking about the knife at all. "After that, the telephone. You had better give me your revolver."

She passed it over. It was only a brushing of finger tips, but I could not move for looking at her. You thought of stuffy parlours with horsehair furniture; and behind these, mistily taking form, the weird glitter of the Arabian Nights. Slowly she reached up towards the chain of the lamp.

"I wear black," she said, pulling the mask down over her face. "That is because—I have never had a lover."

Inscrutable eyes shone for a moment through the holes in the mask. Then the light went out...

When we started for the door, she first motioned me back and glanced into the outer office. Then she nodded, and I followed through a dim room, hung with fantastic rugs, down to the glass-panelled door leading to the passage. In my hand I had the silver key belonging (she had said) to a member who had recently left for America. The murmur of the orchestra grew louder in our ears; it restored that dream-instability of a world peopled with goblins in varicoloured masks. It was growing late, and the revel would nearly have reached its climax...

Now its noise flowed out to engulf us. Down the dark passage I saw the great arch to the hall. Laughter was twined into the hum of people; quick speech, breathlessness, and the clinking of glasses. It was subdued, but that only heightened its fierce tensity. A voice would break out, to be instantly repressed. Across it the orchestra rolled music in thick, sickly-sweet waves. We were inside, now; inside tall arches of black marble, with mirrors cunningly arranged so that the parade of arches seemed to extend itself endlessly. I had again that illusion of an undersea twilight, as at the waxworks. But now the dusk swam with goblins. Black masks, green masks, scarlet masks; figures split weirdly by the mirrors. Figures arm in arm, moving, black broadcloth and rustling gowns; or figures seated in corners, multiplied by the mirrors, with cigarette-ends palely glowing.

I glanced at Marie Augustin, whose arm was hooked in mine. She was spectral also. In a mirror near me there appeared a disembodied arm. It tilted a swathed bottle, and somebody laughed. There were alcoves where low round tables with glass tops were lighted from within; these lights shone up on the pale colours of wine in glasses, with bubbles rising; and they shone on the lower faces, smiling or intent, of the people who sat motionless there…

Leaning against one pillar was a white-mask. The figure had its hand in its inside pocket. Another white-mask went slipping along the aisles. By the mirror-trick, it seemed to move miles among the arches. The pound and thunder of the orchestra was almost over our heads now…and the orchestra, peering goblin-like from behind palms, all wore white masks…

I felt Marie Augustin pressing my arm tightly. Her nervousness steadied me as we walked slowly across the hall, but I seemed to feel the white-masks staring from behind. What would it be like to be shot in the back, with a silencer on the pistol? Under this noise, not even the faint *plop* could be heard. They could fire, and you could be carried out, quietly and unobserved, as a drunk, after you had fallen.

I tried to move slowly. My heart was pounding heavily, and the brandy I had taken seemed now only to muddle my head. Would a bullet in the back be clean and almost painless, or would it stab like a hot iron? Would—

The noise was diminishing. I could smell flowers now, above the heat and perfume, from the passage at the other end. We moved out into the lounge. I stared straight across at the faces of two white-masked *apaches* who still sat in their alcove, eyes on the door. In the scarlet-and-black flicker of light from the bronze satyrs there, the white-masks rose...

I gripped the butt of the pistol in my pocket.

They sauntered forward. They peered at us and went on...

Down the lounge towards the foyer, a slow progress. It was not real; it could not be real! The palms of my hands were clammy, and once my companion's step faltered. If they found *her* assisting me. *Knock-knock*; it was our footsteps, or my heart, or both...

"Your key, monsieur?" said a voice at my elbow. "Monsieur is leaving?"

I was prepared for it, but, even so, that ominous "Monsieur is leaving?" seemed to be delivered with a delighted leer. "Monsieur will not leave," it seemed to say; "Monsieur, instead, will remain indefinitely." I held out my key to a white-mask.

"Ah," it said, "Monsieur Darzac! Thank you, monsieur!"

Then white-mask shrank back as Marie Augustin lifted her own slightly; he recognized her, and hurried across to open the door out of here. A last glimpse of the marble pillars in the foyer, of the heavy blue decorations, of white-mask grinning; then the hum of the orchestra died and we were out...

For a moment I felt weak. I put my head against the bricks of the wall, feeling the coldness of the passage blow deliciously under my cloak.

"Good child!" whispered Marie Augustin.

I could not see her in the dark, but I could feel her body pressing against my side. Triumph went singing and bounding along my veins. We had Galant now! Oh, we had him!...

"Where to?" I heard her murmur.

"The waxworks. We must look for that knife. Then I'll phone Bencolin. He's waiting at the Palais de Justice... I suppose we must go around to the front to get in the waxworks?"

"No. I have a key for the passage door. It's the only one, though. The rest of the people must go out the other way."

She was leading me up towards the back door to the museum. I felt sweat running down from under my arms, and my wound pounded anew; it was beginning to bleed once more. But the triumph of escaping gave pleasure even to that. It was an honourable scar. I said:

"Wait. I'll strike a match."

The match flame sputtered up. Suddenly Marie Augustin's fingers dug into my arm...

"O my God!" she whispered, "what's *that*?"

"What?"

She was pointing to the door which led into the back of the museum. It stood ajar.

We stood there staring at it until the flame crumpled up and went out. Open. You could see the gleam of the catch, and a stuffy air blew out into our faces. Some intuition told me that we were not yet through with horrors for this night. The door even swung and creaked a little, suggestively. It was here that the murderer had stood last night when he launched himself at Claudine Martel. I wondered whether we should see a green light suddenly spring up there, and, silhouetted against it, a head and shoulders…

"Do you suppose," she whispered, "there's somebody—?"

"We can see." I put one arm round her, drew the revolver, and pushed the door open with my foot. Then I went through into darkness.

"We'll have to get the lights on," she was insisting in a tense voice. "Let me lead you. I know every step of the way in the dark. Up to the main grotto… Watch the steps, now."

She did not even grope as we went through the door, through the cubbyhole, and out on the landing. In thick darkness I felt the edge of the satyr's robe brush my wrist, and I started as at the touch of a reptile. Our footfalls scraped on the gritty stone; the damp and musty air had an almost strangling quality. I stumbled on the stair. If there were anybody else about, that person must certainly have heard us.

How she picked her way along in the dark I do not know. I had lost all sense of direction after climbing the stairs and heading towards the grotto. But you could feel the presence of all the wax figures, indefinably sinister, as you could smell their clothes and hair. I remembered old Augustin's words, touching my ears as though somebody had just murmured there, "If any of them ever moved, I should go mad…"

Marie Augustin let go my arm. There were a clink of metal and a rasp of a switch thrown into place. Green twilight illuminated the main grotto, where we stood now. She was smiling at me, very white.

"Come on," she muttered. "You wanted to go down to the Gallery of Horrors and look for the knife…"

Again we traversed the grotto. It was just as it had looked the night before, when I found the body in the satyr's arms. Our footsteps scraped and echoed in the enclosed staircase.

No matter how cautiously you approached, the figure of the satyr always seemed to appear as with a spring at you. It was in place again, the green lamp burning behind it in the corner. I shuddered when I remembered its robe brushing my hand...

The Gallery of Horrors. I could see coloured coats, and wax faces peering out, in a dimness which was even more eerie than the dark. We were close to the Marat tableau now, yet for some reason I hated to look at it. Dread kept my eyes fixed on the floor. Something seemed to whisper, with little words which were as the tapping of hammers on my ear-drums, that I should see a ghastly thing... I raised my eyes slowly. No. It was the same. There was the iron railing in front of it. There was Marat, naked above the waist, lying backwards, his glass eyes glaring at me upside down. There was the serving-woman in the red cap, shouting to the soldiers at the door, and seizing the wrist of pale Charlotte, the murderess. I saw the dim, pale September sunlight drooping through the window... *No!* Something was wrong. Something was missing...

In the heavy and unnatural silence, Marie Augustin's voice boomed.

"The knife is gone," she said.

Yes. There was his bluish hand clutching at a chest thick with blood, but no knife protruded from it. My companion's breath whistled through her nostrils. We did not think; we knew that we were very close to murder which was not done in wax. The weird yellowish light seemed to grow even more dim... I ducked under the iron railing and went up among the figures of the tableau, and she followed me...

The boards in the flooring of that mimic-room creaked under my feet. A little shiver seemed to run through the figures there; I noticed that the serving-woman's foot was almost out of the cloth slipper she wore. By passing inside that railing, you actually seemed to step into the past. The waxworks was blotted out. We were in a dirty brown-painted room high up in old Paris of the Revolution. There was a map hanging disarranged on the wall. Through the window, past the brick wall where dead vines hung, I thought I could see the roofs of the Boulevard St.-Germain. We, like the figures, were simply frozen after the horror of a murder committed here. I turned, and the serving-woman leered at me, the soldier's eyes were fixed on Marie Augustin.

All of a sudden Marie screamed… There was a creak, and one of the window-panes swung open. *A face was pushed through, looking at us.*

Framed in the window, it showed huge white eyeballs and irises pushed up under the upper lids. Its mouth hung open in a sort of hideous grin. Then the mouth was obscured by a gush of blood. It gurgled, its head twitched sideways, and I saw that there was a knife projecting from the neck. It was the face of Etienne Galant.

He uttered a sort of whimpering moan. He plucked once at the knife in his throat, and then pitched forward over the sill into the room.

17

THE KILLER OF THE WAXWORKS

I STOP HERE, MOMENTARILY, IN THE WRITING. EVEN THE tracing down of that scene on paper brings it back so vividly that it shakes my nerves and I feel only the exhaustion I felt then. As the climax of all that night's events, I think that it might have broken steadier nerves than mine. Ever since I had entered the club at eleven-thirty, the terrific race had steadily mounted until almost anybody, I believe, would have been at the breaking-point. For weeks afterwards, Galant's face rode my nightmares, as I saw it in that single awful instant before he crashed through the window at our feet. A leaf, brushing my window at the dead of night, or even the sudden creak of a casement, would bring it back with such clearness that I shouted for lights...

So I hope I shall not be accused of weakness if I say that I remember nothing very clearly for some half an hour. Later, Marie Augustin told me that everything was very quiet and orderly. She says that she shrieked and ran, falling over the iron railing; that I caught her and carried her upstairs, quietly; and that we went in to telephone Bencolin. Our talk was to discuss, with the utmost seriousness, what a bad bump on the head you could get if you tumbled on that railing and hit the stone floor...

But I don't remember that. The next thing which comes back with any clearness is the frowsy room with the horsehair furniture, and the shaded lamp on the table. I was sitting in a rocking-chair, drinking something, and across from me stood Bencolin. In another chair, Marie sat with her hands over her eyes. Apparently I must have told the whole story, rather clearly, to Bencolin, for I was just describing Galant when memory returned. The room seemed to be full of people. Inspector Durrand was there, and half a dozen *gendarmes*, and old Augustin in a wool nightshirt.

Inspector Durrand was looking somewhat pale. When I had finished, there was a long silence.

"And the murderer—got Galant," he said, slowly.

Again I found myself talking, in a coherent and even normal way. "Yes. It simplifies things, doesn't it? But how he got down there, I don't know. The last time I saw him was up in his room, when he set his thugs on me. Maybe an appointment..."

Durrand hesitated, gnawing at his underlip. Then he came forward, put out his hand, and said, gruffly:

"Young man...shake hands, will you?"

"Yes," said Bencolin. "It wasn't bad, Jeff. And that knife... Messieurs, we were all fools. We have Mademoiselle Augustin to thank for showing us."

Leaning on his stick, he looked at her. Her face was pinched as she lifted it, but she met his gaze mockingly. The flame-coloured gown was disarranged.

"I owed it to you, monsieur, from last night," she said, coolly. "And I think you will have to accept my analysis of the crime, after all."

Bencolin frowned. "I am not sure that I can go all the way with you, mademoiselle. We shall see. In the meantime—"

"Have you looked at the body?" I demanded. "Was he stabbed with the knife from the wax figure?"

"Yes. And the murderer took no trouble to hide fingerprints. The case is complete, Jeff. Thanks to you and mademoiselle, we now know everything, including the details of Mademoiselle Duchêne's death." He stared sombrely at the lamp. "*Hic jacet* Etienne Galant! He will never settle his debt with me now."

"How the devil did he get behind that window? That's what I can't understand."

"Why, it seems fairly clear. You know that enclosed stair, between the walls, which goes down from the cubbyhole *behind* the various tableaux from the Gallery of Horrors?"

"Yes. You mean the place where you go to fix the lights?"

He nodded. "The murderer stabbed Galant either in that cubbyhole or close to it. Galant must have started to run; he tripped and fell down the stairs, and then he must have crawled behind the tableaux, trying to find a way out. He was just at the end of his rope when he found that window in the Marat group. And he died before we got here."

"The—the same person who killed Claudine Martel?"

"Undoubtedly. And now... Durrand!"

"Yes, monsieur?"

"Take four of your men and get into the club. Smash the door, if necessary. And if they feel like putting up a fight—"

A tight little smile went over the inspector's face. He squared his shoulders and pulled his hat farther down. In a pleased tone he asked, "What then?"

"Try the tear gas first. If they still feel nasty, use your guns. But I don't think they will. Don't put anybody under arrest.

Find out when and why Galant went out tonight. Search the house. If Mademoiselle Prévost is still there, bring her here."

"May I request," said Marie Augustin, still coolly, "that you do this, if possible, without alarming the guests?"

"I am afraid, mademoiselle, that a certain amount of alarm is inevitable." Bencolin smiled. "However, it will probably be best to dismiss all the guests before getting down to business, Durrand. All servants are to be held. Under cover of the exit, you ought to be able to locate Mademoiselle Prévost. She may still be in room 18. That's all. Try to be quick about it."

Durrand saluted and beckoned to four of his *gendarmes*. One of the others he stationed in the vestibule, and sent the sixth out to the street. Then there was a silence. I settled back in the chair, nerves twitching, but blissfully at peace. Anything now, I thought (oh, very wrongly!) must come in the nature of an anticlimax. There was pleasure in everything: in the ticking of a tin clock, in the coal fire burning beneath an old black-marble fireplace, in the shaded lamp and the worn tablecloth. Sipping hot coffee, I glanced at my companions. Bencolin, gaunt in his black cloak and soft dark hat, poked moodily at the rug with his stick. Marie Augustin's shoulders gleamed in the lamplight; her big eyes were fixed on a sewing-basket with a sort of cynical, pitying look. You couldn't feel anything now. I couldn't, at least. There was a sort of numbness of shock which prevented thoughts, or emotions of any kind. We were spent. There was only the fire snapping, and the friendly tick of the clock…

Then I became aware of old Augustin. His grey flannel nightshirt stretched almost to his feet and gave him an absurd appearance. On top of a long, scrawny neck his head was bent forward; the fan of white whiskers wagged, and the red eyes kept blinking and blinking with an expression of solicitude. Tiny and bobbing, he flopped across the room in a pair of leather slippers much too large. In his hands he had a black dusty shawl.

"Put this round your shoulders, Marie," he urged, in his piping voice. "You'll catch cold."

She seemed on the point of laughing. But he was very serious. He arranged the ugly thing on her shoulders with a nicety, and her amusement died. "Is—is it all right, Papa?" she asked, gently. "You know now."

He gulped. Then he turned his old eyes on us with some savagery.

"Why, of course, Marie. Anything you do—is all right. I'll protect you. You trust—your old daddy, Marie."

Patting her shoulder, he continued to defy us with his eyes.

"I will, Papa. Hadn't you better go to bed?"

"You're always trying to send me to bed, *chérie!* And I won't go. I'll stay and protect you. Now, now!"

Very slowly Bencolin removed his cloak. He put hat and stick on the table, drew out a chair, and sat down, his fingers tapping his temple. Something in the look he directed at Augustin attracted my attention...

"Monsieur," Bencolin said, "you are very fond of your daughter, are you not?"

He spoke idly. But Mlle. Augustin reached up and grasped the old man's hand with an abruptness, as though she were thrusting herself before him. It was she who said:

"What do you mean?"

"Why, certainly he's right!" piped the old man, tightening his thin chest. "Don't press on my hand, Marie. It's swollen. I—"

"And no matter what she might have done, you would always shield her, wouldn't you?" the detective continued, still idly.

"Yes, naturally! Why do you ask?"

Bencolin's eyes seemed to be looking inward. "The standards of the world," he said, "should be at least understandable. I don't know. They are altogether mad, sometimes. I wonder how *I* should feel…"

His voice trailed off, rather puzzled, and then he passed a hand across his forehead. In a steady, rather vicious voice Marie interposed:

"I don't know what this means, monsieur. But it would strike me that you had business of more import than sitting here talking about the 'standards of the world.' Your business is to arrest a murderer."

"That's just it," he agreed, nodding in a preoccupied way. "My business is—to arrest a murderer."

He spoke almost sadly. The ticking of the tin clock seemed to have slowed down. Bencolin examined the toe of his shoe, moving it about on the carpet. He observed:

"We know the first part of the story. We know that Odette Duchêne was enticed here, and we know by whom; we know that she fell from a window, and then was stabbed by Galant… But our real, terrifying killer? Mademoiselle, who stabbed Claudine Martel and Galant?"

"I don't know! That is your affair, not mine. I have told Monsieur Marle why I think it was a woman."

"And the motive?"

The girl made an impatient gesture. "Isn't that clear enough? Don't you agree that it was vengeance?"

"It was vengeance," said Bencolin. "But a very extraordinary sort of vengeance. I don't know whether any of you could understand, or even whether *I* understand. It's an odd crime. You explain the theft of the key by saying that a woman—who was avenging the death of Mademoiselle Duchêne by killing Claudine Martel—used it to enter the club. H'm…"

There was a knock at the door. It had an almost portentous effect.

"Come in!" said the detective. "Ah...good evening, Captain! You know all the people here, I think?"

Chaumont, very straight but somewhat pale, entered the room. He bowed to the others, cast a startled look at the bandage round my head, and then turned towards Bencolin with an exclamation on his lips...

"I took the liberty," said the detective, "of summoning Monsieur Chaumont here after I heard from you, Jeff. I thought he would be interested."

"I—I hope I don't intrude?" Chaumont asked. "You sounded excited over the telephone. What—what has happened?"

"Sit down, my friend. We have discovered a number of things." Still he did not look at the young man, but kept his eyes on his shoe. His voice was very quiet. "For example, your *fiancée*, Mademoiselle Duchêne, met her death at the direct instigation of Claudine Martel, and of Galant also. Please don't get excited, now..."

After a long pause Chaumont said: "I—I'm not excited. I don't know what I am... Will you explain?"

He stumbled into a chair, where he kept running his hat round in his fingers. Slowly and carefully Bencolin proceeded to tell him everything I had learned that night. "...So you see, my friend," he concluded, "Galant believed you were the murderer. Are you?"

He asked the question carelessly. Chaumont was stricken dumb. Long ago he had dropped his hat and gripped the arms of the chair, but he was merely incoherent. He tried to stammer something; his brown face grew even more pale... Abruptly his words tumbled out:

"They suspect *me? Me?* O my God! See here, do you think I'd do anything like that? Stab a girl in the back, and—!"

"Softly," murmured Bencolin. "I know you didn't."

A coal dropped with a rattle from the grate. The stupor of my nerves had begun to wear off; Chaumont's protests jabbed like lancets. I felt that the coffee was burning my throat…

"You seem to think," Marie Augustin snapped, "that you *do* know who is guilty. And you've overlooked—everything of importance."

There was a wrinkle between Bencolin's brows. He said, deprecatingly:

"Well…not exactly everything, mademoiselle. No, I should hardly say that."

Something was going to happen. You sensed it, though you did not know what direction it would take. But I could see the small vein beating on Bencolin's forehead, as though in time to the tick of the tin clock.

"There is just one flaw, mademoiselle, in your theory that the killer stole Mademoiselle Martel's key in order to get into the club." The detective mused. "Well, well—let us say two flaws."

The girl shrugged.

"First, mademoiselle, you can give no earthly reason why the killer should have wanted to go into the club after the stabbing… The second point is simply that I know your theory is wrong."

He rose to his feet slowly. All of us instinctively tried to move backwards, though he was still very quiet and his look was almost absent. The clock ticked loudly…

"Say whatever you like about my stupidity, mademoiselle. I grant it! I came very close to bungling this case altogether. Oh yes. It was only this afternoon, very late, that the whole truth came to me. I take no credit for it. The killer deliberately gave me clues; the killer gave me an even chance to guess. That is why this is the strangest crime in my experience...

"Fool!" His eyes suddenly glittered. He straightened his shoulders. I shot an uneasy look round the circle...

Chaumont sat hunched back in his chair. Marie Augustin leaned forward into the lamplight; her underlip was turned down, her eyes were as ebony in the light, and her grip tightened on old Augustin's arm...

"Fool!" Bencolin repeated. His eyes again became vacant. "You remember, Jeff, my telling you this afternoon that I should have to find the jeweller? Well, I have done so. That was where he got the watch repaired."

"What watch?"

He seemed surprised at the question I flung at him.

"Why...you know those particles of glass, tiny ones, we found in the passage? There was one sticking to the bricks of the wall..."

Nobody spoke. The pounding of my heart choked me...

"You see, it was almost inevitable that the murderer had that happen, particularly in such a cramped space. He smashed the crystal of his wrist watch when he stabbed Claudine... Yes, it was almost inevitable, because..."

"What the hell are you talking about?"

"Because," Bencolin told me, thoughtfully, *"Colonel de Martel has only one arm."*

18

STABBING AS A SPORTING PROPOSITION

BENCOLIN WENT ON IN AN ORDINARY TONE: "YES, THAT was how he killed his daughter. And I shall never forgive myself for being so stupid as not to see it. I knew she was standing with her back to the wall; I knew that in such a narrow space the murderer must have hit his hand there when he withdrew the dagger, and broken his watch crystal... What I couldn't understand was how he came to be wearing the watch on the *same hand* as that which held the knife."

I heard his voice from a distance. My brain was still repeating the words, "that was how he killed his daughter." I stared at the blaze in the fireplace. The statement was so unreal, the import so incredible, that at first I had not even a sensation of shock. All I could think of was a dim library with the rain splashing down the windows, in a garden of the Faubourg St.-Germain. And there I saw an old stocky man, with a heavy moustache and a bald head, standing rigid in his fine broadcloth, his hard eyes fixed on us. Colonel de Martel.

A voice cried out sharply. It broke the illusion into little pieces. "Do you know what you're saying?" Chaumont demanded.

Bencolin went on, still musingly: "You see, a man invariably wears a wrist watch on his left hand, unless he is left-handed. If left-handed, it is on the right one—that is, always the hand *opposite* the one with which he writes, throws, or...strikes with a knife. So I couldn't understand that watch being on the same wrist as that with which he stabbed the girl, whether he was right- or left-handed. But, of course, a man who had only one arm..."

For some weird reason, the very thought of Colonel de Martel seemed to lend dignity to Bencolin's words, even though you thought of him as a murderer. It was no longer (as it had seemed during those mad antics in the club) a sort of meaningless bad dream. But Chaumont, who had a rather witless expression on his face, yanked Bencolin's arm.

"I demand," he said, shrilly—"I demand some excuse or apology for saying—!"

Bencolin woke from his abstraction.

"Yes," he said, nodding—"yes, you have a right to know all about it. I told you it was a queer crime. Queer, not alone in motive, but because that magnificent old gambler actually gave us a sporting chance to guess it. He was not willing to give himself up voluntarily. But he threw clues in our faces, and if we *did* guess, he was prepared to admit his guilt." Quietly Bencolin disengaged his arm from the young man's grip. "Softly, Captain! You needn't act that way. He has already admitted it."

"He...*what?*"

"I talked to him on the telephone not fifteen minutes ago. Listen! Calm yourself and let me tell you exactly how the whole thing happened."

Bencolin sat down. Chaumont, still with his eyes fixed, walked backwards until he stumbled down into a chair.

"You are quite a showman, monsieur!" Marie Augustin said. Her face was still white; she had not relaxed her grip on her father's sleeve, and she exhaled her breath with a sort of shudder of relief. "Was all this necessary? I thought you were going to accuse Papa."

The voice sounded shrill and vicious, and her father's red eyes blinked at her uncomprehendingly as he clucked his tongue...

"So did I," I observed. "All that talk awhile ago—"

"I was only wondering how a rational father would behave. *Tiens!* it's still incredible! But this afternoon—I realized then that it must be true."

"Wait a minute!" I said. "This whole thing is crazy. I still don't understand it. But this afternoon, when you had that brainstorm and suddenly burst out with *'If her father knew, if her father knew—'*" The whole scene was coming back now. "You were talking about Mademoiselle Augustin, it seemed to me."

He nodded. A film was over his eyes. "So I was, Jeff. And that was what made me think of Mademoiselle Martel. Also to think what an incredible, gigantic, unpardonable dunce I had been for not seeing it before! I tell you again I bungled the whole case. Last night Mademoiselle Augustin could have told us who the murderer was, for she must have seen him come in. But I—great God! I was stupid enough to think the killer was a member of the club, whom she would protect! My own insufferable conceit (and that is all) prevented me from asking the obvious question and getting descriptions! The most ignorant patrolman in the service would have done better."

He was sitting slumped in the chair, spasmodically opening and shutting one hand, staring at it as though some lost magic had been there. His eyes were weary and bitter.

"Intricate plans—avoid the obvious—*bah!* I am running on senile decay. Well, mademoiselle! I tried to be so damned clever and circuitous, and ended by making a fool of myself; but I ask you the question now."

Sitting up with abrupt energy, he glanced at her.

"The Comte de Martel is about five feet ten inches tall, and very stockily built. He has a big bald skull, a thick moustache of a sandy colour, very penetrating eyes with overhanging eyebrows, and carries himself almost unnaturally straight. He wears an old-fashioned stock, eyeglasses on a black ribbon, a box-pleated cape of large dimensions, and a rather wide-brimmed hat. You would not likely notice the absence of one arm, on account of the cloak... but he is a man of such distinguished appearance that you could not fail to remember him."

Marie Augustin's eyes narrowed, and then flashed.

"I remember him perfectly, monsieur," she said, mockingly. "He bought a ticket last night about—oh, I don't know!—some time after eleven. I didn't see him go out of the museum, but then that is not a matter for wonder; I shouldn't have noticed... Why, this is delightful! I could have told you long ago. But, as you say, monsieur—I am afraid you suffer from too much subtlety."

Bencolin inclined his head.

"At least," he said, "I can tell you about it *now*."

"Monsieur," Chaumont interposed, earnestly, "I tell you you don't know that man! He is—why, he is the proudest, the most fierce and unyielding aristocrat who ever—"

"I know it. That," Bencolin said, grimly, "is why he killed his daughter. You would have to go back to the history of Rome to find a parallel motive. Virginius stabbing his daughter; Brutus condemning his son to the block... It's morbid and mad and damnable. No rational father would do it. I used to think that those tales of Roman fathers and Spartan mothers were sheer fables. But here... Will you shade that lamp a little, mademoiselle? My eyes..."

As though hypnotized, the girl rose and spread an open newspaper across the lamp. The room was dimmed with weird glowing blotches, where white faces were motionless round the detective's chair. The fire crackled drowsily.

"...And, by the living God," Bencolin suddenly snapped, "he is going to be judged by the standards he applied to his daughter.

"You know the Martels, Captain. Jeff has met them. A lonely man and a deaf woman, with pride buttoned up around them. They live in a great gloomy house, with few friends except old men who remember the Third Empire, and no diversions. Dominoes for a gambler!

"They have a daughter who grows up hating all this. She is far from their generation; she loathes their stuffy dining-rooms, their formal meals, their stiff receptions, their whole embalmed world. It is not enough for her that Disraeli took tea on that lawn with Napoleon the Third when her father was a boy. It is not enough for her that not the slightest scandal was ever breathed in connection with any member of her family. She wants to dance all night at the Château de Madrid, and see the dawn come up over the Bois. She wants to drink queer concoctions in bars decorated like a plumber's nightmare; to drive fast cars, experiment with lovers, and have a flat of her own. And—she discovers that they do not watch her. Once outside her own home, she may do as she likes so long as they never discover it."

He paused. His eyes moved slowly over towards Mademoiselle Augustin, and he seemed to be keeping back a smile. He shrugged.

"Well—we can understand it, can we not? She seizes at anything new which comes her way. They do not guard her allowance. They do not supervise her friends, except in her own home. She is obliged to live two separate lives. And, gradually, as she contrasts this glittering outside world with her own home, she grows even more dissatisfied. Where before she had merely hated restraint, now she comes to hate everything for which her family stands. She rages within herself. *They* are so placid, so stodgy, so maddeningly strait-laced; and she hates them for this.

"She has a friend, Mademoiselle Prévost, who shares her ideas. Say, rather, that these ideas were first nourished by Mademoiselle Martel. Together they see a friend of theirs, Mademoiselle Duchêne, growing up much in the tradition *they* were supposed to have followed…"

He made a slight gesture.

"Do I need to explain further the events which led up to the tragedy? For Monsieur Chaumont's information, we need only say that Odette Duchêne was lured here—never mind how!—and that she died. But Colonel de Martel! Ah, that's different. How did he learn about what his daughter was doing and had done?… I will tell you, because the colonel told me.

"Her activities were good blackmail material for Etienne Galant. Galant waited until he had much to tell, for which a family might readily pay hush money. Then he went to her father.

"Of course, all this occurred some time before the Odette Duchêne episode—even before Claudine Martel conceived the idea of making game of her. I can imagine Galant sitting in Monsieur de Martel's library, and telling, in that deprecating way, certain things…

"What happened? What sudden black horror took hold

of his host then? For many years he has sat there alone with his ghosts. He remembers the day when men fought duels because of the slightest slur on a woman's name. He looks round at those rows of books, he feels solidly under him his ancient house, and he tries to understand what his red-nosed guest is telling him. And he cannot understand. This daughter...

"His only thought is—blankness. Did he have Galant thrown out of the house? Did he want to batter the smug face and mash that red nose to a bloody sponge? Did his whole universe come down with a crash and roar? I don't think so. I think he only rose, possibly pale and a little more rigid, and told his butler to show Galant to the door. And then I can imagine him sitting alone at his table, patiently building up houses of dominoes, while the clock went on chiming through the night.

"It cannot be believed. It buzzes in his brain like a mosquito; he slaps at it, tells himself it means nothing, and yet that insane *whir* keeps on in his ears. And such thoughts would be dangerous, even deadly, to a man who spends all of his time alone. The ghosts come round again. They prod him with the reminiscence of each Martel. He cannot speak to his wife; he cannot speak to anybody—least of all, Claudine.

"Oh, he does not yet think of murder! But I fancy him walking in his melancholy gardens as autumn comes on and the leaves fall, with his gold-headed stick biting into the ground; and this poisonous droning keeps on in his ears... *And what happens?*"

The crackle of a coal in the grate made me jump slightly. Bencolin was gripping the arms of his chair.

"Why, I should have guessed it long ago! Claudine Martel prepares her trap for Odette Duchêne. We know what happened. We know that Galant actually stabbed the girl, when she had tripped and fallen from the window. But Claudine Martel thought that it was the fall, with a fractured skull—perhaps rightly!—which had killed her friend, and she knew that *she* was responsible.

"Her poor little vicious cosmos is wrenched apart. She no longer feels that she is the gay, cynical adventuress who can seize at any pleasure because pleasure is the chief end of life. She goes home that night sick and frozen with terror. She goes *home*—as children do.

"She creeps up that great staircase in the moonlight. She can think of nothing but that the police, big men with insignia on their caps, and harsh hands, are after her. She has defied her household gods. She has emitted a last puerile screech at the things she hates; and, in uttering it, she has caused the death of an inoffensive girl who never did anybody the least harm. Did she see Odette Duchêne's face in the moonlight? I don't know. But her mother was awake. Her mother came into the room and tried in a clumsy way to find out what was the matter.

"So what happens? She does not dare tell anybody. Yet she must have a confidante, she must talk to this horror, or go mad. So, in a low voice, she speaks there in the darkness, with her mother's arm round her... She speaks to a deaf woman! She knows that her mother is not hearing the confession; but it is a comfort to clutch somebody and pour it out. All of it. All the things come rushing back over her, while her mother pats her, and babies her soothingly, and does not hear a single word!

"Yet another person has been attracted by this hysteria. Her father, still trying to understand, still bothered to madness by these voices whispering in his brain, overhears."

Chaumont uttered a groan. It trembled in the silent room; but nobody looked at him, nobody could for a moment understand what *he* felt. We were all thinking of an old man standing in the moonlight, rigid...

"Had he been sitting in his library, patiently piling up dominoes and listening to the clock? Had he been sitting with an old book, and an old glass of wine—knowing that he must not doubt a Martel by even suspecting Claudine, and yet still hearing the voices? Before that, he could doubt. Now he can be sure. He hears the story of the club, he hears that his daughter is not merely one who has hurt her name with a scandal. It is not alone that she has caused the death of a harmless girl. She is, instead, only a kind of procuress, a kind of brothel-keeper. She is mean, and vicious, above all.

"I do not need to trace it. Colonel de Martel has offered to supply us with a statement. Still, I do not think he considered—considered, that is, as a definite plan—the killing of his daughter. He might have felt an impulse to walk into that room and strangle her on her bed in the moonlight. But the coldness of his fury keeps him numb. I think he sat until dawn, looking at the window.

"Then the next night...he hears the telephone conversation. He knows that these two girls, his daughter and Gina Prévost, will meet at the club again. They *must* have news; they must know what Galant has done with the body; they must be assured that they are safe. So, punctually at nine-thirty he puts on his great cape and takes up his gold-headed stick to go out as he has done for forty years—as though he were going to the home of his friend to play cards. But he does not go, this time.

"What he did before he went to the waxworks nearly two hours later we may never know. I think he merely walked, and, the longer he walked, the more grimness came to him. He knew about the two entrances to the club—Galant had mentioned that long ago—but he did not know whether his daughter would come by way of the boulevard or the waxworks. Probably even at that time he merely intended to face her *there*, with her confederate, and show that he knew everything. I am not sure that he had any plan at all—for, you see, he carried no weapon.

"Presently he looked at the neighbourhood of the rue St.-Appoline. He saw the tawdriness, he heard the banging music, and suddenly he saw for the first time the sort of world his daughter enjoyed. It was the worst poison of all. He walked, very straight, into the waxworks—and the madness was on him fully. Then the twilight. Then the great dead of France, modelled in wax all about him...

"Do you understand it?" cried Bencolin, crashing his fist down on the arm of the chair. "Monsieur Augustin was right. The waxworks throws a spell over the imagination; it is a world of illusion. It takes us with terror, or mirth, or sublimity, according to our natures. But on nobody did it exercise a more powerful influence than on this old man who lived always in a dusky twilight of his own. He had heard the past. Now he saw the past. I fancy him going down into the Gallery of Horrors. It was deserted. I see him standing there alone, and for him—it was not a Gallery of Horrors at all.

"He saw people who killed, or were killed, for an abstract ideal. He saw cruelty or madness acquire a sort of terrible grandeur. He saw the Terrorists, unsmiling, watch heads drop into the guillotine basket. He saw the Spanish Inquisitors, unpitying, burn heretics for the glory of God. He saw Charlotte Corday stab Marat, and Joan of Arc go to the stake, for the sake of an ideal, a terrible code, which must never yield!

That was what *he* saw, alone among all the people who have visited there.

"I see him standing straight in the green light, in his black cloak, with his hat off. All the weight of the things he believes is on him. He remembers what his daughter is, and what she has done. The museum is deserted. In a moment, though he does not know it, the lights will be extinguished. Presently his harlot-murderess-bawdy-house-keeper (so he sees her) will be coming there. He hears a last roll of drums, a stamp of the great past marching from its grave…

"Thy Will be done! He walks forward slowly with his hat still off, and wrenches the knife from Marat's chest."

19

ONE CARD FOR CYANIDE

BENCOLIN SAT SILENT FOR A MOMENT, STARING AT THE carpet. Nobody spoke. We all felt the presence of a mad, stocky old man with a gold-headed cane; we all saw the tight line of his jaw, and his unwavering eyes.

"Is it strange, then," the detective asked, softly, "that he should continue this symbolism of his? That, after he had stabbed his daughter, he should put her body into the arms of—*the satyr?* He was offering her there as a kind of sacrifice. He had seen the satyr when he came down those stairs. He knew of the dummy wall, and the door to the passage. Even the lights extinguished did not destroy his plan. You know what happened. It was decreed that Mademoiselle Augustin should put on the lights again when his daughter was in the passage; he saw her, he struck, and Mademoiselle Prévost opened the boulevard door just then. Oh yes, you know all that.

"But do you see now why he took the silver key from her and why he was searching for it? Because the Martel name must be preserved! He could offer his daughter to his own blind gods. He could dump her there in the satyr's arms, for the world to see; left in a dingy waxworks as befitted her. But the vengeance must be a thing between himself and his blind gods solely. He had avenged the ghosts. But the world must not be allowed to know why. It was his secret. If the silver key were found, the police would trace it. It would be blazoned forth to the world that a Martel woman was a whore and a procuress…"

Bencolin smiled grimly. He passed a hand over his eyes, and now his steady voice grew a little bewildered.

"Explain it? I don't try, beyond what I've told you. He killed Galant because he naïvely fancied that Galant was the only person who might ever betray what was known about his daughter, and brand her publicly. So—again I merely quote what he said over the telephone—he sent a note to Galant. He asked for an appointment, and said he was prepared to pay to protect his daughter's name. He arranged to meet Galant in the passage, after which (he said) Galant could take him into the club to the office for payment. And Galant's shrewd, prudent soul remembered that appointment even when his *apaches* were searching for Jeff there; even when an informer was present, Galant must take time off to go and see this man…

"Monsieur de Martel hid in the waxworks once more. And once more he left by the boulevard door, shortly before you, Mademoiselle Augustin, and you, Jeff, escaped. The same knife avenged both crimes."

Chaumont said, hoarsely: "I believe it. I have to believe it. But his telling you this over the phone!—Do you mean to say he deliberately confessed, when he'd done all this?"

"That comes under the head of what I still believe to be the wildest part of this crime." Bencolin had sat with his hand shading his eyes; now he whipped it away and turned to me. "Jeff, when we visited his home this afternoon, did you realize that all the time he was deliberately giving us an even chance—a gambler's chance—to guess?"

"You've said that before," I muttered. "No, I didn't."

"Well, and there's the glory of it! He was waiting for us, waiting with a full stage set. Think back, now… You remember how unnaturally poised he was, how motionless, how he greeted us literally with a poker face? And do you remember what he was doing? He sat there and twisted in his hand, full under our eyes—what?"

I tried to remember. I saw the lamplight, the rain, the man's frozen glance, and in his hand…

"It looked," I said, "like a piece of blue paper."

"It was. It was a ticket to this museum."

The appalling realization struck me between the eyes. The blue tickets! which I had thought about ever since I thought of Mademoiselle Augustin sitting in her glass booth…

"There, in front of our eyes," Bencolin explained, carefully, "he flourished a proof that he had been here to this museum. He was working again according to his code. He would not tell us. But the code said he should not strike, like a thug, and slink away. He would place before the police sufficient evidence. If they were too blind to see it—he had done his duty. I said before, and I say again, that he is the strangest murderer within my experience. But he didn't stop with that. He did two other things."

"What?"

"He told us that he had been accustomed to going, every week, for forty years, to the home of a friend to play cards. He said that he went there on the night of the murder. All we needed to do was to *check* that statement, and we should have found it false. It would have been proof complete, an absence which his friend could not conceivably have failed to notice. But I, dunderhead, never thought of it then! And then, to finish it, he offered us the most subtle suggestion of all. He knew we must have found those bits of glass from the broken wrist watch in the passage. And do you remember what he did?"

"Well? Go on!"

"Think back, now. We were just about to leave. What happened?"

"Why...the grandfather clock began to strike..."

"Yes. And he glanced at his wrist, on which there was no watch. Then, to emphasize that fact, he frowned, and looked up at the grandfather clock. Jeff, no plainer piece of pantomime was ever described. A habit—he looks at his watch, finds it gone, and naturally raises his eyes to the clock."

The thing was so blatantly, glaringly plain as I looked back; as I considered those carefully weighed answers, all calculated to tell us just enough; all a part of a huge gambling game which he had played...

"Several times," continued Bencolin, "he almost weakened. That was when his wife would burst out wildly. It took an almost superhuman self-control to sit and listen to that from the mother of his daughter...the daughter he had stabbed. At the end, he had to dismiss us rather abruptly. Even he could stand just so much."

"But what are you going to do?" demanded Chaumont. "What have you done?"

"Just before I came here tonight," Bencolin said, slowly, "after I had heard what had happened, I telephoned Monsieur de Martel. I told him I *knew*, I told my evidence, and I asked him to supply certain gaps."

"Well?"

"He complimented me."

"Isn't there a limit," snapped Marie Augustin, "to your showmanship, monsieur? Aristocracy, bah! The man is a murderer. He has committed as callous and brutal a crime as any *I* ever heard of. And do you know what you have done? You've given him a chance to escape."

"No," said Bencolin, calmly. "But that is what I am going to do."

"You mean to say—!"

Bencolin got to his feet. His face wore a thoughtful and deadly smile.

"I mean," he said, "that I am going to subject this gentlemanly gambler to the worst test I have ever imposed on anybody. It may cost me my office. But I told you I would judge him by his own standards. I will judge him by the Martels… Mademoiselle, has your telephone an extension cord? Can it be brought out here and put on this table?"

"I don't think I understand."

"Answer me! *Can it?*"

She rose stiffly, tightening her lips, and went to a curtained archway at the back of the room. In a moment she was back with a telephone, yanking after it savagely a length of wire. She set it down on the table beside the lamp.

"If monsieur," she said, frigidly, "will condescend to tell us why he could not himself go into the other room and—"

"Thank you. I should like you all to hear this. Jeff, do you mind letting me sit in that chair?"

What was he up to? I rose and backed away, but he motioned us all close to the table, and twitched the newspaper off the shade of the lamp. The faces of my companions sprang out of gloom, Chaumont bent forward, his arms hanging limply and his eyes screwed up; Marie Augustin rigid and waxen pale; her father mumbling incoherently to some dream behind his red-rimmed eyes.

"Allo!" said the detective, leaning back in his chair with the phone. "Allo! Invalides twelve—eighty-five…"

His half-shut eyes were fixed on the fire. One leg swung with a rhythmic motion. Outside, a car whirred past in the rue St.-Appoline. There were a screech of gears, the slur of another car skidding past it, and a burst of profanity. The noises were intensified in this stuffy room; they beat through the thick curtains with a kind of hysteria.

"That—that's the Martel number," Chaumont said.

"Allo! Invalides twelve—eighty-five? Thank you. I should like to speak to the colonel…"

Another pause. Augustin brushed the sleeve of his night-gown across his nose; his snuffle was very loud.

"He will be sitting alone in his library now," the detective said, musingly. "I told him to expect this message… Yes? Colonel de Martel?… This is Bencolin speaking."

He held the instrument away from his ear. The place was so very quiet that you could hear distinctly the reply from the telephone. There was something eerie, something ghastly and disembodied, about that voice. It was small and almost squeaky, but very calm.

"Yes, monsieur?" it said. "I was waiting for your call."

"I spoke to you awhile ago…"

"Yes?"

"I told you that I should be compelled to order your arrest."

"Naturally, monsieur!" The voice was rasping, rather impatient.

"I mentioned the scandal which must attend your trial. Your name, your daughter's name, and your wife's kicked around in the dirt, and gloated over; yourself telling all your knowledge and your decision in a crowded courtroom, with flashlights going off, and workmen eating sausage while they gaped at you…"

He had spoken still thoughtfully. The rasping voice cut him short:

"Well, monsieur?"

"And I asked you whether you had any poison in the house. You replied that you had cyanide, which is swift, monsieur, and painless. You also said—"

He held the telephone up so that the cold voice grew even louder.

"And I say again, monsieur," snapped Colonel de Martel, "that I am prepared to pay for what I have done. I am not afraid of the guillotine."

"That is not the question, Colonel," the detective said, gently. "Suppose you gained my permission to drink instant oblivion…?"

Marie Augustin took a step forward. Bencolin turned with a fierce exclamation on his lips; she fell back, and he went on quietly:

"You have won the sportsman's right to do so—if you will take a sportsman's chance."

"I do not understand."

"If you were to drink that cyanide, Colonel, you would have atoned. I could keep the whole thing quiet. The connection of your daughter with that club, her past deeds of all kinds, your own acts—in short, *everything* pertaining to the affair—would never be known. I swear it. And you know that my word is good."

Even over those miles of wire you could sense a hiss of indrawn breath. You could feel the bulky old man stiffen in his great chair.

"What—what do you mean?" the voice said, rather hoarsely.

"You are the last of your great line, Colonel. The name would still mean honour for all of those who have borne it. All of them! And if I, the representative of the police, told you that you had satisfied justice—that you had left your name, Colonel, your *name*"—his words were cool, pointed like little sharp knives—"high and clean against all attack... whereas, otherwise, how they could chuckle and leer in all the little houses! How the shopkeeper would smack his lips over the harlotry of your daughter..."

"For God's sake," Chaumont whispered, starting forward, "stop torturing him!"

"...The harlotry of your daughter, her mean little part as a white-slaver and pimp... And I could save you all this, Colonel, honourably and easily, if you would still take a gambler's chance!"

The voice was breaking. It said, huskily:

"Still I don't see..."

"Well, let me explain. Have you that cyanide at hand?"

The voice whispered: "It is in my desk. In a little bottle. Sometimes in the last months I have thought..."

"Take it out, Colonel. Yes, do as I say! Take it out now, and set it on the desk in front of your eyes. Instant death, honourable death, is there. Look at it for a moment."

There was a pause. Bencolin's leg had begun to swing faster; his tight smile broadened, and his eyes smouldered.

"You see it? A flash, and you die. A father, grieving with sorrow over the death of his daughter, has died and left for all of them a great name. Now—have you a deck of cards there?... No, I am not joking!... You have? Excellent. Now, monsieur, this is what I propose...

"You shall draw two cards at random. The first for me, the second for you. You are there alone. No one shall ever know what these cards are—but you shall tell me over this phone…"

Chaumont let out a gasp. The monstrous significance of this dawned on me suddenly.

Bencolin went on: "If the card which you draw for *me* is higher than your own, you shall lock up that cyanide and wait for the arrival of the police. Then—the horrors of the trial, the mud, the scandal, and the guillotine. But if *your* card is the higher, you shall drink the cyanide. And I swear on my oath that no single word of this whole affair shall ever become known… You were a gambler before, Colonel. Do you dare to be one now?… Remember, as I say, that I take your word. Not a living soul will ever know the cards you draw."

For a long time there was no reply. The little nickelled telephone hung there in Bencolin's hand, became now a terrible thing. I pictured the old man in his dusky library, his bald head gleaming in the lamplight, his tight jaw buried in his collar, and the shaggy-hung eyes staring at the bottle of cyanide… The tin clock ticked steadily…

"Very well, monsieur," the voice said. You could sense a breaking-point close at hand. The voice became dry, hardly audible: "Very well, monsieur. I will accept your challenge. A moment until I get the cards."

Marie Augustin breathed: "You devil!… You're—"

She was clasping her hands together. All of a sudden her father let out a sort of giggling laugh which was horrible. His red eyes goggled with admiration, and you could hear the joints crack in his fingers as he rubbed his hands together. His head continued its bobbing; he seemed to be nodding in appreciation…

More dragging ticks of the clock, another coal that rattled in the fireplace, and the distant cry of an auto horn…

"I am ready, monsieur," the voice from the telephone squeaked, loudly and clearly.

"You shall draw, then, for me—and think what it means."

(Gardens of the Faubourg St.-Germain, rustling tattered leaves in the night. The gleaming backs of the cards, and a hand fumbling at them.)

I almost jumped out of a crawling skin when the voice announced:

"Your card, monsieur, is the five of diamonds."

"Ah," said Bencolin, "not very high, Colonel! It should be easy to beat that. So very easy. And now think of all I have told you, and draw for yourself."

His half-closed eyes travelled up mockingly to mine…

Tick-tick, tick-tick, terrible little tin blows on the silence. Gears of a car screamed and whizzed past the windows; Augustin cracked the joints in his fingers…

"Well, Colonel?" asked the detective, raising his voice slightly.

There was a rasp in the telephone. Chaumont whirled with a pale face.

"*My card, monsieur—*"

The squeaky voice faltered. You could hear a gasp… Then there was a little tremble, as of breath through lips curled in a smile; and a small crash of glass dropped on hardwood.

The voice, clear and firm and courteous, rang out:

"My card, monsieur, is the three of spades. I shall await the arrival of the police."

THE END

THE MURDER IN
NUMBER FOUR

I

DURING THE NIGHT RUN BETWEEN DIEPPE AND PARIS, on a haunted train called the Blue Arrow, there was murder done. Six passengers in the first-class carriage saw the ghost; one other passenger and the train guard failed to see it, which was why they decided the thing was a ghost. And the dead man lay between the seats of an empty compartment, his head propped up against the opposite door and his face shining goggle-eyed in the dull blue light. He had been strangled.

This *Blue Arrow* has an evil name. At twelve o'clock the channel boat leaves New Haven. With good weather, it arrives at Dieppe about 3 a.m. On a wintry night of sleet and dull-foamed waves it is the atmosphere for ghosts. The great echoing customs shed, hollow with steam and the bumping of trunks, the bleary lamps, the bedraggled passengers filing silently up the gangplank, set an imagination running to things weird. Sickness, loss of sleep, the bobbing eerie boat floundering in against the pier, had made a wan crew of these eight people on the night of December 18th. Thus, after a six-hour crossing on which the vessel several times lost the

Dieppe light and staggered helpless in the gale, they boarded the *Blue Arrow* for Paris.

Superstitious porters have many tales about this train. Its engine is misshapen, and sometimes there rides in the cab a blind driver named Death. Along the moonlit waste people have been ground under the wheels, with no sound save a faint cry and a hiss of blood on the firebox. On this run, too, there was once a fearful wreck; they say that on some nights, when you pass the place, you can see the dead men peering over the edge of the embankment, with their smashed foreheads, and lanterns hanging from their teeth.

The testimony of eight witnesses was to be had about the tragedy, on this night of December 18th when the murder was committed. Nobody had particularly noticed the victim; he travelled alone, and in the boat he had sat in a corner of the lounge with his hat pulled over his eyes, speaking to none of them. Sir John Landervorne, on his way to Paris to see his old friend M. Henri Bencolin, had asked this mysterious person what time the Blue Arrow arrived there, but he received only a shrug. Mr. Septimus Depping, another Englishman, had asked him for a match; the stranger merely muttered, "*Je ne parle pas Anglais.*" Miss Brunhilde Mertz, militant feminist, clubwoman, and tourist from the United States of America, had tried to engage him in conversation about the inestimable advantages of prohibition (as she did with everybody), and had been highly incensed when he merely turned his back.

On the *Blue Arrow*, he went into a compartment by himself and pulled the door closed. He had not changed the blue night lamps; those who passed in the corridor could see his back as he sat staring out of the window. The guard had got his ticket from his skinny outthrust hand while his back was turned. Even during the examination of passports before they boarded the train, although Miss Brunhilde Mertz had earnestly tried to look over his shoulder, nothing was seen. Then there was a dispute in the customs shed, because Miss Mertz shrilly refused to open her trunk ("Do you think I'm going to let that nosy man look at my underwear?"), until, after she had shrieked "No key! No key!" in ever increasing volume, with the idea that the louder she yelled in English the more easily would she be understood, the weary inspector merely sighed and passed her. Under cover of this disturbance, the dark man disappeared into the train.

Now here occurs a random bit of information of which nobody made much. Two of the passengers professed to behold something. These two were M. Canard, one of the most fiery of the French journalists, and his companion, Mademoiselle Lulu, who played a harp. They said that by one pale light on the edge of the pier, they had seen a man standing motionless at the line of the smoky whitish water. He had not been on the boat. He merely stood there, his cloak blown around him, leaning on a cane, and one of his hands clasped over the cane held a cigarette. The next moment he vanished, almost as though he had jumped into the water.

In the train, the midmost compartment was occupied by the man who was to die. That was number four. In number one were M. Canard and Mademoiselle Lulu. In number two, Mr. Septimus Depping and Miss Brunhilde Mertz. Number three was vacant. In number five, Sir John Landervorne. In number six, Villefranche, the proprietor of a café in Montmartre of not too good reputation. In number seven, Mr. Charles Woodcock, a travelling salesman from America. Number eight was vacant.

A drowsy hush settled on the train when it started, a drugged chill of spirits and bodies, for the heating system would not work. The blue night lamps flickered a little in the draughty corridor. At one end of this corridor, by the door, stood Sir John Landervorne, tall and grey, leaning against the railing and smoking. The train swayed ever so little in a creaking rush: that was the only noise. At the other end of the corridor, from the second of the two doors opening from the car on that side, appeared the train guard.

Somebody screamed. It was Mademoiselle Lulu. She had had an altercation with M. Canard, and in tearful dignity she had swept out of compartment number one and planted herself in the vacant one, number three. Her cry was dreary and chilling in that cold place, as though produced by nightmare; for she had seen a face pressed against the glass of the door giving on the corridor, a bearded face which looked as though it had its nose chopped off. It disappeared in an instant; she put her head against the cushions in terror.

Someone else gave an exclamation. When everyone came tumbling into the corridor, it developed that the face had looked in at every compartment, as the testimony of witnesses showed later. *Yet neither Sir John Landervorne, who had been standing at one end of the corridor, nor the train guard, who stood at the other, had seen anybody there, though, at the moment Mademoiselle Lulu cried out, they were looking at each other from opposite ends of the car.*

Then Miss Brunhilde Mertz, while they all stood out there shivering, happened to glance into compartment number four. They saw the dark man stretched out between the seats, and he did not move. Then, while they looked at each other with that sinking panic of horror piled on horror, Sir John tried to open the door. It had been bolted on the inside.

Saulomon, the train guard, pulled the emergency cord. With the train stopped on a dismal waste five miles from

Dieppe, they investigated. They went round to the other side of the train; it had no door there, but three windows set level together. One of these windows was down halfway, but secured there by its snap; it would go no further. The others were up and locked.

When the corridor door had been pried open, the occupant of compartment four was found with face discoloured by strangulation, eyes blood-filled and staring out, the bruises of thick hands on his throat. He was dead.

Now, this man had been seen entering the train, he had been seen sitting at the window, and Saulomon had collected his ticket some ten minutes before. The door was not bolted then. But the door was bolted now, and no murderer could have gone through that door. Nor could a murderer have come through the window. One of the windows was down some inches, but no human being could have squeezed through that space, even if anyone could have reached the window—for it was twelve feet from the ground, and the idea of a murderer clinging to the side of a train was impossible. The other windows were locked.

Two days later, the Parisian police discovered the murdered man's identity. He was travelling under a forged passport as a lawyer from Marseilles; his real name was Mercier, and he was probably the deftest diamond smuggler in Europe.

II

There was a conference of puzzled people in the office of M. Villon, he of the great, bald mechanical head and small body, who may be remembered as having worked with M. Henri Bencolin in the LaGarde murder case. He had never forgiven Bencolin for tricking him into smoking the cigarette which held the identity of the woman spy Sylvie St. Marie; but that was all meaningless ancient history now. For M. le Comte de Villon was now promoted to the position of *juge d'instruction*, the most dreaded police official in France, whose cross-examination of suspects is a process which even American third-degree experts are forced to admire. And now Bencolin was away; for some months he had been in the United States on a police mission. Villon was in sole charge of the *Blue Arrow* mystery; very spiteful in his quiet, ponderous way, with his pinpoint eyes and big flabby hands.

He sat behind his broad desk, blinking slowly. With him were Sir John Landervorne and Saulomon, the train guard, each bright-featured under a reading lamp in the gloom of the great room.

"It is curious," Villon said slowly to Sir John, "that you should be coming to France to see M. Bencolin, monsieur. He has been away some time. Surely you would know of that?"

Sir John was little greyer, a little more irascible; the rust had got into his voice and the rime on his features. He seemed to be made of wire and iron, gaunt in the leather chair, and the sharp cheekbones threw odd shadows up over his eyes.

"See here," he said. "I have had the honour to be associated with the French police many times, my dear sir. I was with Bencolin when he dug the truth out of that Fragneau stabbing in England, and the Darworth business too. I have yet to be a suspect myself... It's rather a shame Bencolin isn't here now. Would you accept him as a character witness?"

Villon muttered, "Bah! Bungler!" under his breath, and shifted, and played with a penholder. But he continued smoothly: "Monsieur, this is not a question of character witnesses. You must realize that both you and M. Saulomon here tell an extraordinary story. You say that you were at opposite ends of this corridor, and that neither of you saw a person there who was plainly seen by six people in the various compartments." He spread out his hands.

Saulomon, who was tall, smooth-shaven and rather threadbare, ill at ease in Villon's ponderous presence, made a protesting gesture.

"M. le Comte," he remarked, "is justified in calling it extraordinary. But it is true. I swear it is true! I do not lie, I. For ten years I have served—"

"Oh, let him talk! It's true enough," Sir John said irritably.

"Nothing? You saw *nothing*? Come now, my friend: The dim light, the possibility that you might have looked away... eh?"

"Nothing! The light was clear enough for me to see this

man Saulomon at the other end. I wasn't looking away, because I was waiting for him to get my ticket."

"But if I may ask, what were you doing in the corridor?"

"Great God! Can't a man step out for a cigar if he likes?"

"You could have smoked in your compartment, if I may mention it. *Peste*, but no matter! You could not have mistaken each other, possibly?"

"No, we could not. Both of us are over six feet; I have a beard, but it isn't black, and neither of us went near the compartments at the time this woman screamed. You want a small man with his nose chopped off. But why concentrate here? If *I* may mention it, why not discover how the person who killed this fellow Mercier killed him, anyway? I had only been standing in the corridor five minutes or so. How did the murderer get in and out?"

"He didn't go through a bolted door," said Villon, smiling. "He must, therefore, have come through the window."

"Wriggling a normal body through five or six inches of space while the train was in motion?"

"Well, he might have been a very small man."

"A dwarf, yes. Where does your dwarf come from? And how is he able to strangle a man?"

"Why, from the roof of the carriage, possibly. They do it frequently in the American moving pictures." Villon's face was a strange caricature of an intelligent man being stupid: the dull-smiling lips and suspicious eyes strikingly naïve. For Villon was baffled, and he was maintaining anything he could think of. Sir John could hardly restrain his bubbling anger, but he asked:

"And the motive for this crime? This phenomenal dwarf who slides down from train roofs, strangles a large man, walks through a bolted door without disturbing the bolt, and parades up and down the corridor to show his beard and his chopped-off nose—what's his motive, if any?"

"His motive," answered Villon with sudden ringing clearness, "was robbery. I have examined the customs officer who looked at the man Mercier's passport. Mercier took his credentials out of a large wallet. The officer saw that the wallet was filled with thousand-franc notes. When the body was examined, the wallet was empty."

Villon got up from the desk. His big head seemed to drag down the weight of his body, and he was peering at them shaggily.

"Messieurs, I don't suspect you. Don't be under a misapprehension. I want to find out who knew this Mercier, and therefore I must see everybody. The other passengers are coming here tonight." He touched a bell. "No; be still, please."

Then Villon went over to the window. Lights were strung over the naked city, following the dark curve of the river and the toy bustle on the Pont Alexandre. He shivered. For a while there was silence. Villon's next remark startled them with its dreary frankness.

"I must confess to failure. I do not seem to handle things the way Bencolin did. He saw to everything. But I'm only human; I have too much work! Work, work, nothing else, and I'm only human, yes... I should have caught this man Mercier. I didn't set the nets, and I should have done so. We were on the watch for him. He had diamonds. This will cost me my position, I fear, messieurs...

"*Bien*, you shall know everything," Villon continued, with sudden doleful helplessness. "Mercier had been in America. He had smuggled six uncut diamonds of great value past the English authorities; he arrived at Southampton two weeks ago on the liner *Majestic*. Scotland Yard lost track of him, but we were warned to watch the channel ports. He had a confederate. It is not known where this confederate is now; it is not known whether the confederate is man or woman. We do not even know whether Mercier was carrying the diamonds, or whether he disposed of them in England, but this latter is considered unlikely. They were not on his person when he was killed, nor were they in his hand luggage. And you should know this. The tide of diamond smuggling has turned to Europe now; the United States has become so rigorous that it is impossible for even the cleverest of them— like Mercier—to do it safely. I did not set the nets. It will cost me my position."

Slowly Villon turned round.

"A few things only are to be known as possible clues. The compartment has been tested for fingerprints, both on the glass of doors and windows and on the woodwork near the windows. The only fingerprints are those of Mercier. His luggage, consisting of a small portmanteau, was found rifled and scattered near the station; it had not been carried into the train. Do you make anything of that? Well, I will go on. Sir John, you were the first to examine Mercier after the murder. Did he wear a beard?"

"Why, yes—a brown beard. It was—"

Saulomon abruptly lifted his head.

"But—that is—are you *sure*, monsieur?" he demanded. "I recall distinctly that the man in compartment four had no beard when I took his ticket."

"Exactly!" Villon cried. "And he had no beard when he was before the passport examiner; the passport picture shows a clean-shaven face. But when he was taken to the morgue after the murder, he was bearded. The attendant doctor discovered that the beard was false. It had been hurriedly put on with spirit gum between the time he left the passport examiner and the time he entered the train. *Why?*"

After a lengthy silence Sir John observed, "He might have been intending to meet somebody in Paris…" Then he stopped, and began drumming on the chair arms.

Villon went to the desk and leafed through some papers.

"Here are our reports. We had six people on that train, aside from yourselves. Four of them we may eliminate as having no probable connection with this affair. They are useful only as corroborating the evidence. With M. Canard I am personally acquainted; in fact, I may say that I am one of his closest friends. He had never before set eyes on this man Mercier, nor had his *petite amie*, Mademoiselle Lulu. M. Villefranche and Mr. Woodcock, the American salesman, you yourself have eliminated, M. Landervorne. As you will see by the records, they occupied compartments where they were under your eye the whole journey until the time of the murder—and we shall be forced to accept you as a reputable witness. Besides, thorough inquiry nets no possible connection between either of them and Mercier, or our agents would have discovered it. *But*, by a curious coincidence, both Mr. Septimus Depping, the Englishman, and Miss Brunhilde Mertz, the American lady, had seen Mercier before; they must have seen him. All three of them travelled to England on the *Majestic* two weeks before." He picked up two typewritten sheets. "Here are their records. With your permission, I will read:

"Depping, Septimus. R., Loughborough Road, Brixton, London. Business: jeweller, Bond Street, London. Age, fifty years, appears in comfortable circumstances. Recently returned from the United States. In Paris now on business for firm of Depping & Davis. Occupied compartment number two with Miss Mertz. Testimony: I was asleep most of the time, when I could, because the woman kept talking a lot of damned drivel about women's rights, and poked me in the ribs with an umbrella when I dozed off. Once I went out to see whether I could get a drink; that was shortly after the train started, and about ten minutes before we saw the man look in the window. I couldn't get the drink. Yes, I saw the man look in the window, but not very well; I was sleepy. I don't remember the time. All I remember was that that asinine woman talked loud enough to wake the dead, and complained about everything, and said the American trains were comfortable and much faster than anything she's seen over here. Address in Paris: Hotel Albert 1*er*, rue Lafayette.

"Mertz, Brunhilde Nation. R., Jinksburg, Missouri, U.S.A. Author of 'Woman, the Dominant Sex,' 'What Europe Owes to Uncle Sam.' Age stated as none of our business. Touring the Continent for the purpose of lecturing about it in America. Testimony: 'It's a pity you can't ride on a train in this abominable country without getting murdered! And such service! Did you ever hear of the checking system for baggage?' Examining magistrate: 'Madame will pardon me if I ask her to confine herself to the essential facts?' Witness: 'Well, if that isn't essential, I'd like to know what is—such cheek! I want you to know I'm an American citizen, and you can't bully me, young man, or our ambassador will—' Examining magistrate: 'Madame, I beg of you—' 'Well, what do you want to know? *I* didn't kill the man; I sat right in my compartment the whole time. Certainly I saw the measly, stupid little rat's face that looked in...'"

"And so on," said Villon, putting down the paper. "Miss Mertz was a somewhat difficult witness, as you will perceive. That is all."

He sat down. In the stillness his chair creaked. Taxis hooted along the quai below. Leaning forward, Villon rested his head on his clasped hands.

"It would almost make one think wild things," Saulomon said in a low voice. "If you were aboard the Blue Arrow night after night, you would feel it. Thieves, murderers, ghouls ride it, streams of them, and we don't know them; we hardly see them, in the mist. But their evil remains, like a draught out of a cellar." He looked up suddenly. The sharp features, the long, powerful hands, the eyes of a mystic, made him incongruous in his role. But in the next instant stolidity closed over him, and he stared down at the floor.

It was as though the imagination of all three, focused on a weird train and a strangler's hands, brought a little of the blue mystery of it into that room. A sense of remoteness added to their feeling of nearness to a dead man in a false beard—which somehow made it all the more horrible. A sudden noise would have startled them. They were looking at murder, through the distorted magnifying glass of an eyewitness.

III

I￼T WAS SOME MOMENTS LATER THAT MISS BRUNHILDE Mertz arrived, escorted by Mr. Septimus Depping. They sat in chairs so that a semicircle was formed round Villon's desk. Miss Mertz leaned forward, a heavy stuffed woman, staring down over the icy bulges of her figure through glasses which made her eyes terrifying in size; she carried her grey hair like a war banner, and spoke with the baffled ferocity of a saint who knows he is right but can convince nobody. A hat resembling a duck under full sail rode aggressively over one eye. Mr. Depping, on the other hand, was uncomfortable; he fidgeted, polished his monocle, stroked his ruddy face, smoothed at the creases of the immaculate trousers on fat legs.

"Er…well?" said Mr. Depping.

"…and furthermore," said Miss Mertz, "if you think you can bullyrag me, I want to tell you you've got another thing coming!" She shook her finger, and the duck wagged ominously. "The very idea of this outrage, *the very idea*! Now, none of your parleyvooing on me, sir; you speak English.

Everybody ought to speak English over here; the idea of this foolish talk, widdgy-widdgy, and waving your hands, like a lot of crazy people! It isn't natural, *I* say! And—"

"Madame," said Villon, rather awed; he stumbled, and added deftly: "Mademoiselle, of course! I do not wish to offend you. We are merely trying to get at the truth of this matter, you see. Just a few questions."

"Questions! Bah! If you were half a police force, you would have solved this thing long ago. The idea!"

"Perhaps mademoiselle has some ideas?" Villon asked politely.

"*I have found the murderer*," said Miss Mertz.

There was such an abrupt and appalled silence that Miss Mertz enjoyed the full savour of it before she went on. Then she became theatrical. Flustered, pompous, with glasses and hat coming askew at the same moment, she got up.

"Let a real intelligent person show you how to act, you slow-pokes!" she cried. "I want to tell you, if you had more people from the good old U.S.A. around, you'd soon know how to handle these things—wouldn't they, Depping?"

"Er…of course," said Mr. Depping.

"Now I'll tell you how I did it. I was coming down the elevator in the lobby at the Ambassador tonight and right over by the door that runs into a little alcove, I saw a man sitting, and I knew who it was. It was the same one who looked in the compartment at us on the train; I'd swear to it on a stack of Bibles. Well, *I* knew what to do, and I didn't waste any time. I got my porter, and he got a policeman. The porter speaks English, and I told 'em what to do. You never can tell what they'll do against Americans in these foreign cities; if we jumped on the man, he might start a rumpus, and maybe we'd get a knife in us, the way they do in these foreign cities.

So I just had the porter call him in the corridor that runs out to the street right by the hotel. They jumped on him, and stuffed a handkerchief in his mouth so he couldn't yell for his friends and maybe get me killed; and I told the policeman I'd be responsible—to bring him right around here with us, and I'd present you with the murderer." Triumphant and breathless, she pointed toward the door. "They've got him right out there now, and your flunkies all round here are trying to keep him quiet."

Villon rose heavily, as though lifted by a sort of slow explosion. His mouth was partly open, and he merely stared. Depping was fumbling to adjust his monocle.

"Bring him in!" shrilled Miss Mertz.

Everybody in the room scrambled up, turning a hodge-podge of astonished faces. An apologetic *agent de police* escorted through the door a very quiet little figure, who was spitting out a handkerchief with gurgles of disgust.

Villon bawled, "Lights! Turn them on over by the door!" When the lights came on, Villon's mouth opened still further. The prisoner gently disengaged his arms from the grasp of the policemen. He stood looking over the group slowly and sardonically—a small man, whose lips were pursed mock-ingly under his pointed black beard, eyebrows raised in quiet amusement. His careful evening dress was slightly rumpled under the long cape, and he held a silk hat under his arm.

"Oh, my God," Villon said slowly and tonelessly.

"Mademoiselle," explained the stranger, "is not oversup-plied with brains."

"Brains? *Brains?*" cried Miss Mertz, glaring around her at the group. "What do you mean, brains? Do you know who I am?"

"Why, naturally," the stranger replied, smiling. "If I may

be so bold as to say so, you are the meddling shrew who has nearly ruined a somewhat important piece of work, and I, mademoiselle, am Bencolin, the prefect of police of Paris."

IV

BENCOLIN WENT OVER TO THE DESK. HE PUT DOWN HIS hat, removed his opera cloak, and put that beside it; then he pulled off his white gloves—quietly, in perfect stillness. Villon had not moved.

The prefect of police faced them, his fingertips spread out on the desk. Under the light of the hanging lamp his head was sharply outlined, with the glossy black hair greying at the temples and parted in the middle; the pouches under the quizzical black eyes, and the wrinkles around them; high hooked nose; curling moustache and short pointed beard—with Bencolin, the caricaturists had always a chance for Mephistopheles.

"I am sorry that I have had to resort to this deception," he said. You noticed not a little of the aristocrat in the back-thrown head, the slow, graceful speech, the faint and dominant contempt with which he faced Miss Mertz. "I have been in France for several days, but few people knew it. I was not prepared to have my presence smashed in on you in such an abrupt fashion, but I had no choice." He smiled suddenly, and exhibited the gag he still held. "Chiefly, my apologies go to

M. Villon. But since I am here, I must make my arrest before I should have chosen to do so."

Mr. Depping had the monocle in his eye, and was frankly staring. Sir John's face wore a curious smile. Saulomon was casually searching after cigarettes. Miss Mertz still had her arm extended in the dramatic gesture; she had not straightened the hat over her eye.

"Bencolin," cried Villon, "you were the man in the corridor, then?"

"Yes. That is why I owe you so many apologies. Won't you sit down, Miss Mertz? I have much to explain.

"When I arranged this elaborate bit of deception," he went on, "I did not know that I should have to cope with murder. My intent was to trap the accomplice of the man Mercier. We of the police cannot be content with knowing the identity of our guilty men. Unlike the detectives in fiction, we must have proof. My friends, two months ago I went to America to assist in running down a league of smugglers—that story does not belong here. Four of them are now in the hands of the New York police. The fifth, Mercier, escaped us, and came to England. The sixth and last is here, in this room.

"Please do not interrupt. I knew who he was, I knew that Mercier would meet him, and Mercier walked into my trap. For Mercier sold in England the diamonds he had brought with him from the States. I know to whom he sold them, and I knew that when Mercier came to France and divided his gains with his last confederate, we should be able to arrest that confederate. For Mercier carried marked money.

"There was a trustworthy man in whom I confided, privately; he watched Mercier in London, and followed him on the channel boat, which I met at Dieppe. Of course, Sir John Landervorne's connections with Scotland Yard ceased long ago, but he remains no less valuable for that. I met the boat at Dieppe. *I must not be seen*; if I were seen, it was necessary that my presence be denied. I had confided in Sir John. I also confided in M. Saulomon, the train guard, because I recognized his intelligence, and also because it was such an ironical joke that I should confide thus in the man who murdered Mercier...M. Saulomon," he said quietly, "you are caught. I trust that you will make no resistance."

It would have relieved the tension had anybody exclaimed, or moved, or cried out. Instead, there was such a deadly matter-of-fact calmness in the room that the whole proceeding seemed unreal. Saulomon was lighting a cigarette; his big hands did not tremble, his face was wooden, but under the harsh light the veins were throbbing in his head.

"Proof, monsieur?" he asked.

Abruptly the thought shot through Sir John's mind: "God, something's going to happen!"—the stiffness of Bencolin's pose, the tensity like the sound of drums slowly rising.

"Your strongbox at the Credit Lyonnais," answered Bencolin, "contains the marked money you stole from Mercier's wallet when you killed him. You said that you took Mercier's ticket; you did not, because you never went into the compartment. I found it on him when the body was examined at the morgue. They found none of your fingerprints at the scene of the crime; nevertheless, they were found on the metal clasps of Mercier's rifled portmanteau."

It was rather like handling a bomb. By his shiftings in the chair, the struggle that reddened and pulled his face, they thought for a moment that Saulomon would act. Then, soothingly, the struggle ceased. Saulomon inclined his head.

"I did it, monsieur," he said.

"Let us reconstruct, then. You knew Mercier was coming

over, but you did not know on what day to expect him. At Scotland Yard we did not arrest him; we deliberately forced him over on that boat, letting him think he was distancing us, because we wished to use him as stalking horse for you. Mercier and you had been working cleverly. Consider! A train guard, who there in that dimly lighted place could pass for a porter, could take a man's luggage and abstract smuggled stones from them before the luggage went to the customs. A clever plot. But this time Mercier did not play the game. He wanted to get away from you with the money he had gained in England. The false beard? Exactly! He put it on after he had left the passport inspector; he did not turn on the full lights in the compartment, hoping thus to deceive you and slip past. Well, you could play such a game yourself, eh?

"Now! Mercier is already in the train, and you know who this bearded gentleman is. He has bolted his door so that those who got into the train would not enter and see there a man wearing a beard—he did not wear a beard on the boat. You could not enter by the door. But *outside*: the train is waiting there by its platform, and as usual, it is a high platform above the tracks, so that one passing by the train finds the train windows on a level with his breast. Inside one compartment, near the window, which is halfway down, sits Mercier, opening the wallet which contains his winnings. You see him. You are a tall man—your hands through the open window in an instant, there in the darkness of the platform. Mercier sees only two hands, which flash in at his throat. He is still gripping the wallet when the life has gone out of him. Had it fallen on the floor, you would have been baffled, for you knew the money was not in the portmanteau, which you had already rifled. Look! His knees are drawn up in a death agony which is grotesquely like that of a sitting man. Here is an alibi. Mercier propped against the window, sitting there as though he were peering out, with his back to the door—you saw the possibility. Nobody could see that he was dead. He would tumble down, of course, after the train started and the movement dislodged him, but if it could be proved that he was alive when the train started, your alibi could be strengthened all along—it was almost perfect. Your error lay in saying that you had taken his ticket, for you wished to keep him alive as long as possible, and you did not want to discover the body—there might be embarrassing questions."

Bencolin sat down on the edge of the desk and pulled up his trouser leg. He regarded Saulomon thoughtfully.

"I also made a mistake, M. Saulomon. I should not have gone into the train at all. But looking through the window outside and seeing Mercier on the floor, I was not unnaturally startled; I came in to see what had happened, and found the door bolted. Then I began to realize what had happened. I wanted to see who was on the train, and when I foolishly exhibited myself at the corridor window, I had to get Sir John and M. Saulomon to swear that they had seen nobody. Why? Well, was it not good tactics? If I revealed myself to the murderer as the prefect of police, got him in the league with me, and threw myself on his mercy for silence, was it not rather good evidence to him that I suspected nothing? Otherwise he would hardly have been so secure in his position, and he would not have deposited in a bank that marked money which will send him to the guillotine."

Saulomon stood up. His eyes were brilliant, he smoothed at his pale hair, and suddenly he laughed.

"It was admirable, M. le prefect. Well!" He glanced towards the policeman in the doorway.

"I could kill you, Bencolin," said Villon venomously. "If for nothing else, I could kill you for that absurd masquerading as a ghost. Why? Why must you look in and scare everybody to death?"

"That statement," said Bencolin, "is not flattering. Besides, I did not have my nose chopped off; I merely pressed it against the glass." He contemplated the speechless Miss Mertz, raised his eyebrows and chuckled faintly. "Give me pardon for a little curiosity, my friend. I wanted to see whether Miss Brunhilde Mertz had succeeded in getting through the French customs the one of Mercier's diamonds which she had bought from Mr. Depping in London."

V

BENCOLIN AND SIR JOHN LANDERVORNE LEFT VILLON'S
office in the Quai d'Orsay. There had been a somewhat
hectic scene, in which Miss Mertz was remembered to have
struck somebody with an umbrella. In the midst of it Sir
John remembered most distinctly Saulomon's tall, pale figure
standing unmoved among the shadows, on his face a dim
smile of wonderment and pity.

Muffled in their greatcoats, Bencolin and Sir John crossed
over and stood by the embankment at the river. A faint snow
hovered in the air, like a reflection of the weird pale carpet of
light which flickered on the dark water, and, beyond, on the
dull shine of the Place de la Concorde. A necklace of lamps
on a soft bosom which shivered with the cold; windy spaces
and low grey buildings, twinkling, muttering; the lighted
arch of the bridges; farther on, the closed bookstalls where
the river curved away. To Bencolin, every house held a quiet
mysterious beauty, every street stone was a shining miracle.
He leaned on the balustrade and sniffed the sharp wind.

"A pretty enough chessboard, isn't it?" he remarked after a

while. "A chess game can be a terrible and enthralling thing, when you play it backwards and blindfolded. Your adversary starts out with his king in check, and tries to move his pieces back to where they were at first; that's why you can't apply rules or mathematical laws to crime. The great chess player is the one who can visualize the board as it will be after his move. The great detective is the one who can visualize the board as it *has been* when he finds the pieces jumbled. He must have the imagination to see the opportunities that the criminal saw, and act as the criminal would act. It's a great, ugly, terrific play of opposite imaginations. Nobody is more apt than a detective to say a lot of windy, fancy things about reasoning, and deduction, and logic. He too frequently says 'reason' when he means 'imagination.' I object to having a cheap, strait-laced pedantry like reason confused with a far greater thing."

"But look here," said Sir John, "suppose you take this business tonight. You gave a reconstruction of that crime, all right, and perhaps that was imagination. But you didn't tell us how you knew that was the way it happened. Reason told you that. Didn't it? How did you get on to the murder, anyhow?"

"It's an example of what I was trying to say. There is so much elaborate hocus-pocus around the whole matter of criminal detection that it makes a detective wonder why people think he acts that way. The fiction writers want to call it a science, and attach blood pressure instruments to people's arms, and give them Freud tests—they forget that your innocent man is always nervous, and acts more like a guilty one than the criminal himself, even his insides. They forget that these machines are operated by the most cantankerous one of all, the human machine. And your psychological detective wants to pick out the *kind* of man who committed a crime;

after which he hunts around till he finds one and says, 'Behold the murderer,' whether the evidence supports him or not. I hope you'll permit me to say damned nonsense. There is no man who is incapable of a crime under any circumstances; to say that a daring crime was necessarily committed by a daring person is to argue that a drunken author can write on the subject of nothing but liquor, or that an atheistical artist could not paint the Crucifixion. It is frequently the tippler who writes the best temperance essay, and the atheist who finds the most convincing arguments for religion.

"And your so-called 'reason,' in an intricate crime, convinces you of exactly what is untrue. It reduces the thing to the silly restricted rules of mathematics. In this Mercier murder, for example, reason said to me Mercier was alive when the train started, because he was seen sitting by the window, and the guard took his ticket; also, somebody must have been in the compartment with him, since no man could have strangled him from outside while the train was in motion. This was perfectly elementary logic, and quite false. Imagination asked me these questions: Why did not Mercier make an outcry when somebody attacked him? Why did he not struggle; does a person sit quiet and unmoving when he is assailed? Why no resistance, then? *Because Mercier did not see the murderer*, a thing impossible if anybody were in the compartment. What does it suggest? Hands through the window, obviously; confirmed by the fact that though Mercier's wallet was robbed, his pockets were not rifled—the murderer's arms would not be long enough to do this through the window. Discount the testimony for an instant, says imagination, and see whether this would have been possible at any time. Yes, before the train started. Did anybody speak with Mercier after this time, or see him move? Nobody except the train guard. Yet this sole witness first says that the man's back was turned when he took his ticket; later he announces that Mercier was wearing no beard. How did he see that, if the man's back were turned and the lights were so dim that you who examined the body face to face could hardly distinguish the features? Then see whether the guard did take the ticket. If not, he lied, and the evidence of the only person who spoke to Mercier after the train started is discounted. I found the ticket.

"Well, then. Who fits all our specifications for the guilty man? We know him to be a confederate of Mercier; it seems likely that he is also the murderer. Who else? Two others on the train had been associated with Mercier. On the boat from New York he had made arrangements with Mr. Depping to sell Depping his diamonds. (I also was on that liner, and it was I who threatened Depping with the law if he did not pay Mercier in marked money.) Moreover, Miss Mertz had bought one of the diamonds. Both these people were on the train. Neither had reason to kill Mercier, so far as I knew, and it was physically impossible for either to have killed him. Depping was too small to have reached that window; Miss Mertz had not the strength."

Bencolin paused, and smiled. "*Voilà!* I'm getting as verbose as a detective in fiction," he said. "I dragged you over here to Paris, and I don't mean to talk shop all the time. Suppose we go somewhere and have a drink. *Taxi!*"

If you've enjoyed *The Corpse in the Waxworks*,
you won't want to miss

The Lost Gallows

by John Dickson Carr,

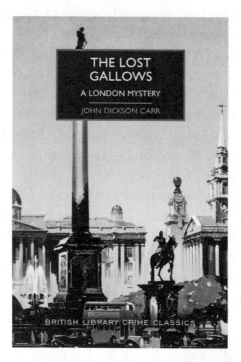

the most recent BRITISH LIBRARY CRIME CLASSIC

published by Poisoned Pen Press,
an imprint of Sourcebooks.

Praise for the
British Library Crime Classics

"A wonderful rediscovery."
—*Booklist*, STARRED Review, for *The Sussex Downs Murder*

"First-rate mystery and an engrossing view into a vanished world."
—*Booklist*, STARRED Review, for *Death of an Airman*

"A cunningly concocted locked-room mystery, a staple of Golden Age detective fiction."
—*Booklist*, STARRED Review, for *Murder of a Lady*

"The book is both utterly of its time and utterly ahead of it."
—*New York Times Book Review* for *The Notting Hill Mystery*

"As with the best of such compilations, readers of classic mysteries will relish discovering unfamiliar authors, along with old favorites such as Arthur Conan Doyle and G.K. Chesterton."
—*Publishers Weekly*, STARRED Review, for *Continental Crimes*

"In this imaginative anthology, Edwards—president of Britain's Detection Club—has gathered together overlooked criminous gems."
—*Washington Post* for *Crimson Snow*

"The degree of suspense Crofts achieves by showing the growing obsession and planning is worthy of Hitchcock. Another first-rate reissue from the British Library Crime Classics series."
—*Booklist*, STARRED Review, for *The 12.30 from Croydon*

Poisoned Pen
PRESS

poisonedpenpress.com